HOMECOMING

ALSO BY BERNHARD SCHLINK
The Reader
Flights of Love
Self's Punishment
Self's Deception

HOMECOMING

Bernhard Schlink

Translated from the German by
Michael Henry Heim

Weidenfeld & Nicolson
LONDON

First published in Great Britain in 2008
by Weidenfeld & Nicolson

1 3 5 7 9 10 8 6 4 2

Originally published in German as *Die Heimkehr*
by Diogenes Verlag AG, Zurich © 2006
Translation © Michael Henry Heim 2008

A CIP catalogue record for this book is available
from the British Library

ISBN 978 0 297 84468 6 (cased)
978 0 297 84472 3 (trade paperback)

Printed in Great Britain by Clays Ltd, St Ives plc

Weidenfeld & Nicolson
An imprint of the Orion Publishing Group
Orion House, 5 Upper St Martin's Lane, London WC2H 9EA

www.orionbooks.co.uk

Part One

I

WHEN I WAS YOUNG, I spent the summer holidays with my grandparents in Switzerland. My mother would take me to the station and put me on the train, and when I was lucky I could stay put and arrive six hours later at the platform where Grandfather would be waiting for me. When I was less lucky, I had to change trains at the border. Once I took the wrong train and sat there in tears until a friendly conductor dried them and after a few stations put me on another train, entrusting me to another conductor, who then in similar fashion handed me on to the next, so that I was transported to my goal by a whole relay of conductors.

I enjoyed those train trips: the vistas of passing towns and landscapes, the security of the compartment, the independence. I had ticket and passport, food and books; I needed no one and had no one telling me what to do. In the Swiss trains I missed the compartments, but then every seat was either a window or aisle seat and I didn't have to fear being squeezed between two people. Besides, the bright wood of the Swiss seats was smarter than the red-brown German plastic, just as the gray of the coaches, the trilingual inscription "SBB—CFF—FFS," and the coat of arms with the white cross in the red field were nobler than the dirty green with the inscription "DB." I was proud to be half Swiss even though I was more at home with both the shabbiness of the German trains and the shabbiness of the city my mother and I lived in and the people we lived with.

The station of the city on the lake, the goal of my journey, was the end of the line. The moment I set foot on the platform I couldn't miss Grandfather: he was a tall, powerful man with dark eyes, a bushy white mustache, and a bald pate, wearing an off-white linen jacket and straw hat and carrying a walking stick. He radiated reliability. I thought of him as tall even after I outgrew him and powerful even after he had to lean on the walking stick. As late as my student days he would occasionally take my hand during our walks. It made me uncomfortable but did not embarrass me.

My grandparents lived a few towns away on the lake, and when the weather was fine Grandfather and I would take the boat there rather than the train. The boat I liked best was the big old paddle-steamer, the one that let you see the engine's glistening oil-coated bronze-and-steel rods and cages in the middle at work. It had many decks, covered and uncovered. We would stand on the open foredeck, breathe the wind in, and watch the small towns appear and disappear, the gulls circle the ship, the sailboats flaunt their billowing sails, and the water-skiers perform their tricks. Sometimes we could make out the Alps behind the hills, and Grandfather would identify the peaks by name. Each time I found it a miracle that the path of light cast by the sun on the water, glistening serenely in the middle and shattering into prancing slivers on the edges, followed along with the boat. I am sure that early on Grandfather laid out the optical explanation for it, but even today I think of it as a miracle. The path of light begins wherever I happen to be.

2

IN THE SUMMER of my eighth year my mother had no money for a ticket. She found a long-distance truck driver—I have no idea how—to take me to the border and hand me over to another driver, who would drop me off at my grandparents' house.

We were to meet at the freight depot. My mother was busy and could not stay. She deposited me and my suitcase at the entrance and ordered me not to budge from the spot. I stood there anxiously watching each passing truck, relieved and discouraged in turn as they passed. They were bigger and made more of a roar and stink than I had realized: they were monsters.

I don't know how long I waited. I was too young to have a watch. After a while I perched on my suitcase and jumped up whenever a truck seemed to slow down and want to stop. Finally one did stop. The driver hoisted me and the suitcase into the cabin, and his mate placed me in the bed behind the seat. They told me to keep my mouth shut and my head below the side of the bed and sleep. It was still light, but even after it got dark I couldn't sleep. At first the driver or his mate would turn and curse me if my head stuck up above the bed; then they forgot about me, and I could look outside.

My field of vision was narrow, but I was able to watch the sun go down through the passenger-seat window. I caught only fragments of the conversation between the driver and his mate: it had to do with the Americans and the French, deliveries and payments. I was almost lulled to sleep by the regularly recurring sound, the regular, restrained tremor of the truck as it passed over the large slabs forming the surface of the Autobahn in those days. But the Autobahn soon came to an end, and we drove over bad, hilly country roads, where the driver could not dodge the potholes and was constantly shifting gears. It was an uneasy journey through the night.

The truck kept stopping: faces would appear in the side windows, the driver and his mate would climb in and out, let down the tailboard, shove the cargo around and restack it. Many of the stops were factories and warehouses with bright lights and loud voices; others were dark filling stations, rest areas, and open fields. The driver and his mate may well have combined their official duties with a bit of business on the side—smuggling or fencing—which lengthened their time on the road.

In any case, by the time we reached the border the truck I was supposed to meet had left, and I spent the dawn hours in a town whose name I do not recall. The main square had a church, a new building or two, and many roofless buildings with empty windows. As it began to get light, people came to set up a market, hauling sacks, crates, and baskets on large, flat two-wheeled carts, to which they had hitched themselves between the shafts with loops over their shoulders. All night I had been afraid of the captain and his helmsman, of being attacked by pirates, of having to pee. Now I was afraid both of being picked up by someone who would do as he pleased with me and of going unnoticed, being left to my own devices.

Just as the sun grew so warm that I began to feel uncomfortable on the fully exposed bench, from which I dared not stray, a car with an open top stopped at the side of the road. The driver remained in the car, but the woman beside him got out, put my suitcase in the trunk, and pointed to the backseat. Whether it was the large car, the fancy clothes the driver and his companion wore, the self-assured and nonchalant way they had of moving, or the fact that just over the Swiss border they bought me my very first ice cream—for a long time thereafter I pictured them whenever I heard or read about the rich. Were they smugglers or fences like the truck drivers? I found them equally creepy, though they were young and treated me with consideration, like a little brother, and delivered me to my grandparents in time for lunch.

3

THE HOUSE MY grandparents lived in had been built by a globe-trotter of an architect: it had eaves supported by artfully hewn wooden struts, a formidable mezzanine bay window, a top-floor balcony adorned with gargoyles, and windows framed by round, stone-in-stone arches—a combination colonial country seat, Spanish fortress, and Romanesque cloister. Yet it held together.

The garden helped to make it a whole: there were two tall fir trees to the left of the house, a large apple tree to the right, a thick old box hedge in front, and wild vines climbing up the walls. The garden was spacious: there was a veritable meadow between the street and the house; there were vegetable beds, tomato and bean plants, raspberry, blackberry, and currant bushes, a compost pile to the right of the house, and, to the left, a wide gravel path leading to the rear entrance, which was framed by two hydrangea bushes. The gravel would crunch underfoot, and by the time Grandfather and I had reached the entrance Grandmother would have heard us coming and opened the door.

The crunch of the gravel, the buzz of the bees, the scratch of the hoe or rake in the garden—since those summers at my grandparents' these have been summer sounds; the bitter scent of the sun-drenched boxwood, the rank odor of the compost, summer smells; and the stillness of the early afternoon, when no child calls, no dog barks, no wind blows, summer stillness. The street where my mother and I lived was full of traffic. Whenever a tram or truck drove by, the windows rattled, and whenever the machines used to demolish and reconstruct the neighborhood buildings bombed during the war went into operation, the floors shook. There was little or no traffic where my grandparents lived, neither in front of the house nor in the nearby town. Whenever a horse and cart drove past, my grandfather would tell me to fetch a shovel and pail and we would coolly collect the dung for the compost pile.

The town had a train station, a landing stage for boats, a few shops, and two or three restaurants, one of which served no alcohol, and my grandparents sometimes took me there for Sunday lunch. Every other day, Grandfather made the rounds of the dairy, the baker's, and the cooperative grocer's, with occasional side trips to the pharmacy or shoemaker's. He wore his off-white linen jacket and a likewise off-white linen cap and carried a notebook in his pocket, one that Grandmother had made by sewing together bits and pieces of blank paper and that he used for shopping lists. He held his walking stick in one hand and my hand in the other. I carried the old leather shopping bag, which, since we made the rounds every other day, was never so full as to weigh me down.

Did Grandfather take me shopping every other day just to make me happy? I loved going shopping: the smell of the Appenzeller and Gruyère in the dairy, the scent of the fresh bread in the bakery, the variety and quantity of food in the grocery. It was so much nicer than the small shop my mother sent me to because she could buy on credit there.

After our shopping expedition we would walk to the lake, feed the swans and ducks with stale bread, and watch the boats sail past or take on and let off passengers. I felt the stillness here as well. The waves beating against the seawall—that too was a summer sound.

Then there were the sounds of the evening and the night. I was allowed to stay up until the blackbird had sung. Lying in bed, I heard no cars and no voices; I heard the church bell toll the hour and the train rumble along the tracks between the house and the lake every half hour. First the up-lake station would ring a bell to signal to the down-lake station that the train was leaving; several minutes later a train would pass, and several minutes after that the down-lake station would signal the train's departure. Since the latter station was farther away than the former, I could barely hear the second bell. Half an hour later the train would come from the down-lake station, the sounds repeating in reverse order. The last train ran shortly past midnight, after which I might hear wind in the trees or rain on the gravel. Otherwise it was perfectly still.

4

LYING IN BED, I never heard footsteps on the gravel: my grandparents did not go out in the evening, nor did they have company. Not until I had been with them for several summers did I realize that they spent their evenings working.

At first I gave no thought to how they earned their keep. I could see that they did not earn money like my mother, who left the house in the morning and came back late in the afternoon. I could also see that much though not all of what graced their table came from their garden. I knew by then what pensions were, but never heard my grandparents lament, as I heard elderly people at home lamenting their low pensions, so I never thought of them as pensioners. I never thought of their financial situation at all.

My grandfather left his memoirs when he died. Only after reading them did I learn where he was from, what he had done, and how he had earned his living. Much as he liked to fill our walks and hikes with stories, he rarely told stories about himself. He would have had many to tell.

He could have told stories about America, where his father had emigrated in the 1890s after a landslide devastated his house and garden and soured him on village life. He took his wife and four children, intending to turn the latter into fine upstanding Americans. They went by train to Basel, by ship to Cologne, and on to Hamburg, New York, Knoxville, and Handsborough by train, ship, and cart. The memoirs recorded Cologne Cathedral in all its glory, the expanse of the Lüneberger Heath, the sea both calm and stormy, and the welcome given them by the Statue of Liberty and by relatives who had settled in America and either thrived or come to grief. Two of my grandfather's siblings died in Handsborough, and a hard-hearted relative granted them burial space only next to, not in, his cemetery. I finally understood why the photograph hanging in my grandparents' bedroom showed a small, attractive cemetery surrounded by a cast-iron grill with a stone gate and two shabby graves set off by boards. The emigrants landed on their feet but were not happy: they were homesick, an illness that can be lethal. Back home in the village church the cause of death of those who had died in Wisconsin or Tennessee or Oregon was again and again announced or recorded as homesickness. Five years after the six emigrants had set off, four returned with the large trunks the village carpenter had made for them.

My grandfather could also have told stories about Italy and France. After apprenticing as a weaver and spinner, he worked for many years in Turin and Paris, and again his memoirs reveal the interest he took in the sights he saw and the countries and peoples he came to know, the miserable wages, the wretched living conditions, the superstitions of the Piedmontese workers, men and women alike, the conflict between Catholicism and secularization, and the growth of nationalism in France. The memoirs likewise reveal how often he suffered from homesickness. But having assumed the management of a Swiss spinning mill, taken a wife, and founded a family, and having bought a house on Swiss soil, he finally felt he was living in accordance with, rather than at odds with, his nature.

When on the eve of the First World War he switched over to a German mill, he did not have to abandon his homeland: he commuted back and forth over the border until the postwar inflation slashed his income, first in Germany, then, even more, in Switzerland. He tried to spend it immediately on items of lasting value, and I still have one of the indestructible woolen blankets that he acquired in great numbers from a disbanded German horse hospital. But horse blankets hardly nourish a woman who must be strong and healthy to conceive and give birth, and so Grandfather started managing another Swiss mill. He remained true to the Germans, however. He was always moved by the fate of Germans abroad, perhaps because he thought they were as homesick as he so often had been.

He would help Grandmother with the cooking, and one of his duties was to take the round metal sieve with freshly washed lettuce leaves outside and swing it until the leaves were dry. Over and over he failed to come back in, and Grandmother would send me out for him. I always found him standing in front of the door staring down at the drops speckling the flagstones. "What's the matter, Grandfather?" The drops reminded him of the Germans scattered over the world.

It was not until after my grandparents had made it through the Great War, the influenza epidemic, and inflation, and after my grandfather had turned the mill into a successful operation, that the son arrived. From that point on there is an occasional snapshot glued into the memoirs: my father with a folded paper cap on his head and a hobbyhorse between his legs, the family seated around the table in the gazebo, my father in suit and tie on his first day at the Gymnasium, the family astride bicycles, each with one foot on the ground and the other on a pedal, as if just about to ride off.

Some pictures are simply lying loose: my grandfather as a school-child, as a newlywed, as a pensioner, and a few years before his death. He is invariably staring straight ahead with a serious, sad, lost look, as if he could not see anybody out there. In the last picture a skinny old-man's neck topped by a furrowed face is sticking out of an oversize collar like a tortoise head out of its shell; the eyes are timorous now, reflecting a soul ready to retreat behind stubbornness and a fear of people. He once told me that all his life he had suffered from headaches stretching from the left temple via the left ear to the back of the head, "like a feather in a hat." The word "depression" never came up, and he probably had no idea that a patient claiming to be sad, lost, and fearful might well be diagnosed as having such a condition, though who knew that at the time? Still, it rarely reached the stage that kept him from getting out of bed and working.

He retired at the age of fifty-five. The mill had been merely a way of putting bread on the table: his passions were history, society, politics. He and some friends purchased a newspaper and became its publishers. But their position vis-à-vis Swiss neutrality ran counter to that of public opinion, and their limited financial resources made them vulnerable to the competition. The venture gave him and his friends more pain than pleasure, and after a few years they were forced to abandon it. But his activities as a newspaper publisher had brought him into contact with book publishers, and the last project he undertook—and worked on every evening with my grandmother—was to edit a collection of short fiction he called *Novels for Your Reading Pleasure and Entertainment.*

5

HE LIVED FOR the history he read in books and recounted to me on our walks. No stroll, no hike, no march, as he liked to call them, was complete without a story from Swiss or German history, especially military history. He kept an all-but-inexhaustible trove of battle maps in his head and would draw them in the ground with his walking stick: Morgarten, Sempach, Sankt Jakob an der Birs, Grandson, Murten, Nancy, Marignano, Rossbach, Leuthen, Zorndorf, Waterloo, Königgrätz, Sedan, Tannenberg, and many others I have since forgotten. He had the gift of bringing a story alive.

I had my favorite battles, stories I wanted to hear over and over. The Battle of Morgarten. Count Leopold leads the cream of Austrian knighthood into battle as if it were a hunting party, expecting an easy victory and quick spoils from the supposedly poorly armed, defenseless Swiss. But the Swiss are battle-tested and battle-ready; they know what they are fighting for: freedom, home, hearth, wife, and children. They know too where Leopold will make his move: a knight by the name of von Hünenberg, a good neighbor and friend of the young Swiss Confederation, has shot an arrow with an admonitory parchment into their camp. When the narrow street is jammed with Austrian knights and progress is slow, they rain rocks and tree trunks down upon them, thereby driving a good number of them into the lake and, weighed down as they are by their armor, a watery grave. Then they descend upon the rest in person, and a massacre ensues.

I was impressed by the valor of the Swiss, but I was also worried by von Hünenberg's arrow. Wasn't he a traitor? Didn't his betrayal tarnish the glory of the Swiss?

"Your father asked the same question." Grandfather nodded. "Well?"

"Von Hünenberg was a free man. He didn't need to side with the Austrians; he could side with the Swiss or with no one."

"But he wasn't fighting for the Swiss. He was underhanded about it."

"He couldn't have helped the Swiss any more if he had fought with them. If you can do the right thing only by being under-handed, being underhanded doesn't make it wrong."

I wanted to know what had happened to von Hünenberg. But my grandfather did not know.

The Battle of Sempach. Once more the Austrians trust to their heavy armor; once more they underestimate the prowess and courage of the peasants and shepherds. At first the Swiss are unable to wedge their way into the Austrians' front, bristling as it is with spears, but by noon—it is the hottest day of the year—the sun has made the knights' armor red-hot and heavy, and when Arnold von Winkelried seizes all the spears he can and buries them with his dying body, the Austrians are too exhausted to put up any resist-ance. Once more they are totally defeated.

My first reaction was one of astonishment: How could Arnold von Winkelried, in the midst of his heroic feat, find time to say, "I wish to pave the way for freedom, fellow countrymen. Care for my wife and children!"

But my grandfather would not rest until I understood that the Austrians lost because they had failed to learn the lesson of Mor-garten. "Underestimating the Swiss, using heavy armor, ignoring the vagaries of nature—this time sun rather than water—anyone can make a mistake, but no one should make the same mistake twice."

Once I had grasped this lesson, I was ready for its successor: "One must learn not only from the harm one suffers but also from the harm one inflicts." He told me about the English who won battle after battle with their longbows but were at a total loss when the French built their own longbows and turned them to good use.

The Battle at Sankt Jakob an der Birs. The very name of the enemy—the Armagnacs—was enough to terrify the Swiss. Grandfather described the army of thirty thousand: mercenaries from France, Spain, and England steeled by long service in the Hundred Years' War and inured to atrocities and plunder. The French king has no more need of them and is only too glad to offer them and their leader, the crown-hungry dauphin, to the Austrians. The Swiss number fifteen hundred. Sent out to reconnoiter rather than attack but seduced into one skirmish after another, they are finally faced with the entire Armagnac army. They retreat to the Sankt Jakob Infirmary, where they fight bravely into the night and to the last man. The Armagnacs are victorious but suffer so many casualties that they lose their taste for war and sue for peace.

"What's the lesson this time?"

Grandfather laughed. "That there are times when doing something crazy is right, provided you do it all the way."

6

THERE WAS ANOTHER THING about which Grandfather told tale after tale: mistaken verdicts. Here too I had my favorites, ones I requested over and over; here too we discussed the moral implications of the tales. They were momentous. For though mistaken verdicts are unjust by definition, the more famous of them often have a historical significance that goes far beyond injustice and can even transform injustice into justice.

Take the case of Count von Schmettau against a miller by the name of Arnold. The miller refuses to pay the count his quitrent because he says a local official has grabbed the bread out of his mouth by diverting his millrace into a pond for raising carp. The count takes the miller to court. The count wins in the first and second rounds and finally at the Supreme Court in Berlin. The miller writes to Frederick the Great, who, suspecting the favoritism, bribery, and disgraceful hocus-pocus involved, orders the judges thrown in jail, the pond filled in, and the verdict against the miller rescinded. This order was arbitrary and unjust: the miller's millrace had plenty of water, and had he run the mill as he should have done, he would have been able to pay the quitrent. In other words, the miller was a scoundrel. But the case served to establish Frederick's reputation as a righteous king and Prussia as a state in which all—weak and strong, rich and poor—were equal before the law.

The trial against Joan of Arc may not have transformed injustice into justice, but it did give rise to a situation that would hardly have been possible otherwise. Joan, a beautiful peasant girl of sixteen, arrives at the court of a Charles too weak to besiege the English and have himself crowned king of France at Reims. Joan miraculously leads the French into battle and on to victory, captures Orléans, clears the way for Charles' coronation, and marches on Paris. There she is taken prisoner and sold to the English. The king, who could perhaps have had her liberated, does nothing. Joan, steadfast, is tortured and raped, sentenced to death for witchcraft and sorcery by Bishop Pierre Couchon, and burned at the stake. However, the trial and its verdict make her a martyr for the French cause and a symbol of liberation, and twenty years later the English are ousted. Just as without Arnold the miller there would have been no rule of law in Prussia, so without Joan of Arc, France would not have been liberated.

One of the stories, though, had no redeeming features. In 1846 the beautiful daughter of a Protestant tailor in Nancy, Mennon Elkner, and the son of a Catholic executioner, Eugène Duirwiel, fell in love. The executioner, who had learned of their love from a neighbor of the tailor's, wrung a statement from Mennon to the effect that she would break with Eugène. She was doubly despondent: she had lost her beloved and was pregnant. She brought two stillborn boys into the world and buried them in her garden. But the neighbor had been spying again, and Mennon was arrested, accused of double infanticide, and sentenced to death by the sword. One might guess what is to come. But what comes is even more gruesome than one might guess. Eugène had just taken over his father's duties and went to his first execution knowing only that it was a case of double infanticide. When he recognized Mennon in the murderess, he grew pale, his head spun, his knees buckled, and his hands shook. Urged on by his father, who was at his side, and by the other officials present, he delivered two blows with his sword, wounding Mennon on her chin and shoulder, but then flung the sword down and neither would nor could go on with it. There being a schedule to be observed and a family's honor to be saved, the executioner lunged at Mennon with his knife to complete his son's job for him. With each stab, the crowd grew more restless until it stormed the platform.

Grandmother, who would recite poems about the battles of Lützen and Hochstädt, about Arnold and Joan of Arc, also knew a perfectly unpoetic, inartistic poem about the fate of the fair Mennon. Whenever Grandfather came to the point in the story when the crowd revolted, he would stop and say, "Ask Grandmother. She's a lot better at telling how it ends."

I can't reconstruct the entire poem. The last two stanzas went something like this:

> *The executioners were stoned by all;*
> *They died a painful death that very day.*
> *But could Mennon to safety make her way?*

For yet she lived and to her God did call.
They bore her full of hope to a free bed,
But soon thereafter they pronounced her dead.

Five sacrifices form this gruesome tale.
Although from love most true it did arise,
It ended in a bloodbath, woe, and bale.
Who does not shudder at such acts unwise?
Yet there's a happy ending one may proffer:
Perhaps they made their peace in the hereafter.

7

GRANDMOTHER'S ONLY CONTACT with wars, battles, heroic deeds, trials, and verdicts was through poetry. She regarded war as a stupid, stupid game that men were not yet mature enough—and perhaps would never be mature enough—to abandon. She forgave Grandfather his passion for things martial because he joined her in her battle against alcohol, which she considered nearly as great a scourge as war, and for woman suffrage, and because he always respected her other, peaceful, feminine way of viewing and conceptualizing things. It may well have been respect that brought their marriage about and held it together.

One summer, when Grandfather was working in Italy, he had a visit from his mother. She had come to remind him that it was time for him to start a family, and told him about various young women, giving him to believe that he would not be rejected should he propose. Among them was a cousin she had seen at a funeral and taken a liking to. The following summer Grandfather visited his parents, helped to bring in the hay, and roamed the countryside alone, seeking out the fortresses he had read about in his beloved history books. At one point his mother suggested he visit his aunt. There he met the cousin, whom he had not seen since childhood. A photograph taken at the time shows a young woman with luxuriant dark hair, a proud, lively look in her eye, and a mouth whose full lips hold the promise of sensuality and at the same time seem ready to twitch into laughter. It made you wonder what the local young men were waiting for and why she had waited for a man with already thinning hair. His memoirs record a brief conversation at a window and how he was "surprised at her clever thoughts and the placid, resolute—yet never immodest—way she had of expressing them to her rather overbearing cousin." They then exchanged a few letters, "the contents of which I cannot recall," whereupon his proposal, in writing, was accepted, likewise in writing. The engagement was celebrated a year later; the wedding, a year after that.

I don't know whether it was a happy marriage; I don't even know whether it makes sense to speak of the happiness of their marriage or whether they ever thought about it. They lived a life together, took the good with the bad, respected each other, relied on each other. I never once saw them have a serious argument, though they often teased and even poked fun at each other. They took pleasure in being together and showing themselves together, he the dignified personage he had become in his old age, she the beautiful woman she had remained. Yet there was always a shadow over them. Everything about them was subdued: the joy, the joking and laughing, the talks about the things of this world. It was my father's early death that had cast its shadow over them, and the shadow never waned.

That too was something I realized only after reading Grandfather's memoirs. At times my grandparents spoke of my father with such immediacy and lack of artifice that I never had the feeling they wanted to withhold information about him from me. I learned which of Grandfather's stories he preferred, that he had collected stamps, sung in the church choir, played handball, drawn, painted, and been a voracious reader; that he had been nearsighted, a good pupil and law student, and never done military service. There was a picture of him in the living room, a slim young man in herringbone knickerbockers standing in front of a wall, his right arm resting on the ledge, his calves crossed. The posture is nonchalant, but the look behind his glasses is impatient, wondering what is going to come next, ready to turn to something else if it fails to engage him. I found intelligence, resolve, and a bit of arrogance in his face, though maybe only because they were qualities I wished for myself. Our eyes had a certain slant to them, one more than the other. Apart from that, I could see no similarity.

But that was enough for me. My mother never brought up my father and never hung a picture of him anywhere. I had heard from my grandparents that he perished in the war while serving with the Swiss Red Cross. Perished, fallen, missing in action—these formulas of finality I had heard so often as a child that I came to think of them as immutable monuments. The pictures of men in uniform I saw at my friends' houses, some with black crêpe trimming their silver frames, made me as uncomfortable as the pictures of the dead adorning gravestones in some countries. It is as if people refused to leave their dead alone, forced them back into the light, made them keep their composure even in death. If that was how war widows commemorated their dead husbands, then I preferred my mother's renunciation of visual commemoration.

But dead and far away as my father was, we were bound by one thing. Grandmother once told me that my father liked poetry and that Theodor Fontane's "John Maynard" was one of his favorite poems. I learned it by heart that very evening. She was pleased, and over the years she would point out one or another poem my father had liked, and I would set to immediately. She knew many poems by heart herself and may simply have been happy to see me spend my evenings memorizing poetry.

8

ONCE THE SUPPER TABLE was cleared, the dishes washed, and the flowers in the garden watered, my grandparents would set to work on the *Novels for Your Reading Pleasure and Entertainment* series. They worked at the dining table, pulling the ceiling lamp down and reading and editing the manuscripts, the page proofs, and the bound galleys. Sometimes they did some writing as well: they insisted that each volume conclude with a brief didactic essay, and when none was forthcoming they supplied it themselves. They wrote about the importance of toothbrushing, the battle against snoring, the principles of beekeeping, the history of the postal system, Konrad Escher's attempts to control the River Linth, the last days of Ulrich von Hutten. They also rewrote passages in the novels when they found them awkward, unbelievable, or immodest or when they felt they could make a better point. The publisher gave them a free hand.

When I was old enough to stay up after the blackbird had finished its song, I was allowed to sit with them. The light of the lamp just above the table, the dark of the room surrounding it—I loved it. I would read or learn a poem or write a letter to my mother or an entry in my summer diary. Whenever I interrupted my grandparents to ask a question, I got a friendly answer. I was afraid though to ask too many: I could sense their concentration. The remarks they exchanged were sparse, and my questions sounded garrulous. So I read, wrote, and studied in silence.

From time to time I lifted my head cautiously, so as not to be noticed, and observed them: Grandfather, his dark eyes now riveted on the work before him, now gazing out, lost, into the distance, and Grandmother, who did everything with a light touch, reading with a smile and making corrections with a quick and easy hand. Yet the work must have been much harder on her than on him: while he cared only for history books and had a neutral, objective relationship to the novels they dealt with, she loved literature, fiction as well as verse, and had a sure feeling for it; she must have suffered from having to spend so much time on such banal texts.

I was not allowed to read them. If I grew curious when they talked about one or another novel, I was told in no uncertain terms I was not to read it: there was a better novel or a better novella on the subject by Conrad Ferdinand Meyer or Gottfried Keller or another classic Swiss writer. Grandmother would then get up and bring me the better book.

When they gave me the extra copies of the bound galleys to take home as scrap paper, they made a point of reminding me not to read them. They would not have given them to me at all had paper not been so expensive at the time and my mother's income so low. For many of my school years, everything I did not have to hand in to the teacher I wrote on the back of the bound galleys: Latin, Greek, and English vocabulary words, first drafts of compositions, plot summaries, descriptions of famous paintings, world capitals, rivers and mountains, important dates, and notes to classmates a few desks away. The galleys were on heavy paper and nearly a centimeter thick. The books grew thinner and thinner as I tore pages out of them, but the staples held the remaining pages together. I liked the thick pads of thick paper, and because I was a good boy I refrained from reading the printed sides of the pages for years.

9

DURING THE FIRST few summers my grandparents found the life
I was leading with them too isolated, and tried to bring me into
contact with children my own age. They knew their neighbors and
by talking to a number of families arranged for me to be invited to
birthday parties, outings, and visits to the local swimming pool.
Since it took a lot of doing and they did it out of love, I did not
dare resist, but I was always happy when the event was over and I
could return to them.

I had trouble understanding the dialect the children spoke; I
did not understand their allusions. Their educational system, their
school and after-school activities, their social organization were
completely different from mine. Whereas their school provided
after-school activities like sports or chorus or dramatics, my friends
and I were left to our own devices. The gangs we formed and the
wars we fought were harmless, but they had not prepared me for
the civilized, structured games of the Swiss children.

Even pool behavior differed from what I was used to: there were
no water battles; nobody was tossed into the pool or ducked
underwater. They played a kind of fast and fair water polo, boys
and girls together—and equal. The pool was a wooden construction on the lakeshore. Non-swimmers could romp on a twenty-
meter-square surface of boards that sloped under the water from
one meter to one meter seventy, rested on wooden piles, and was
surrounded on three sides by changing cubicles and catwalks;
swimmers who wished to move beyond it to the lake proper had
only to duck under a rope on the fourth side. Once, out of sheer
social frustration, I impressed the Swiss children by climbing onto
the roof of the outermost cubicle and jumping into the lake from
there.

Friendships might have grown out of these contacts had we seen one another more often, but the Swiss children's summer holidays began soon after I arrived, and they would disperse, returning only shortly before my departure. One boy and I bonded over an interest in the conquest of the North and South Poles. Was Cook a con man and Peary a dilettante, Scott great or mad or both, Amundsen filled with a sense of mission or merely obsessed by ambition? The boy's father seemed to like me as well. "You have your father's eyes," he said to me the first time he saw me. He said it with a sad but friendly smile that perplexed me more than the remark itself. Yet despite these promising beginnings, the projected correspondence between the boy and me never materialized.

So I spent my summer holidays without playmates my own age; I spent them taking the same walks to the lake and hikes through a ravine, around a pond, and up a hill with a view of the lake and the Alps; I spent them going on the same excursions to the Rapperswil fortress, Ufenau Island, the cathedral, the museums, the Kunsthalle. These hikes and excursions were as much a part of the summer as harvesting apples, berries, lettuce, and vegetables, hoeing beds, weeding, snipping wilted flowers, trimming hedges, mowing grass, tending the compost, keeping the watering can filled, and doing the watering. Just as these operations recurred naturally, so the recurrence of the other activities struck me as natural. The never-changing evenings at the table under the lamp thus belonged to the natural rhythm of summer.

IO

ONE SUMMER WAS different from the others. For one summer I had a playmate: a girl from a small Ticino village spent the vacation with her great-aunt, our neighbor. Things did not go well. The woman, ailing and barely able to walk, had thought the girl would read aloud to her, play patience with her, and knit. The girl had looked forward to being near the big city. To make matters worse, great-aunt knew next to no Italian, great-niece next to no German.

But Lucia had the gift of simply ignoring the language problem. When she spoke to me through the fence in Italian and I replied in German that I didn't understand, she just kept on, as if I had made perfect sense of her words. Then she stopped and waited until I said something about the school where I was studying Latin. She beamed at me so expectantly and encouragingly that I went on, saying whatever came into my head, trying to turn the Latin vocabulary I had learned in the past two years into Italian words. She laughed, and I joined her.

Then Grandfather would come and talk to her in Italian, and it all bubbled out of her: sentences, laughter, jubilation, pure joy. Her cheeks glowed, her dark eyes shone, and when she shook her head her curly brown locks swung back and forth. I suddenly felt something I could not identify or name; I knew only that it was powerful. It canceled the beautiful moment we had just shared. Lucia had betrayed it; I had been disgraced. I have experienced stronger bouts of jealousy since then, but never have I felt as helpless as I did that first time.

It passed. All summer, whenever Grandfather and I invited her to join us, she would give me to understand that she and I belonged together no matter how much she and Grandfather flirted in Italian. "She's got you under her spell," Grandmother would say with a smile when she saw us prettying ourselves up for an outing with her.

Grandmother came with us on the boat ride to Ufenau as she did every year. She loved Conrad Ferdinand Meyer and knew the several hundred couplets of his poem "Hutten's Last Days" by heart. On the island, she could celebrate her fondness for him, his work, and poetry in general. She too was under Lucia's spell: her wonder, her trust, her gaiety. When on the trip home Lucia and I sat down facing them, Grandfather took Grandmother's hand. It was the only sign of intimacy I ever saw between them. Today I wonder whether they had hoped in vain for a daughter or perhaps even lost one, but then I was simply happy: we had had a nice day on the island, we were having a nice evening on the lake, my grandparents loved each other and the two of us, and on the walk home Lucia had taken my hand.

Did I love her? I had as little a concept of love as I had of jealousy. I looked forward to seeing Lucia, missed her when she was not with me, was disappointed when we wanted to see each other but could not, was happy when she was happy and unhappy when she was unhappy and even more when she was cross. She would grow cross from one minute to the next. When something did not go her way, when I failed to understand her or she me, when I was less attentive to her than she required. Often I thought she was unjustified, but to argue over justice was linguistically pointless: I had barely formed *giustizia* from *iustitia*. And in any case, I suspected Lucia was not much interested in discussions about justice. I learned to submit to her happiness and crossness like the weather, which one could not count on, only accept with joy or sorrow.

We had little time to ourselves: Lucia had to play patience and knit with her great-aunt; she had to massage her head and feet; she had to listen to her. "If she can't understand me, she can at least listen to me," the woman told my grandmother when she once pleaded Lucia's cause. Lucia wanted to do as many of the things Grandfather and I did together—walks, hikes, excursions, gardening—as possible. Once she even took part in a dung-collecting expedition. Sometimes we sat in the tree house we had built in the apple tree with Grandfather's assistance, but building the house had been more fun than playing in it, and we had less of a language problem when we were active. We did not exchange addresses at the end of the summer. What would we have done with them?

I had no concept of beauty either. Lucia's ebullience, her quick-wittedness, her dancing curls, her eyes, her facial expressions, her mouth, her pearly, bubbly, gurgly laugh, her wit, her gravity, her tears—they all fell together: I was unable to differentiate between character, behavior, and appearance. Only her dimple held a unique fascination for me.

How could the forehead above the inner end of the left eyebrow be so smooth, yet suddenly show a dimple? It was a dimple of confusion, embarrassment, disappointment, and sadness. It moved me because it spoke to me when Lucia would not or could not. It would perk me up even when she was cross and even though her being cross made me unhappy and I was afraid to make her crosser by showing her the effect it had on me.

By the time I fell in love with a classmate a few years later, I had developed concepts of beauty, love, and jealousy, and what I experienced with her pushed my concept-free experience with Lucia into the background. I had the feeling I was falling in love for the first time. I had even forgotten Lucia's farewell gift.

On the morning of the day before she was to go home she helped my grandparents and me in the garden as she had occasionally done before. She then took her leave of the garden and my grandparents: she would be spending the rest of the day with her great-aunt and would have time the next morning only for the briefest of farewells. When I took her home, she showed me a door that opened on the steps to the cellar. "Come back at six. I'll be waiting."

It was the door to the laundry. I pushed it open just wide enough to be able to slip in, then pushed it shut. I saw a large copper cauldron, various tubs and buckets, a washboard and a stomper, and I smelled the freshly washed, white linens hanging on

clotheslines. The two windows were large, but the vines growing
along the grating did not let in much light. Everything lay in a
dusky green.

Lucia was waiting for me. She stood on the far side of the room
holding a finger before her lips, so I said nothing and did not
move. After we looked at each other for a moment, she bent and
lifted the hem of her skirt and showed me her genitalia. Then she
gave me a provocative nod, and I understood and undid my belt,
unbuttoned my shorts, pushed them down my legs along with my
underpants, and stood up straight. I had never had an erection,
nor did I have one then. Unlike Lucia, I had no pubic hair. But my
face was burning and my heart pounding, and I was overcome by
desire, though for what I did not know.

We stood there facing each other for a while. Then she smiled,
let go of the dress with her right hand, and walked up to me. She
was still holding the skirt with her left hand, so a bit of her naked
stomach and naked thighs and genitalia were still visible, and I
could not tell whether I should look at them or at her face, in
which I found something that had a similar effect on me as her
nakedness. She took my head in her right hand, pressed her mouth
briefly to mine, and let my body feel a breath of hers. Before I
could come to, she turned and disappeared through the other door
into the house. I could hear her running along the passageway and
up the stairs, and another door opening and closing.

II

WAS IT AFTER THAT that I started reading the forbidden sides of
the proofs? Had the romance I had experienced with Lucia aroused

a desire in me for the romance of literature? Or did it happen later, when I simply had nothing better to do? During a boring class? When I was tired of doing my homework? On the train, having nothing else to read? When I was thirteen, my mother and I moved out of the city to a village where she had bought a small house, and I had to take a train to school.

The first novel I read was about a German soldier who had escaped from a Russian POW camp and braved a number of dangers on the journey home. I soon forgot the adventures but not his homecoming. He makes it all the way to Germany, finds the city his wife is living in, finds the house, finds the flat. He rings the doorbell; the door opens. There stands his wife as beautiful and young as he remembered her through the long years of war and captivity—no, more beautiful and, if a bit older, more mature, more feminine, womanly. But she does not look happy to see him; she stares at him, horrified, as if seeing a ghost. And she is carrying a little girl who can be no more than two, while another one, a bit older, clings to her and peeks out coyly from behind her apron; moreover, a man is standing next to her with his arm around her.

Do the men fight over the woman? Do they know each other from before? Are they meeting for the first time? Does the man with his arm around the woman deceive her and tell her the other man fell in action? Or does he even pose as the other soldier home from the war or captivity? Does the woman fall in love with him without a second thought and put her old life behind her? Or does she take him on without love, out of need, because she is unable to brave her loss and start anew? Because she needs a man to care for her and her first daughter. The daughter by her first husband, who now stands before her in tatters, disbelief, and despair.

I was not to know: I had used the blank sides of the paper the proofs were printed on and torn out and disposed of the first pages. The first pages were the last pages of the novel.

12

I WANTED TO READ the end of the novel the following summer.
I had thrown away the last pages but still had the first page and
hence both author and title. I knew that my grandparents kept
the complete series in their bedroom; it filled shelf after shelf of a
tall, narrow bookcase.

I did not think the novel would be hard to locate. True, the
bound galleys did not have the serial numbers that the finished
copies had and that served to order them in the bookcase, but since
I had been given the bound galleys the summer before and the
novels came out at a rate of two a month, I expected to find the
one I was looking for among the latest twenty-four. I did not.
I knew that my grandparents sometimes altered the titles, so I
looked for it under the author's name. When I had no success there
either, I suspected that they had changed both title and author, and
I looked at the opening passage of each novel. In the end I found
neither the title nor the author nor the opening passage. Not even
after I extended my search to include earlier titles and pulled out
one after another did I find the novel. But I did not work my way
through all the approximately four hundred of them. After the first
sunny week it rained steadily to the end of my stay. My grandparents could not do any gardening, and I could find no excuse to run
upstairs, slip into their bedroom, and continue my search.

By the following summer I had forgotten the novel. It was the
last time I spent the whole vacation with my grandparents. My
friends had started taking trips together or going on exchange visits to England and France. I was asked if I wanted to go on a bicycle trip. I could not afford it. I had been delivering magazines for a
year and earned a decent wage, but needed the money: the pur-

chase of the house had put a financial strain on my mother, and I had to pay for my own clothes and books.

I was disappointed at having to give up the bicycle trip, but I still looked forward to spending the summer with my grandparents. I found it annoying to be babied by my mother and told what to do all the time. At my grandparents' I enjoyed being treated like someone who was free to be himself and was taken seriously and loved. I looked forward to waking up in my bed under Stückelberg's *Girl with a Lizard,* helping Grandmother with the cooking and asking her for a poem while we worked, bringing Grandfather back into the kitchen from his Germans scattered all over the world, and sitting with the two of them at the brightly lit table; I looked forward to the scent of Grandmother's eau de toilette in the bathroom, to the potted linden in Grandfather's study, the plates with the red blossoms around the edges, the cutlery with the ivory handles, the giant cheese dome; I looked forward to the summer quiet, the summer noises, the summer smells.

As a result I experienced everything intensely. Many of my memories of house and garden, of village, lake, and landscape derive from images of this last summer.

During my student years the visits were brief: a few days before or after Christmas, a few after summer semester ended or before the winter semester began. I would send Grandfather the papers I thought might interest him; he would immediately write back an appreciative letter, setting aside the critical questions, of which he had many, until we next met. He in turn collected newspaper clippings for me, mainly about the Germans in Silesia, Transylvania, and Kazakhstan, whom he felt I was insufficiently concerned about. Once a semester I received a parcel with a packet of clippings, a packet of dried apple slices, and a five-mark banknote.

13

THE WINTER BEFORE my comprehensive exam I was nervous about getting through the material and thought of canceling my Christmas visit, but my grandparents insisted on my coming: I didn't need to stay long, they wrote, but I had to come. It was urgent.

They had always kept their house tidy, but during this last visit the tidiness was oppressive. They had parted with everything that they did not absolutely need and that they felt I, their only grandson, would have no interest in. They did not want to go to an old people's home; they wanted to keep their house. But they were making ready for death and could bear nothing superfluous, nothing gratuitous around them.

They went from room to room asking me what I wanted. Many familiar objects had already gone, and the shelves and cupboards they opened were half empty. I wanted everything: everything was full of memories, and everything I took would help me to keep the memory alive. But there was a message in the sobriety with which they were preparing for death: I could take very little. During my university years and early career I would have a small flat and be unable to afford storage costs: I could use only what could fit into one room. Grandfather's desk and armchair, perhaps? His history books? Grandmother's Gotthelf, Keller, and Meyer? The picture of the mill Grandfather had run? I had a lump in my throat; I could not speak; I nodded to everything.

The *Novels for Your Reading Pleasure and Entertainment* were still there, but my grandparents did not offer them, nor did I ask for them. They would certainly have given them to me. I could also have confessed that I had ignored their admonition and read first the novel about the soldier coming home, then others in the series. After giving up their editorship and closing the series, they expressed a certain pride in the novels, which an editor in Bern had praised as the best of their kind. Besides, they were perfectly cheerful about their preparations for death. I was often on the point of tears during my visit; they were not.

When I left, Grandfather took me to the station as usual; as usual he had found me a seat in the right coach and the right compartment. The coach was in the middle of the train because it would be safer there should a collision take place. The other person in the compartment was an elderly woman to whom he introduced me as his grandson and whom he asked to keep an eye on me. As usual he would not let me accompany him back onto the platform after our farewell embrace. I leaned out of the window and saw him alight and walk toward the exit. At the end of the platform he turned and waved; I waved back.

Several weeks later my grandparents were run over by a car. They had been shopping in the village and were on their way home. The driver was drunk and drove onto the sidewalk. Grandmother died before the ambulance arrived; Grandfather died in the hospital. He died shortly after midnight, but I decided that their common tombstone should bear the same date.

Part Two

I

I STILL HAVE Grandfather's desk and armchair. I also have Grandmother and Grandfather's book and the picture of the mill. The desk and armchair first took up residence in my room at my mother's house; they came with me to the first place I lived in on my own—a room with a kitchenette, shower stall, and view of the station—and then to the apartment in one of the dilapidated apartment buildings still common at the time, the kind with high ceilings, molding, and double doors, which my girlfriend and I moved into after she had her child. When we separated and I moved out, I stored the desk and chair with the rest of my belongings.

I had to get away. Away from my beautiful, moody, faithless girlfriend, away from her whining fidget of a son, and away from the city I had grown up in and gone to school and university in, a city where memories lurked around every corner. It took all the courage I could muster, but I quit my job at the university without another prospect in the offing, sold the Swiss bonds I had inherited from my grandparents, and set off.

Actually there was nothing particularly courageous about quitting the job. I had spent six years sweating over a doctoral dissertation I would never finish. I had known it for ages but could not bring myself to admit it. The uses of justice was the topic, a topic worthy of my grandfather and one that anybody could go on reading and thinking about forever. But my thoughts refused to coalesce into a system; they remained random and anecdotal: grand-fatherly thoughts on a grandfatherly topic. I intended to demon-strate that justice is of use only insofar as its claims are formulated and put into practice without concern for social utility. *Fiat iustitia, pereat mundus:* Justice be done though the world perish. Such was the proper motto for justice in my view, and if the world held that obedience to the claims of justice would lead to doom and destruc-tion, it was free to refuse obedience and take responsibility for the result, but justice was under no obligation to mitigate its claims.

I collected example after example, from the cases made by Grandfather and the show trials orchestrated by Freisler and Hilde Benjamin to decisions brought down by our Constitutional Court, which, rather than pursuing justice, had attempted to mediate or mollify political conflicts or otherwise serve a socially useful func-tion. Granted, Frederick the Great, Bishop Pierre Couson, Freisler, Hilde Benjamin, and the judges of the German Constitutional Court had different conceptions of justice, but I believed I could demonstrate that given the political nature of their verdicts they were all aware that they were not serving justice alone—whatever they may have meant by it—but other goals as well. These other goals were as different as their conceptions of justice—the good of the king or the Church, racial purity, class struggle, peace—but they were similar in that they were more important to them than the justice in the name of which the proceedings were carried out and the decisions taken.

So far so good. But how was I to take the good it sometimes did and the damage it caused, the good and damage to justice and soci-ety, the good and damage in the short and long run, and balance and weigh them? In the end what I grew tired of was not so much the topic as my thoughts, incapable as they were of constructing the system they needed to construct. I grew tired of the endless words, the words I read, the words I thought and wrote. I wanted to get away from more than my girlfriend and her son and the city; I wanted to get away from all those words.

Nor was the decision to pick up and go particularly courageous. I intended to spend several months in America, and though I had never been on my own for so long or so far away from home, there were people in New York and San Francisco I could stay with and even the hope of finding relatives in Knoxville and Handsborough on the way to the West Coast. What could go wrong?

Yet the days immediately preceding my departure were pure torture. I was not afraid of planes plummeting or trains derailing: I would not have minded had my journey met a precipitous end. But being in a foreign country, being deprived of what I was accustomed to and familiar with—which suddenly seemed so right, so suitable, so fitting—now became terrifying beyond measure. I had Grandfather's homesickness even before leaving. I nearly asked my girlfriend if we might not get back together. Then, the moment my travels began, the homesickness disappeared.

South of San Francisco I found paradise: a place of luxuriant gardens, open fields, and a handful of buildings that merged with the surroundings and were screened from the road by a wooded area, a series of rocky terraces leading down to the Pacific, all sunny and warm and infused with the aroma of flowers and the sea. The buildings housed a dining hall, meeting rooms, and accommodation for about sixty guests. The meeting rooms and fields were used for yoga classes, tai chi, breathing exercises, and meditation. In group therapy sessions, whose names and methods I no longer remember, the meek learned to rage and the furious learned the joys of silence and humility. On one of the rocky terraces you could lie all night in a pool of hot sulfur spring water, gazing up at the stars with nothing but the sound of the ocean in your ears. Before long your thoughts would slow down, then cease; then even your dreaming ceased and you were at total peace with yourself.

Had it not been so expensive, I would have succumbed and stayed another week, another month, another year. But after laying out half my savings in three weeks, I decided to go to a school I had learned about there, a San Francisco massage institute where in three months I could train to be a masseur. Of all my experiences in paradise I had been most impressed by massage. I had had no idea that contact without words—or sexuality or eros—could reach so deep, that hands could do so much good, that bodies undergoing massage could become so beautiful, and that massaging a happy person could make one happy. I wanted to feel at home in this corporeal world. The fee was moderate. My contact in San Francisco, a painter with a large apartment, let me stay with him free. When I expressed sadness at having to leave paradise, my instructor comforted me by saying that instead of being sad to leave I should be happy at the prospect of returning.

I put in my three months at the massage institute: I massaged and was massaged; I went to lectures on anatomy and on the ethical and economic aspects of massage as an occupation; I spent the weekends memorizing the Latin names for bones and joints, muscles and tendons, and practicing their American pronunciation; and in the evenings of the last few weeks I studied for the final. I passed. I was happy to have learned what I learned, happy that my bad English kept me from trying to sound clever and witty, that words played no role whatsoever in what I was doing. I had inhabited a new world and found the distance I had been seeking from the old one. Only the jabs of the painter, by the end of my stay a good friend, occasionally spoiled my good mood. The way I went about learning the trade, he said, was all work and discipline. I was a monster: super-German, super-Protestant. What had my mother done to me? What had I done to myself?

2

ON MY FLIGHT BACK to Germany I toyed with the idea of making a life for myself as a masseur in California. But on the train ride from the airport to my hometown, a route that ran through an overdeveloped landscape strewn with tidy cities crisscrossed by sparkling-clean rain-washed streets of well-tended houses with well-tended gardens and fences, I became painfully aware of how false a world it was, yet how much a part of it I was, so much so that I could never leave it. It was simply out of the question.

I stayed with my mother for the first few weeks. We hardly saw each other: she left the house early, came home late, and was soon in bed. She was a private secretary. She had started working for her boss when he was an underling and came up in the world with him. She always kept abreast of the latest secretarial techniques, secretarial practices, and secretarial styles. When her boss broke off their affair, which had gone on for barely a year, she went back to being just a secretary, though she was ready to help when a woman's touch was required. That she was always there for him he took for granted. In his own way he was as loyal as she: not only did he take her with him as he climbed the ladder; he made sure she received an off-scale salary.

That made her proud. She had hoped to study medicine but could not qualify because her education had been interrupted by compulsory labor during the war. After the war she had me to care for and hence a living to earn. Her parents had been well-to-do but were picked off by a low-flying aircraft while fleeing at the war's end. By the time she received her payment for war losses, it was too late for her to study, so she used the money to buy the house in the village we moved to. Did she blame me and my birth for having spoiled her plans? She would have been a good doctor: she was precise, she had a good eye for what mattered and what did not, and she kept on top of things. What she lacked in warmth, she would have made up for in vigilance and commitment: her patients might not have liked her, but they would certainly have felt they were in good hands.

She lived a life that was all duty, much as if she had been a doctor. Perhaps she hated herself for having devoted all her energy and discipline to the pursuit of money and nothing higher. I grew up with the refrain that school was a privilege and if she had to work so hard for her salary I could do the same or more for the privilege of studying. She was disappointed, even annoyed, that I had given up on my dissertation, but she had never made things easy for me: I had had to go on delivering magazines even after the monthly installments for the house were no longer a burden for her, and to supplement the meager allowance she gave me when I was at university. She had disapproved of my trip to America, and she was unhappy about my taking the first job that came along upon my return.

Fortunately the job was not long in coming. I found a position as an editor and enjoyed it from day one. The publisher was looking to expand his list of legal titles and also charged me with starting up a journal and a series of textbooks. I had often been frustrated by the existing journals and textbooks, and I could make full use of my teaching experience to better them. I was sure I knew what students needed.

The publishing house had its office in the neighboring city, and I moved into a place nicer than any I had lived in before. The three stories of a private house built in the twenties had been remodeled into three apartments, and mine, the middle one, had two small rooms and a large one with a balcony overlooking a field lined with fir trees that hid the neighboring houses. I moved in Grandfather's desk and armchair, a bed, the kitchen items my girlfriend had rejected, and a mountain of cardboard boxes. Day after day I came home from work to sit on the floor of the large room and unpack clothes, sheets, towels, dishes, books, various drafts of my dissertation, notebooks and drawings, letters and diaries, stuffed animals, Bakelite cars, papier-mâché cowboys, Indians, and soldiers, plus such other childhood treasures as teeth, marbles, magnets, an oil lamp stolen from a construction site, and an American helmet found in a bombed-out lot. I wanted to make a new start by getting rid of all the dross, keeping only the essentials, the way my grandparents had done.

In the course of their battles the cowboys, Indians, and soldiers had lost their arrows, feathers, and weapons and even their arms and legs. I reviewed the troops' last parade, and while trying to recall their names and deeds, my hands recognized the thick paper I had wrapped them in years ago. It was printed on one side, and I began to read. After a few sentences I realized I was reading the story of the soldier making his way home. I collected the pages and strips of pages, smoothed them out, and arranged them in order. Sometimes I found a sequence of a few pages, sometimes just a single page. I also went through the paper I had used to pack the Bakelite cars and other items, but came up with nothing more. The first page, the page with author and title, I didn't find.

3

I READ THE FOLLOWING:

faster than he had thought. Karl shouted, "Now!" and they all jumped over the railway embankment with him: the count, the grenadier, Gerd,

Jürgen, Helmut, and the two Silesians. Two more jumped after them as they hastened down the slope. They jumped too late. Their cry when the wheels met them was overpowered by the locomotive's whistle.

The train had come faster than Karl expected, and was shorter. It had passed before they reached the small wood, and the guards were standing on the embankment, shooting. The first bullet hit Helmut; he flew a few meters through the air before falling to the ground. The next bullets hit the two Silesians. Then Jürgen screamed but kept running. Karl tripped and turned a somersault. He rolled until he reached the bushes between the first trees. The others too made for the wood and flung themselves into it.

The bullets went on whizzing for a while, but the guards were no longer aiming. They could not follow them. To do so they would have had to leave the other prisoners.

Karl and his companions lay low until they stopped hearing shots, shouts, and commands, until only the birds were singing, the crickets chirping, and the bees buzzing. "Karl," whispered the

want to die? Karl looked at him as if one answer were as meaningless as another, though he did need to know. "If you don't want to die, it's got to go."

Jürgen was leaning against the tree, staring at his left hand, which was as thick as a bazooka, had turned a gray-purple green, and stank. He shook his head slowly. Then he looked at the others with his childlike eyes and said with his childlike voice, "Else sings, and if I can't accompany her anymore . . ."

"But there's no way around it!" Gerd said, he too shaking his head. He stood and went over to Jürgen as if about to pick up his plow and make a long, straight furrow. Then gently stroking his head with the left hand, he gave him a powerful punch in the chin with the right, caught him as he collapsed, and laid him carefully on the ground. "Silly boy."

Karl gave the commands. Wood on the fire, one knife in the fire, the other in the boiling water, the shirt torn into strips, Jürgen held down. Then he cut. He drew his lips back and bared his teeth, his eyes gleaming with the desire to make the gruesome but urgent operation as precise as possible. Jürgen came to and let out a squeaky, childlike scream, then fainted again. When the hand fell off, the blood bubbled out as if from a mountain spring. Karl removed the glowing-red knife from the fire and pressed it against the stump. It hissed and smoked and stank. The count threw up.

"Will he make it?"

"How should I know?" Karl spat. "I'm no doctor." He bound the stump.

"Then how did you know he would die if you didn't . . ."

Karl looked up. "Did you smell that hand?" he asked, laughing in their faces. "You couldn't have stood that smell much longer. You'd have left him behind. Abandoning him here on the island—would that have been the right thing to do?"

Something new was gleaming in his eyes, a hardness, a coldness, a disdain that sent shivers down their spines. Then he tossed the knife into the boiling water and said, "In ten minutes we'll be on our

only for the eye, only a picture, the bones still cold and stiff. Then the red disc rose slightly higher. The only good minute of the day had arrived.

Enjoy it. Enjoy it while you can. The sun will turn yellow soon. It will soon start pricking instead of warming. You will soon have to wind rags around your head, leaving only slits for the eyes and the swollen, inflamed, mosquito-bitten eyelids. And the mosquitoes will soon be back, a swarm for each of you, with no respite until the cold of night. And neither your clothes nor the rags around your head nor the shoes on your feet will give you shelter. And the bites will not merely itch, they will plague you like a leper's boils.

Enjoy it. Your bones warm up; the tundra smells its sweetest: the miserable bits of moss, the meager plants and weeds, the stunted conifers emit the bewitching promise of fragrance. The air is full of the aroma of home—its woods and heaths—and of foreign lands: herbs you have never tasted, flowers you have never seen.

The friends' hearts are heavy with homesickness and wanderlust. They sigh, sigh in blissful yearning. They stretch—amazed, because in the cold of the night they did not think their bones would ever serve them again—and sit up. The grenadier hands out what is left to hand out: a few berries plus perhaps a scrap of dried fish or, as long as they last, half a potato. Then off they go, while they can, before the good time has passed. But even if it has in fact passed, they get under way without a moment's hesitation, without a murmur. They are going home.

Only the morning after they camped with the Lochen tribe had things been different. Jürgen just lay there. At first Karl thought he was dead, but then he saw him smile. Gerd and the grenadier pulled themselves up and sat back to back, looking around as if luxuriating at a resort. But there was nothing to see. The place where the Lochens had been was empty.

"They promised to come back and take us with them." His hand shielding his eyes, the count searched the horizon. "We mustn't move from the spot."

"It's so nice here," Gerd said.

"Why did we think we had to keep going all these weeks?" the grenadier wondered.

And Jürgen just smiled at the stump of his hand.

Karl drew his lips back and showed his teeth. Should he move on without them? Many were the times he had wished he were alone, many the days they had been an albatross around his neck. The day might come when they would really bring him down. Nor did he care for them: not Jürgen, the child who would never grow up; not the silly, arrogant count; not the grenadier, a war machine who could no sooner be converted into a viable civilian than a tank could be converted into a tractor; or Gerd, whose naive and upstanding peasant ways got on his nerves. Yet he knew that he would do everything in his power to jolt them out of it, that they would mewl and whine and refuse to budge, that he would kick them in the rear until whatever it was the Lochens had given them yesterday was out of their system. He would stay on their backs until they came to see again that they were on their way home.

"Good-natured people, the Lochens," thought

4

HAD I READ BEFORE about the putrid hand or the good-natured Lochens? I could not remember. I skimmed on through adventure after adventure. Then I skipped forward to see what of the end had remained, and read the final pages:

on and on, stopping just short of Moscow, then up and up, in the Cauca-
sus. But after Stalingrad we stopped hearing from him.

Karl shook his head. "He'll be back. He'll be back to rebuild the shop
and the house."

The old man gave a derisive laugh. "Wouldn't that be nice, but don't
count on it. We've heard from all them others taken by the Russians." He
looked Karl up and down. "They get you too? Looks like you been through
a lot and still got a lot to go. You can sleep here in the warehouse till you
find something better."

"Is his wife alive?"

"Yes." The man looked straight ahead. "But she moved away." He lifted
his arms and let them fall. "Women are having a hard time of it."

"I'd like to give her a message from her husband. Where . . ."

"From her husband?" The man shook his head and stood. "You get some
sleep. I'll wake you in the morning."

And so Karl spent his first night home amidst the stock of his shop. He
walked through the warehouse checking what was left: a lot of chairs, a
few wardrobes and chests of drawers, the first model of the desk he had
designed before he had been called up. He still liked it: he had done well to
design the desk for writers and scholars rather than factory managers and
party bosses. He was grateful to the faithful old man for having watched
over the warehouse and saved the stock. He was nearly blind, hard of hear-
ing, and all but lame. It must have been an enormous strain on him, and

he would not have made the effort had he not believed there was at least a possibility that his young employer would return. Should he have revealed his identity to him?

Whatever it was that prevented him from doing so then was still at work the following morning: he merely thanked him. Then he went to the local register office. The upper stories were gone, but the odor of officialdom in the basement and on the ground floor was as strong as if nothing had happened. It could not have been simpler: his wife lived in the neighboring city. Kleinmüllerstrasse 58. He stood at the side of the Autobahn, and before long a small three-wheeled van picked him up. It set him down in the city center twenty minutes later. He wandered through the streets in amazement: houses intact, gardens in bloom; rubble, debris, bomb craters nowhere to be seen; the bells in the double-steepled church tolling noon; the market well stocked with potatoes, vegetables, apples . . . Peacetime conditions, he thought. He was glad his wife did not have to live amidst the wreckage.

For a long time he stood staring at the house from across the road. Red sandstone, a door that looked as if it were keeping somebody prisoner, a balcony that seemed made for cannons, a number of large windows but a number of narrow, embrasure-like windows too, a massive building, and gloomy despite the garden surrounding it. Then he crossed the road, opened the garden gate, and went up the

Too bad. I would have liked to read again about what happened when he rang the bell, the door opened, and his wife stood before him. And I would have loved to know what happened after that. But even though I didn't expect to learn more than I had when I read it the first time, I found it exciting, as if this time I could read on to the end.

5

AFTER SETTLING into the apartment, I settled into the city. I knew it: it was the fair sister of my ugly native city, and early on my friends and I started making excursions into its elegant Old Town, whose cafés, bars, and wine cellars had a lot more going on than the ones we were used to. Later many of those friends chose its university over ours: it was older and more attractive. I would have gone there as well had I not been offered a student job at the university in my hometown.

I visited the Saturday markets, a new one each week. The markets had little merchandise but many small stands manned by peasants from the surrounding countryside or their wives or grandmas. They sold homegrown fruits and vegetables, honey from their hives, homemade marmalade, freshly squeezed juice. Different markets had different stands, of course, but the selection was similar, as were the overall picture and smell and the cries in broad dialect praising their chard and fresh strawberries. What differed most was the clientele, and it was at the markets that I became acquainted with the city's various neighborhoods: here a self-contained enclave of longtime petit bourgeois inhabitants, there a well-manicured section where old and new wealth coexisted, and, farther on, a neighborhood in transition: crumbling gray edifices and family-run shops next to smartly gentrified houses along traffic-free streets whose intersections were inlaid with granite cobblestones. It was 1980. German cities were recovering from the tear-down and build-up mania of the fifties, sixties, and seventies and regaining a certain self-respect.

The Friedrichsplatz neighborhood was a case in point. Some of the private residences, many of which boasted Renaissance and art nouveau elements, had been remodeled; most of the older, plainer, more or less standardized houses were still waiting their turn, though here and there they, too, were covered with scaffolding. The twin-steepled, red-sandstone and yellow-brick Church of Jesus towering so majestically over the chestnut trees and the bustle of the marketplace must have been cleaned out not too long ago. The street along the nearby school was already closed to cars, and the confusing network of one-way streets leading to and from it was meant to scare drivers away. I enjoyed shopping at the market there and, when I was through, sitting at a restaurant that had tables and chairs outside.

6

BEFORE I COULD decipher what was being described in the novel of the soldier on his way home, I had to dream about it. I dreamed that, like Karl, I had come from afar, that, like Karl, I had walked amazed through the streets of a city, and that, like him, after crossing a marketplace, I had stopped in front of a massive, gloomy, inhospitable building of red sandstone. Then I awoke to realize that I knew the building, that I had seen it while sitting in the market but failed to single it out.

I drove there after work. The name of the street bordering one side of Friedrichsplatz was not Kleinmüllerstrasse but Kleinmeyerstrasse, and the number of the building not 58 but 38. Still the red sandstone, the prisonlike door, the cannon balcony, and the embrasures matched perfectly. The building was dark and did not stand out. Its façade looked east and was in shadow when I arrived, but I could imagine it looking more inviting in the morning sun. I would get to the bottom of things. I would get to the bottom of everything.

I opened the garden gate, walked up the steps to the door, and read the names next to the bell. Karl had climbed at least one flight of stairs, so his wife had to have lived in one of the upper stories. None of the names struck a chord. I jotted them down so I could write to them or phone.

Karl had hitched a ride in a small, three-wheeled van. The ride took twenty minutes. He must have lived and worked in the city I grew up in, and his wife must have moved to the city in which I now lived and worked. The novel did not mention where his warehouse was. Near where I used to live? I had been born by the time he came back. I might well have been playing outside when he walked past.

I laughed over my near-miss meeting with a fictional character. But I also began to wonder how my grandparents had come by the manuscript. Could the author have been a friend of my mother's whom she recommended to them? Or was it all a matter of chance? I was aware that the *Novels for Your Reading Pleasure and Entertainment* series featured German authors as well as Swiss. Why not one from my hometown? And why not one who, instead of making up cities and buildings, stole them from reality?

7

BACK HOME AGAIN, I read on:

river was wide, wider than any they had ever seen.

"That must be the Amazon," Jürgen said reverently. "I've read . . ."

"The Amazon!" the count said with a sarcastic laugh.

"Shut your trap!"

The grenadier pointed upstream. "What's that?"

It was not a ship. Passenger or cargo. Nor was it a string of barges such as Karl was used to seeing on the Rhine. It looked like an island swimming down the river, an island with a house and fence on it. Karl knew immediately that this floating island was their only chance: they would never make it across the river, but they might be able to reach the island and from there the other shore. He tore off his shoes, trousers, and shirt and tossed them into the bag. Knowing that the others would not accept an explanation but would follow him, he jumped into the river.

They made it. Even Jürgen, who thought he had to keep his stump above water; even the count, who had an irrational fear of getting water up his nose. In a half hour they were sitting on the logs that constituted the island, dangling their legs in the water while they caught their breath.

"What's that?" The grenadier was pointing to the fence and the house.

"We'll find out soon enough," Karl said, standing up and nodding to the grenadier. "Follow me."

They walked around the fence, found the entrance, and were admitted and taken to the leader.

"Germans," he said with a laugh, "soldiers. You've lost nothing here in Russia, in Siberia."

"We're not looking for anything. We want to go home."

"Ha ha," he went on laughing and slapped his thigh. "You're in luck. You're in luck because you've found Aolsky. If you're willing to work, I'll take you on until they forget you on the shore." Then he pointed to both banks and said, "That is the Soviet Union, and that is the Soviet Union, but this is a free country. No Party, no commissars, no soviets. I've got six sons and six daughters, and if each child has eight children the free country will soon have a great and free people. Long live free Aolistan."

"What will happen when the journey comes to an end?" Karl did not know what river they were on or where it flowed, but the lumber would have to be delivered somewhere this side of the border.

The leader gave him an ill-humored, suspicious look. He was a bear of a man. For a moment Karl thought he meant to crush him with his paws, but then he laughed again and slapped his thigh again.

"So the clever German wants to know what will happen when the journey comes to an end? Well, free Aolistan will break asunder and the wind will blow us away. But when it sets us down, we'll put free Aolistan back together again."

He went over to a flat, wide, roughly hewn structure and opened the gate. There was a seaplane inside.

Karl wondered how the great free Aolistani people would manage to fly back to the upper reaches of the river in such a small plane, but if the leader had it in him to get hold of a small plane he might be able to get hold of a large one too. Maybe even one that the wind could blow back home or at least across the border.

They stayed a whole month. Every night the leader, his wife, and his children had a party, and they were invited. Every morning they got up with the sun and did the leader's

giants would have overtaken them and tried to do away with them. Stones rained down as if hurled by a thousand mighty arms; the trees they had camped under split like matches in a toy forest constructed by children; the ground shook as if about to sink. Karl, who had taken shelter behind a rock and was unharmed, heard the cries of his comrades amid the falling stones and cracking trees. He recognized Jürgen's voice, squeaking as it had when he amputated his hand; the count's, gurgling and nasal; the grenadier's, bellowing as if, hit and wounded, he were flinging himself on the foe with his bayonet. He could not hear Gerd but then spied him in the pale moonlight, a step away, but safe for the second he needed to reach out and pull him behind the rock. There they lay, panting, while the giants' fury gained the upper hand and the cries of the others weakened and died out.

When they ventured out from behind the rock the next morning, they no longer recognized the place. Gerd picked up a few stones in an attempt to find his comrades, but soon gave up. The maze of roots, branches, and stone they were standing on was a good two meters higher than the ground they had camped on the day before. They would have needed an excavator to recover the bodies.

"First the airplane accident—and so near the border—now this. Can there be a jinx on us?"

Karl gave a derisive snort. "A jinx? Anything is better than the mine. The worst day here in the open is better than the best in the mine." Then, having pondered his words, he added, "Even death here in the open is better than the mine."

Gerd shook his head. "I know you're right, but God seems to be playing games with us."

"We've got to get out of here."

"Wait a minute." Gerd took Karl's arm. "Can't you feel it? Can't you feel them taking leave of us and willing us to take leave of them?" He put his other hand to his ear as if listening to something.

Karl tried to master his impatience by counting. I'll give him to fifty, he said to himself, then went on to a hundred and a hundred and fifty. Still counting, he heard Gerd hum "I Once Had a Faithful Comrade,"

8

I COULD NOT REMEMBER having read about the putrid hand and the good-natured Lochens; nor did Aolistan and the giants' fury come back to me; not even the meeting with the faithful old man had left a trace in my memory, much as I was concerned how it ended. Yet despite my failure to recognize what I had once read in what I was now reading, it felt familiar. Familiar, though alien: something was missing. And I kept feeling the missing link was water: I remember water playing a bigger role in Karl's adventures.

There was more than a wide river; there were lakes and oceans, islands and coasts, Lake Baikal and Lake Aral, the Caspian Sea, the Black Sea.

I was nonplussed by the tricks my memory was playing on me. While writing my dissertation, I had worked for a while with some colleagues on a computer program for resolving court cases. The program was meant to determine whether a plaint was justified, a claim well grounded, a payment required—that kind of thing. We soon realized that the problem was not programming, memory, or computation time; the problem was that we were insufficiently clear as to how lawyers go about resolving cases. As long as we were unclear about that, we could not simulate it on the computer. We had plenty of ideas about what they *should* do, but precious few about what they *did*. One of the few we did have was that, as with medical diagnoses and chemical analyses, the establishment of patterns played a decisive role. My job was to interview lawyers about the role of pattern recognition in their work.

"Déjà vu is a sense of recognizing something one has not in fact experienced," a retired judge told me. "The older I got the more often I found myself thinking I recognized an old case in a new one. I would resolve it with the assurance of a sleepwalker, but when I went to file it with the old one there was no old one to file it with."

"How do you explain . . ."

"Patterns. Isn't that what we're talking about? Over the years the patterns of past cases and resolutions are not merely stored in the brain; the elements that make up the patterns combine to form patterns of their own. These new patterns are what we call déjà vu."

"Do they combine by themselves?"

"Well, presumably you've run the pattern through your head while working on a case. Napoleon is supposed to have had a déjà vu on the morning of the Battle of Austerlitz. I can see why. He had more on his mind than the battles he had known and fought; he had all the battles that had ever gone through his head, pattern after pattern made up of elements like soldiers, infantry and cavalry, cannons, terrain, positions . . . One of them was the Austerlitz pattern."

It was ambitious and costly enough for our program to come up with existing patterns; now we had imaginary ones to consider as well. What were the elements that made up our juridical patterns? And if we succeeded in identifying them, how should the program combine them into imaginary patterns, patterns that were fair, not random? Or even fair and unstained by considerations of utility.

I solved none of these puzzles; I simply presented the results of my interviews. One of the reasons I was happy to move into publishing was that I could leave the puzzles behind. Handling authors, evaluating manuscripts, predicting whether a book will sell—that is all puzzle-free.

But now I had another puzzle to deal with, a déjà vu whose basis I might well have remembered. What had the elements of the novel done behind my back? What patterns had they combined to form?

9

I READ THE REST:

was lively and gay, with tired eyes and a sad mouth. "Everything's in ruins, destroyed: the house, the shop, everything."

"Then we'll build them back up."

"Like the crèche," his mother said with a smile, and Karl remembered

how at one Christmas a cousin had smashed their old crèche and all its fig-
ures with his new ball and he and Mother had put it back together. He was
about to return her smile, but noticed it was gone. "Everything's in ruins,
destroyed: the house, the shop, everything."

He did not want to repeat himself but had nothing else to say. That a
house is only a house, a shop a shop? That being alive is all that matters?

"Everything . . ."

"Quiet!"

He said it so loudly that he awoke with a start.

"Anything wrong?" Gerd asked.

He nodded. "Sorry to have woken you."

"Dreaming of the mountain? Every night I dream I've got to push that
dump truck up it. You remember, the heavy dump truck that crushed the
Westphalian when he couldn't push it anymore and it rolled back on him?"

Karl nodded. "Go back to sleep, Gerd. Stop thinking about the dump
truck. Stop thinking about the dead. Think of home."

"Do you think they'll still want us?" Gerd asked after a pause.

"I don't think I'll ask." Karl sneered.

and if they didn't pay up, his curse would be upon them. Then he let
them go.

They set off. Karl in the lead, then Gerd. The ground was stony, but
already the sand, which they were not supposed to expect until the fourth
day, had lodged itself between their teeth. The wind never stopped, never
stopped blowing the sand into their mouths and hair and clothes and ears
and nose and eyes, which they pinched into slits. The mountains seemed as
far off on the evening of the first day as they had that morning. Ditto the
second and third day. By the fourth day they had lost interest in the moun-
tains. They came to the fountain. Though prepared for the worst, they were
disappointed: the water stank.

"He said it was good water."

"Listen here!" Karl said, hot under the collar. "When there's no choice,

there's no point in sniveling. We'll drink the water and take some with us. We'll pay for it too." There were a few coins in the hollow behind the stone that had been described to them, and he added the sum he had promised.

The water had a foul taste to it, but it was water. It gave them back their lips, mouths, and throats; it gurgled in their stomachs; it moistened their faces and hands. "It's good," Gerd said reverently. "It's good."

They filled their bottles and moved on. Karl said nothing about the dark cloud forming at one edge of the mountains. No matter what was brewing up ahead, they could only move on. The cloud soon left the horizon for the sky above the mountains and eventually took up half the sky.

Now Gerd saw it too. "Looks like rain."

Karl shook his head. He watched it growing and growing. It was no simple cloud; it was a living thing, like a swarm of mosquitoes, of bees, of birds. It spun on its axis, circulating something, spitting it out, then reincorporating it to spur its growth. And all the while it made a whirring noise Karl had never heard before and never wanted to hear again. It reminded him of the sound made by high-tension wires. There was a flash of lightning, but not the lightning he knew. The sudden streaks were a glistening network of light, like the pattern of veins on the hand of a terrifying, raging, punitive god. It was a roaring electric storm. Karl could hear the air crackle and feel his hair rise. Then he heard a horrible cry, a knife blade of a cry, a gaping wound of a cry, and saw Gerd flare up for a second, then fall, turn head over heels, roll next to his feet, and lie there, black. Even the image of the black, grinning face lasted only an instant; then everything went black and the wind broke loose and whipped up the sand, forcing Karl to his knees.

This is the last judgment, he thought. If I survive this, I will survive everything. He felt the sand rising higher and higher up his sides. I must not remain here. I must not let the sand engulf me. I must not be buried here. He stood and moved on, step by step. He had no goal and no strength; sheer defiance dragged him forward. They might get him in the end—the sand, the desert, death—but he would not give himself to them. Three times he collapsed and felt the sand engulfing him; three times he got to his feet and moved on. Then he stopped moving and was moved, shoved, carried, hurled. The cloud no longer wished to engulf and bury him; it was inhaling and exhaling him, lifting him up and bearing him away, blowing him over the ground, making him its plaything, having its way with him. He could do nothing, nothing at all but register he was still alive.

Then, all at once, he could see again: the raging sand had died down; the sky was shining bright blue again, arrogant, indifferent to the insult of having been so rudely overrun. After the darkness Karl greeted the sun, which he had so often cursed during his march across the desert, as a friend. He saw that the storm had brought him to the edge of the mountains, saw a small hut perched atop one of the gray slopes, and knew it was the goal the storm had in mind for him.

As he was nearing the hut, the door opened and a woman emerged and came up to him. She has the bearing of a queen, Karl thought, and was afraid. All his strength and will were gone; he was weak. He was in dirty, ill-smelling rags. She would waste no time in calling her men and having them chase him away like a mangy dog. She was beautiful, he saw: she had curly hair, strong shoulders, full breasts, rounded hips, and long legs. As she approached, he also saw a friendly question in her eyes and a smiling mouth. But all he could manage was a croak. And then he stumbled and tipped over. His last thought was that he should have fallen at her feet.

When he came to, he was lying in a bed. He felt a linen cloth on his forehead. After all these years it was like clear water or fresh bread. He heard singing and opened his eyes to see

won't stop you. I'll give you my father's long coat and large pouch and pack enough food to get you over the mountains and into the valley where the border runs."

Karl did not know if he should believe her. "I . . ."

"Don't say a word," Kalinka said, flinging her arm around his neck and laying her head on his breast. "If thoughts of home weigh so heavily on

you . . . thoughts about her . . . Will she be good to you? Will she sing to you when you sleep? Will she know the herbs to use when your old wound smarts? Will she bury your head between her breasts when you dream of the mine and awake with a start? Oh, how I should like to keep you for nine more months and yet nine more. How I should like to keep you forever."

Kalinka freed herself from him and went inside. Gazing out into the distance, over the desert and the mountain slopes and up to its peaks, he felt none of the sadness he had so often felt standing here. Sorry as he was at the thought of leaving, the joy of setting off was greater.

After a while she called him in. She had laid out the coat and packed the pouch. She had made him their usual supper and made love to him as she had on other nights. When he got up and set off, she feigned sleep, but then she went to the doorway and watched him climb higher and higher.

Nine months! He arrived at Kalinka's on page ninety-three and set off on page ninety-five, and for nine months he had done nothing but eat, gaze sadly into the distance, and make love. Nine months when he was unable to move on? No, nine months when for all his desire to see house, home, and wife he did not wish to move on.

I was surprised that my moral grandparents had let that through. Though perhaps they punished him by putting another man beside his wife when he got home. If the novel amounted to a punishment of its protagonist, Karl's wife would not fling her arms around him with a shout of joy after recovering from the shock of seeing a man presumed dead standing before her. The man beside her would have no reason to steal away after being shown up as a liar and a cheat, and if Karl ventured to challenge him he would suffer an ignominious defeat.

IO

THAT WEEKEND I visited my mother. When the village on the Neckar we had moved to became a suburb, she moved into a village on the edge of the Odenwald. She would say hello to all and sundry and chat in the general store but otherwise kept to herself. She had always enjoyed driving and started driving sporty convertibles as soon as she could afford it. She would get stuck in traffic on the way to work, but since she worked late into the evening the drive home was fast. In summer she would put the top down, let the wind ruffle her long blond hair, and, at traffic lights, bask in the admiring glances of men she had absolutely no interest in. She would have been a beautiful woman had it not been for the contemptuous lines around the mouth and had she not been so aloof, but such things were invisible at traffic lights. Sometimes the contempt and aloofness disappeared, though perhaps that was the twilight on her terrace or the candlelight in a restaurant.

I visited her once every four or five weeks, and we occasionally met to see a film or have dinner together in town—effortless and mildly boring encounters. My mother always had a not-quite-unloving but highly formal way of treating me. She valued formality in any case, but with me it came out more than usual, because she felt it would introduce a note of manliness into my upbringing. Tenderness, intimacy, regret over things gone wrong or gone by, vacillation over making a decision—these were all foreign to her, or she had buried them so long ago and so deeply that they no longer dared to surface. We informed each other of the events in our lives without much commentary. Her criticisms of me did not subside; she merely couched them in pointed questions: "Do you ever think of your dissertation? Are you still seeing the person you introduced to me that time?"

Sometimes I brought all the ingredients and cooked. My mother did not like to cook and was not good at it: I was raised on bread, cold cuts, and warmed-up canned foods. Seldom did I see her so happy and gay, so girlish, as when I was at work at the stove and she was doing some unimportant task for me or was simply on her first glass of champagne. Taboo topics remained taboo: not a word about my father, her relationship with him, her relationships with other men and with her boss. But she did sometimes talk about her childhood and the new start after our flight from the bombs: the foraging at local farms, the Care packages, the dishes that could be made from stinging nettles . . .

"You cooked nettles?"

"Believe it or not."

"Did you take me on your foraging trips?"

"I was the small, brave blond woman, babe in arms. You started earning your keep early."

I asked her about *Novels for Your Reading Pleasure and Entertainment*. She had never come with me to see my grandparents or—so far as I knew—gone on her own. Even as a child I kept at her until she explained that they had never forgiven her their son's having fallen in love with her and married her, and therefore having stayed in Germany and been killed there. She said she understood their grief but did not see why they placed the blame on her. I responded with the heavy but proud heart of a child: if that was the case, I would no longer go either. Oh no, she replied. I shouldn't have to suffer, nor should I hold it against them: they loved me and I them; they were good people; they just couldn't get over their grief.

"Remember the series of novels Grandmother and Grandfather published after the war? Did you ever recommend authors to them? Friends or acquaintances who wrote?"

"We communicated only about the essentials: when your train

was getting in, how long you'd be staying. I never recommended any authors to them."

"Do you happen to know a sandstone building near the Church of Jesus, Kleinmeyerstrasse 38, Friedrichsplatz?"

"Is this an interrogation? May I at least be informed of what I stand accused?"

"It's no interrogation. I'm just trying to find out something about one of the novels in the series." I told her about my two readings—many years ago and several days ago—of Karl's adventures and how I had located the house. "The author must be from here."

"Don't you have anything better to do?"

"You mean my dissertation? I'd never have got to the bottom of it. I can't tell you how happy I was to let it go. Sometimes I enjoy thinking about one or another of the issues involved, but I'd much rather get to the bottom of Karl's story."

"There are any number of ways for that story to end. You have no idea how many homecoming stories were told and published after the war. Homecoming novels were a genre all their own, like war novels or romances."

"Can you give me one way it might end?"

She thought awhile, quite a while, then said, "She stays with the other man. She had been told Karl was dead, and she mourned him. But then she met the other man and fell in love with him. Karl just stands there while she tells him. Then he asks her and the other man to swear on their daughter's life that they will tell nobody he is alive. She can't understand why, but he insists, so she swears, and the other man does too. Then Karl leaves."

II

DON'T YOU HAVE anything better to do? My mother was good at making me feel guilty. It was the way she brought me up to be good in school, to do my house and garden chores, to deliver my magazines on time, and to see to the needs of my friends. The privilege of getting an education, living in a nice house with a nice garden, having the money to pay for necessities (let alone extras), enjoying the company of friends and of a loving mother—all this had to be earned; moreover, it had to be earned with a smile: my mother had solved the conflict between duty and desire by decreeing that I was to desire to do my duty.

I often made fun of it later. And I thought I had broken free of it all when I blithely gave up the dissertation. But the moment Mother asked those questions, my guilty conscience was back, and again there was no evil deed behind it: I had a guilty conscience even though I had done nothing wrong.

Seek and ye shall find. In my California paradise I made up my mind to be a good friend to my former girlfriend and her son should they need one. I had only the best intentions. Veronika was chaotic and did need a friend: her son, Max, whose father had never paid any attention to him, had grown close to me after eight years under my roof and let me, more than anyone, talk him out of at least some of his shenanigans. I did not want Max to suffer just because I did not wish to run into the man Veronika had taken up with before our separation.

He wasn't around anymore, but I ran into his successor. Veronika was not interested in my offer of friendship: she said she had needed me when the last one left her, but now she could manage on her own. Max, however, was happy to see me, and we took up our old habit of going to the movies together every two weeks.

Sometimes we did not even wait till the end of the film to go out for pizza or curry wurst with French fries and one Coke after the other.

Now I had something better to do, once every two weeks, anyway. Not only that, it was not long in giving me a clue to the end of Karl's story, and I took this as a sign that I should lay aside my guilty conscience and move on with my search.

One day Max and I went to see the adventures of Odysseus with Kirk Douglas, and suddenly everything was clear: it was not the Caspian or Black Sea I was after; it was the Aegean. The model for Karl and his companions, for their wanderings, their adventures, the dangers they succumbed to, was none other than *The Odyssey*.

I had read the adventures of Odysseus as a child in a collection of Greek tales. In school I had translated excerpts of *The Odyssey* from Greek and had even learned the first ninety-six lines by heart in the original. I had never forgotten Polyphemus, the Sirens, Scylla and Charybdis, Nausicaa, Penelope, Odysseus' revenge on the suitors. That very night I took it up again. I started with the end. I had thought Odysseus found home and happiness intact on Ithaca with his Penelope; instead I learned that he had to take leave of her once more and set to wandering with an oar on his shoulder until he came to a land in which the people had no idea what an oar, a ship, the sea, or even salt was. From there he was allowed to wander back, but since he was to die far from the sea and Ithaca is an island in the sea, death would befall him far from his home. Thus had Tiresias prophesied in Hades, and Homer assures us at the end of *The Odyssey* that Tiresias' prophesy came true.

Homer's mention of Tiresias led me from the end to the earlier book in which Odysseus descends into the underworld and learns of the future from Tiresias. In the same book he alights in the land of the Laestrygonians, giants who devour many of his companions and destroy their ships. Before that he is taken in by Aeolus' fourteen-headed family on a floating island, and even before that he must drive his companions on by force because, treated to lotus by the good-natured Lotus Eaters, they have forgotten their homeland. In Hades, Odysseus speaks not only to Tiresias but also to his mother. Later his companions lay hands on the sun god's sheep and cattle and perish in a storm by way of punishment, and Odysseus is washed ashore on Calypso's island, where he remains for nine years before she lets him travel on.

Then there are the encounters with the cyclops Polyphemus and a happy year with the goddess Circe, the tempting song of the Sirens, and the journey between the whirlpool of Charybdis and the rock of Scylla. Presumably my novel's author too had turned them into adventures, adventures depicted on the pages I no longer had. Perhaps the encounter with Polyphemus had been transformed into Karl's having to sneak his comrades out of a cave past Russian rescue teams; perhaps Circe had been transformed into a Siberian shamaness or the Sirens into a KGB choir. Whirlpool and rock could remain as is, though they might as well have shown up as a narrow mountain pass or high waterfall. The author had let his imagination soar: Aolsky, though lord of the winds no longer, was the proud possessor of an airplane and possibly helped Karl to acquire the one with which Karl's comrades wreaked as much havoc as Odysseus' companions with Aeolus' sack of winds; there were no giants, but the forces of nature raged as if they were giants; Karl's mother met him in a dream rather than in Hades; and Gerd had not stolen cattle and sheep from the sun god but presumably coins from the owner of the well. Sandstorm for storm at sea—why had the author rejected the Caspian or the Black Sea? Were the nine months with Kalinka that replaced the nine years with Calypso a function of the increased tempo of our times or the fact that the novel was written after the war?

The prototype for Jürgen's putrid hand may have been Philoctetes' putrid foot, and Eumaeus the swineherd, who was the first person Odysseus met at Ithaca and who helped him to take revenge on the suitors, lived on in Karl's faithful old watchman, though such prowess was hardly to be expected of a man nearly blind, hard of hearing, and all but lame. In fact, the last part of the novel showed too many discrepancies with the model to allow me to use the model as the solution to the riddle of the ending. Karl had no son, no Telemachus; Karl's Penelope had not stood up to the suitors; she had chosen one and had had a child—if not two— by him. Striking him dead was not as indicated as Odysseus' frenzy in the presence of the brazen band that pressed, plagued, and plundered Penelope. No, neither Kleinmüllerstrasse nor Kleinmeyerstrasse had been the scene of a massacre.

12

WHY HAD THE AUTHOR deviated from his model at the end? Though the analogous question is equally as interesting: Why had he followed the model until the end?

It was not as if the author had mechanically transposed adventure after adventure from the world of the saga to Karl's: the story was too playful for that. No, he felt compelled to tell a soldier's tale, a tale of homecoming. He knew the jargon, he knew *The Odyssey,* and he took it easy: he did not go to the trouble of researching Siberia's geography or vegetation; he did not care that rivers in Siberia flow north, not south. All he knew was that in the north Siberia has tundra and forests and rivers and in the south it is hot and dry and bordered by a number of countries. Why trouble the reader with detail?

Do we actually want to know? I thought of an old friend who is better at naming and interpreting stars and constellations than anyone you can imagine. He makes it all up, but even if you know he makes it up you enjoy listening to him. Is it because the true names are of as little use to us as the false ones? Because all we care about is bringing the mighty glitter of the firmament down to earth, using names and interpretations to help us feel at home with them?

After *The Odyssey* I read Josef Martin Bauer's *As Far as My Feet Will Carry Me*. I remembered the success it had back in 1955 when it appeared, a success it owed to the impression it gave of telling a true story. It did the German soul good to hear that a German soldier had made his way back from Siberia on his own steam. Clemens Forell's route, like Karl's, took him along and across great rivers and led through tundra and forest and over mountains. Both heroes headed south, following the natural route across the Urals, through Russia and Poland or Czechoslovakia and into Germany. Clemens Forell's itinerary is so precisely marked by the stops he makes, and the circumstances surrounding his arrival in Iran are detailed with such clarity, that the account sounds totally authentic. I started to wonder whether my picture of a playful, imaginative writer was not a bit of an oversimplification. Couldn't the author of Karl's story have told a true or at least probable story, embellishing it only slightly?

The literature on German POWs in Siberia revealed that most German prisoners there had neither the will nor strength, let alone courage, to resist. Very few dared to attempt escape; not one succeeded. By imagining that there was a way out of captivity, that escape was possible, and that the escaped prisoner could eventually make his way back home, the author of *As Far as My Feet Will Carry Me* had domesticated what was otherwise overwhelming, rendering it something people felt at home with.

So my author had simply had a story to tell and made things

easy for himself. How does someone so intimately acquainted with *The Odyssey* come to write a *Novel for Your Reading Pleasure and Entertainment*? Clearly he had had a classical education. He must have been unable to go back to his old job after coming home from the war and was keeping his head above water with hack fiction. Had a Jason volume or an Oedipus or Orestes volume followed his *Odyssey*? And as the times got better, did he start teaching Greek or philosophy or found a theater?

I wrote to the German and Swiss national libraries asking whether they had the *Novels for Your Reading Pleasure* series in their collections and received replies in the negative. Their goal was to collect everything published in Germany and Switzerland, respectively, they wrote, but they might have overlooked publications of smaller presses.

I put the following classified advertisement in the *Neue Zürcher Zeitung:* "Volumes of 'Novels for Your Reading Pleasure and Entertainment' sought for scholarly purposes. Please submit volume title and author and price requested to box no. xy." I received only one reply, which included volume 242, *Midnight Emergency* by Gertrud Ritter, free of charge. From that I learned, if nothing else, that the series had been published by the Rhein-Verlag in Basel and that its logo consisted of a river being crossed by a ferry. My bookseller had never heard of the Rhein-Verlag, but I did find it in the Basel business directory and the name of the owner in the Basel telephone book. I phoned and got the man's son, who had the same name. His father was dead, the publishing house likewise; he was in computers. He remembered my grandfather: when he was a boy, the old man would come regularly to fetch and deliver manuscripts and proofs. No, there were no archives.

13

ONE THURSDAY I DROVE to Kleinmeyerstrasse 38 after work and
rang the second-story bell. I chose the second floor because the
longer I mulled over the vague memory of the novel's ending the
surer I was that Karl had climbed only one flight of stairs. I had
neither written nor phoned in advance: I wanted to climb the
stairs and stand at the door like Karl, unannounced and unpre-
pared for what would happen.

The nameplate next to the bell read BINDINGER. I waited. I
could hear children playing in Friedrichsplatz and the Church of
Jesus bells chiming six. Just as I was about to ring again, I heard the
buzz of the door opener and pushed the heavy door open. The
staircase was large, the stairs wide and deep, the chest-high wooden
paneling with meander relief was obviously well cared for, and the
wall opposite the entrance to the ground-floor apartment was fully
covered by a picture, dark with age, of a man on a horse before a
motley crowd waving flags large and small. I climbed the stairs.

Standing in the doorway was a woman my age, of average
height and weight. She had pale blond hair pulled back and held
with a clip. She was wearing floppy jeans and a loose red sweater.
Her feet were bare. She took the clip out of her hair, shook her
head until the hair came loose, and said, "I've just come home."

"From work?"

She nodded and raised her eyebrows inquisitively.

"I'm on my way from work too."

She smiled. "No, I mean: What brings you here?"

"It's hard to explain. It goes back quite a few years and has nothing to do with you. It has to do with your apartment. Do you
know who lived here after the war?"

"We did."

"You?"

"My parents, my sister, and I. Who are you?"

"My name is Debauer. Peter Debauer."

I put my hand in my pocket and came up with a business card. I gave it to her and said, "May I tell you the whole story?"

She looked at my card, at her watch, into the apartment, and back at me. She nodded and held out her hand. "Barbara Bindinger."

The entrance hall was large and had the same paneling as the staircase. Through an open double door I could see a room with molding and a parquet floor and—through an open double door of glass—a balcony. The fittings were handsome, even lavish, which made the furniture, curtains, and carpets, of fifties and sixties vintage, look out of place. It also looked as if no one had put things away or cleaned up for quite some time.

"Shall we go out onto the balcony?" she asked. "I think it's warm enough."

I began my tale. After a while she got up and brought out a bottle of wine and served it. She was an attentive listener. There was nothing special about the way she had stood in the door, walked onto the balcony, or now sat facing me, but I liked how she'd shaken her hair free, liked her slightly crooked, warm smile. And only now in the bright light of the balcony did I see her pale blue eyes and her complexion, with its hint of pink, yet so pale, so white, so naked as to make me feel I was stealing an unseemly glance at her breasts or genitals. I noticed a small scar on her upper lip, the remnant of an otherwise perfect operation or a fall. Her lips were beautiful.

She smiled again when I finished. Then she shrugged. "I can't recall having peeked out coyly from behind my mother's apron when a stranger came up the stairs. Or could it have been my sister who peeked out coyly and I was the one my mother was carrying? I don't remember any man other than my father, neither then nor later. My parents were happily married, the way people of their generation were happily married. I can't possibly imagine Mother having secrets or a lover. But how can I be sure? My sister has my mother's documents, and they may include a diary with pictures of a lover and letters from him and, between its pages, the pressed rose he gave her or had sent to the hotel after the first night. I certainly wouldn't have begrudged her that, especially during her years as a widow. But that wouldn't bring you any closer to the end of your novel, would it?"

"Can I speak to your sister?"

"She doesn't live here. Though she doesn't live far away either."

I could not tell whether the answer was meant to put me off or encourage me. I did not want to make a thing of it, nor could I, because she took up again immediately. "What fits is the house, the floor, and the two sisters. Maybe the author lived in the building. We could ask around and see whether an indigent Greek teacher moved here after the war. What else did you say? Philosophy professor, theater director? We did have a theater director living on the ground floor—he's the one who hung that reject painting from the props department downstairs—but he didn't move in until the fifties and moved out long ago. Too bad we can't ask Mother."

"Is she no longer with us?"

"She's been dead for three months. I moved in two weeks ago and haven't been able to take care of things after work. Fortunately Margarete took all the stuff that was worth anything; all I have to do is get rid of what's left."

I told her about my still-empty flat.

"An empty flat instead of one filled with things you don't like— that's better, isn't it?"

"I think it's terrific. And for the time being I don't feel like traipsing through furniture showrooms and junk shops."

She asked me if I'd be willing to help her with the clearing operation. She was a teacher, had just come back from six years in Kenya, and all her old friends were gone. "How about Saturday? I'll rent the van and cook a dinner. I'm a good cook. Trust me."

14

ON SATURDAY WE EMPTIED the apartment of her mother's belongings and transported them to the dump. Barbara cooked an African meal. We ate on the floor: the only things Barbara had kept were the refrigerator and stove, dishes and cutlery, and sheets, towels, and blankets. She slept on the floor too. I asked what she'd done with the furniture she'd had in Kenya. She said she had tired of it and left it behind. She was living out of three wardrobe trunks equipped with large drawers and rods for hanging clothes. She'd bought them in Kenya secondhand. "I'm not the domestic type."

But finding the right furniture was important enough to her to send us poking through antique shops each Friday for the next few weeks. At first we limited ourselves to local establishments; then we branched out into the neighboring regions of Spessart, Hunsrück, and Eifel. During the preceding week Barbara would look them up in the local phone books and make the necessary calls, and by the weekend she knew where to go. The best places were the biggest: they had the biggest selection and the biggest mess, which meant you could pick up for a song what in a small shop would be the showpiece in the display window. She had her eye on art nouveau, and the dining room set and the desk with matching chair and the bookcase that she put together piece by piece over the weeks turned out to be perfect for her place. She had taste.

As for me, I was not looking for a specific style. I found a tall

narrow wardrobe with a large oval mirror in the door and a wide
bed, both of cherrywood, and a set of bookshelves with glass doors
that went well with Grandfather's desk and chair. "If we lived
together," she said with a laugh, "we'd have everything we needed."

At first we would set off at two and be back by evening; later we
would stay overnight somewhere, taking a double room: "You
don't mind, do you? We need our money for other things." To tell
the truth, I did mind: I have always had problems with being close
to people at night when I am not intimate with them—on overnight school excursions, in mountain chalets, with friends, with
my mother, even with my grandparents, when they let me sleep in
their room because painters were taking care of some water damage in mine. But I said nothing. Besides, I was amazed at how
easy—and pleasant—it was to spend the nights with her: Barbara's
need to go on reading or suddenly turn out the light, her occasional awakenings in the middle of the night, her noises and
smells, my waiting to use the bathroom and at times our mutual
use of same, her face as she fell asleep, when she got up, in front of
the mirror, and her body with its heavy breasts, thick thighs, cel-
lulite, often displayed in worn, baggy underwear—none of it put
me off, went too far, invaded my privacy. She was so nonchalant
about everything that I, despite my weeks in paradise still rather
timid in matters of the body, found myself following suit. Not
only that, she was so cheerful and witty that at first I thought it was
put on, but in time I was infected by it. She would pose as a
baroque angel, as the Reich eagle and its Federal Republic equiva-
lent, as a bewildered beaver and dying swan. She danced out of bed
to the bathroom and back to the music of the radio alarm clock,
and before long I was dancing with her. When she split her sides
laughing over some witty little poems I knew by heart, I learned
some more. She even had a cheerful—or at least content—way of
saying nothing.

I had never before fallen in love with a woman I really knew. It may not have happened the first time I met her, but the second or third time—or sometime in between—I would wake up with the conviction that I had fallen in love with the woman I had gone out with the previous evening. Things were different with Barbara. When she said that if we were living together we would have everything we needed, I just laughed. Then I thought that we would be good together and eventually that I would actually enjoy living with her. In the end I realized it was much more; it was what my happiness, my whole life depended on: living with her, falling asleep and waking up next to her, cooking and eating with her, spending my day-to-day existence with her, having children with her. After that I thought things would take the course they normally took when I fell in love: I could hold off and wait to decide whether I wanted to jump into this thing or not. But this time I was already in it.

The next weekend we were in the Eifel region, between Bonn and Cologne, in a gigantic warehouse with all kinds of junk, though a few finds as well, from Biedermeier to art deco, including a bed and a leather couch that caught Barbara's fancy. When she started bargaining for the bed, I said, laughing so she could take it as a joke if necessary, "Why not stick to the couch. We've got all the beds we need." She laughed too, dropped the bed, and started in on the couch.

That night she got into bed with me and cuddled up close. Then she sat up, pulled off her nightgown, and said, "You too. I want to feel you." She said it in a voice I had never heard her use. We made love.

15

I TOOK IT AS A SEAL on an unspoken agreement. When she awoke the next morning, her head on my throbbing arm and her arm on my chest, I thought everything would be different now, everything would be right. The first time we were frenetic and bumbling, but we woke up in the middle of the night and made love as easily as if our bodies had been intimate for ages.

Barbara's tenderness was another plus I had trouble believing at first but was soon infected by. We could not keep our hands off each other: in the car, in the street, in shops and restaurants. She was so unbridled in her passion that she swept me away with her, washed away my inhibitions, my stiff, ungainly ways. The voice she used when she wanted to make love made me glow all over, and the small, dark drop of blood that sometimes appeared in the scar on her upper lip burned in my heart. I felt more alive than I ever had before. But what was even more of a miracle than the passion was the tenderness, a tenderness that transformed the day, minute by minute. Yes, everything was different now.

At the same time everything remained as it was. The space the relationship occupied in our lives did not increase. It was limited to our weekend forays and a single, at most, meeting during the week, when either she invited me or I her to dinner. And whereas we had formerly taken leave of each other at the end of the evening, we now spent the night together. If after working late, say, I gave her a spur-of-the-moment call and asked if I could drop in and spend the night, I never got anywhere. Either she was out or was on her way to a parents' evening at school or a meeting with a colleague or she had to prepare her lessons for the next day or correct homework or she was tired or had her period or a headache or a backache. She would be tender about it and laugh and tell me how much she looked forward to next time. Sad as I was, I knew I could use the evening for other things and didn't worry. I didn't want any worries.

If I was unable to increase the space our relationship occupied, I tried at least to refashion it: vary the venues of our weekend visits, bring us together with her new and my old friends, and—besides cooking and eating together—go to films, plays, concerts. Visit her sister.

That was what led to our first quarrel. "Why do you make such a mystery out of her?" I asked. "Since she used to live here and had to report her departure to the residence registration office, I could find out the address for myself."

"What would you tell her?"

"That she comes up in a novel, what the novel is about, that I want to find out if . . . But why am I going on like this? You know."

"How will you explain the way you found her?"

"I'll just . . ."

"Through me. You'll tell her you talked to me and I told you about her. What else will you tell her about me?"

We were at my place. We had finished eating and were having an espresso. I was counting on our moving in together. True, the topic had never come up, but we were now buying only furniture that would make sense in a common flat: she the leather couch, I two leather armchairs with matching table; she a large mirror in a gold frame for her entrance hall, I an art deco lamp for mine, but, as she had pointed out many times over, one that would look perfect in her dining room. Because I had no dining room, we were eating in the kitchen. She was staring daggers at me, the open window a dark square behind her. Suddenly I noticed a dimple above the inner end of the left eyebrow—a Lucia dimple—but a dimple of defiance and anger. It made me laugh, which naturally infuriated her. She stuck out her jaw, parted her lips, and trained her flashing eyes on mine. I barely recognized her.

"I haven't quite thought through what to say to her," I said. "The best thing would be for us to go and see her together, talk to her together. If that won't work, if you've got a problem with her, then just give me your take on how to deal with her."

"Yes," she said, and then raised her voice. "I don't see why I have to come out and say it—you must certainly have noticed it—but since there's no way around it now, I will: I have a problem with my sister. You must certainly have noticed too that I don't want to talk about it. Is that clear?"

"Does that mean we'll never go to see her?"

"Never, never . . . I don't know. We'll have to see."

"And if I went on my own?"

"You've got nothing better to do?"

I laughed. "You sound like my mother. What's so bad about . . ."

But the comparison with my mother got her hackles up. I could not understand it. She had never met my mother, and I had said practically nothing—and nothing bad—about her. Do women have some primordial fear of being identified with their menfolk's mothers? I never had a chance to ask. She blasted my behavior, my character, the way I looked, the way I made love, the way I lived life. I could tell she was working through a tension that had its roots in the mother comparison, the problem with her sister, our talk, even our relationship as a whole, but what the tension consisted of I never found out. Not even after she had calmed down.

"I've always been like that. Even as a girl. It doesn't mean anything. It just happens. Sorry."

16

IT WAS IN AUGUST that I had first rung her bell. School had just started. She had come back from Kenya with her big trunks that summer.

It stayed warm until November. Then it turned cold from one day to the next and began to rain. I loved hearing the rain during the night and seeing it out of my office window. It gave me a cozy feeling. Now is the time for us to move in together, I thought.

On Wednesday, Barbara phoned me at the office to make plans for the weekend. "Let's go to Basel," she said. "I once went there with my parents and liked it. I'd like to take you around."

"I like Basel too, but rain is forecast for the weekend, and all cities are gray in the rain. There's so much we haven't done here yet, and if nothing appeals to you we can always bake Christmas cookies: Christmas is only six weeks off."

"You know I like getting away over the weekend."

"We've gone away every weekend since we met."

"Because we both wanted to. At least I thought it was both of us."

I could hear that tension coming back to her voice and did not want to experience her working through it again. "Oh yes, those were wonderful times."

"Then it's clear: we took those trips because we wanted to. If you want to stay here and I want to go away, you can stay and I'll go. I'll give you a ring on Monday." And she hung up.

I was furious, and disappointed. If that was all we meant to each other, what about my hopes? Move in together? I might as well save my breath. But then why had she played the furniture game with me? Or had she? Maybe it was all my imagination. Yet it had seemed so obvious.

At first I only pretended to be enjoying my weekend alone. I wanted to show her. And myself. Then I actually began to enjoy it. I took Max to the movies, which I had not given up in the previous weeks, though I had cut down on the time I allotted him. This week we went to one place for pizza and another for ice cream, and I listened with a sympathetic ear—and without ranting or giving advice—while he went on about his problems with Veronika's new friend. I tidied up my apartment, which gave me the nice feeling of having tidied up my life along with it. I sifted through bills and paid the ones I needed to, filed them away, and tossed the ones that could wait into the wastepaper basket. I read the manuscripts that had come in for the first issues of the journal I had started and wrote letters to difficult authors. I never seemed to find the time for either when I was at the office.

Then I did something I had been meaning to do for a long time: I put together all my Karl material. There was not much. I had scoured the university library for information on forties and fifties pulp fiction and came up short. What I did find was extensive historical and sociological literature on German prisoners of war and returnees: interesting, but not particularly useful. The National Committee for a Free Germany, the German antifascist groups, the summary justice of various trials and verdicts, the hierarchy in the prison camps that resulted first from the prisoners' military ranks, then from their complicity with the Russian camp administration, and, when the Russians stopped limiting the receipt of packages, from their hawking their contents in the market that arose for that purpose—none of it had anything to do with Karl or his author. The same held for the fate of the late returnees: the trouble they had finding a place to live and a place in society, their marital problems and problems with their children, their alcoholism and pathological reserve, all of which figured prominently in the scholarly literature.

Fiction was potentially more promising. If Karl's author had found the ending of *The Odyssey* unsuitable for his story, perhaps he had gone elsewhere rather than think up his own. Discovering the model would doubtless bring me closer to him. He would perhaps be transformed from a Greek teacher to a Greek and German teacher, from a theater director to a theater director who had made a name for himself with the stage adaptation of a homecoming novel.

I also had to go to the residence registration office—not so much for Barbara's sister as to find out who else had lived at Kleinmeyerstrasse 38 in 1945. In the neighboring buildings too. I had to write to them, visit them, describe the author to them as best I could, and hear what they had to say. I also drafted a letter to Barbara's sister, which I planned to show to Barbara before sending it off.

I took a bath and read Leonhard Frank's tale about Anna, the woman whose husband does not return, and Karl, his friend, who has heard so much about Anna that he not only pictures her but falls in love with her and cannot resist the temptation to assume the role of his friend, whom he has had to leave behind in captivity. If Anna realizes from the start that he is not her husband, why does she pretend he is? If she is unsure but suspects something, why does she never ask? Is it to keep her options open so she can later feign shock and horror and go back to her husband? But she has renounced her husband long before he returns, and she goes off with his friend. I knew the story of Martin Guerre, whose charming—and enterprising—double took over his wife, house, and land and, greedy as he was, sued the family for even more land but was unmasked before the court by the unexpected appearance of the real, long-since-presumed-dead Martin Guerre. In this case I could understand the wife: Martin Guerre had not loved her; he had abused and abandoned her. But in Leonhard Frank's story the husband must have been madly in love with his wife: after all, he had talked about her in such a way as to make someone else fall in love with her simply by listening to him. Or was his talk a form of betrayal? Was that what alienated his wife, what she could not forgive him?

By Sunday my life was mine again. I knew it with a certainty that started out sad, turned defiant, and ended up reconciled. Darkness fell. It was cold and wet out. But my apartment was warm, full of music, and redolent of rosemary.

17

AT FIVE THE DOORBELL RANG. Barbara was at the door. She was wet, her hair looked pasted onto her head, her coat was dripping. "I . . . I ran."

"All the way from Basel?"

"No, moron! From the bridge, where my car gave up on me. I didn't go to Basel; I stayed at home. Have you got anything dry I can put on?"

She took a shower and pulled on the underwear, socks, jeans, and sweater I gave her. Then she sat in the other armchair, using the cup of hot chocolate I had given her to keep her hands warm. "What's that music? It's beautiful."

"Arvo Pärt. It's music without beginning or end. I've been listening to it over and over for hours."

She took a sip and said, "I've got to talk to you."

I waited.

"There's another man. Not here. In Kenya. I haven't seen him since I came back, and hadn't seen him there for months. Since March, to be exact. But he's still in the picture. I can feel it. And he may be coming."

"Do you want him to come?"

She looked at me as if I were torturing her. "He's . . . We're . . . We're kind of married."

"Kind of? I didn't know people could be 'kind of' married."

That tortured look again. "He's a journalist, an American, always on the road. We've never really lived together and didn't really want to get married. It didn't make sense with him here today, gone tomorrow and me in Germany—he doesn't speak a word of German. But then we thought, well, that's the kind of life we led—footloose, unsettled, unsociable—and yet we wanted to have each other no matter where we were. I've always felt unsettled, even here in Germany, even as a child."

I smiled. "Always escaping on the weekends?"

She smiled back. "Always." She took another sip. "In April he went off to Sudan, where the rebels are in power, not unchallenged of course, and they're internally divided as well. That was the last I heard from him. I've heard *about* him, though: that he was captured by the rebels or by government troops, that he took part in the negotiations between the two, that he was involved in emergency relief, you name it. Once before, he stayed away for over a year without a word and then turned up with a fantastic scoop. Maybe you've heard of him. His name is Augie Markovich; he's a two-time Pulitzer winner. I used to worry. Then we promised not to." She shook her head. "There were times when he could easily have kept in touch and didn't, just to give me practice in not worrying."

Again I waited: I did not want to repeat the question I had asked before. But then she might not proffer the answer on her own, and finally, much as I wanted to avoid pressing her, I could not help myself. "Well, what do you want? Do you want him back in your life?"

She gave me a bewildered look. "I don't know. I never thought you and me would . . . It just happened, and it's good. I can't believe how good it is. But at the same time . . ." She shook her head again. "I don't know who I am anymore. Maybe I'm not the footloose, unsettled, unsociable person I used to take myself for. Maybe I'm the same as everyone else, out for a house and garden and dog and friends and kids and hubby, looking forward to home every day and a nice cozy existence. No, that's not what I want. I hate that and always have."

"What if you put the husband and children first, followed it with the friends and dog, and left the house and garden till last?"

She took me seriously. "I see what you mean. I'll give it some thought, okay?"

"Okay."

She finished the hot chocolate. "Will you help me get the car to a garage? And let's go to a movie afterward. And can I stay over tonight? It'll give my clothes a chance to dry."

18

THE NEXT WEEKEND we left town again—the rain had let up, and Basel lay pretty as a picture under a clear, cold, blue sky. From then on, things were different between us. The weekends before Christmas we spent at home. We got together more often during the week and led the normal life of a normal couple. She got to know my friends and colleagues better, and I hers. We went to the opera, though I preferred concerts, and to concerts, though she preferred the opera. We saw every African film that was shown on television or released commercially. We baked cinnamon stars, hazelnut macaroons, and Hilda rolls. We took a yoga course together. She did not want me to introduce her to my mother: she wasn't ready yet. Nor was she ready to go and see her sister with me. As a token of her goodwill, however, she gave me her sister's address.

She remained as witty as she had been from the outset, but was no longer so content, so cheerful. It was as if our relationship had begun as an enclave from which she had shut out her anxieties. Now the enclave had become an integral part of her life and the anxieties had seeped in. Barbara felt guilty about not having visited her mother—or her father—when they were dying. In both cases it would have been difficult but possible, and in both instances it was not a must: when her father went into the hospital, she was an exchange student in Edinburgh and he had made it through other heart attacks, and her mother's cancer would progress so fast just before she was coming home anyway the doctors either had not known or did not tell her. I also learned that Barbara found the large classes, apathetic pupils, and frazzled colleagues a burden after Kenya, that there had been more interest in English and German there, that the cold, wet, gray autumn had got to her more than before, that she had grown away from most of her friends and they from her.

We talked a lot about ourselves. I told her about my grandparents, my parents, about Veronika and Max, the utility of justice and the possibilities of homecoming. She thought I should be asking my mother more about my father, talking more to Veronika about the things that worried me about Max, and turning my ideas on the utility of justice into an essay. She would listen when I went on about my work, and run for a bandage when I cut myself cooking. She did everything to be there for me.

Sometimes she awoke at night with a little cry or woke me because she had not been able to fall asleep for hours even though her eyes kept closing over her book. Sometimes she cried at night. I would take her in my arms, and when she had a nightmare she would tell me what she remembered of it; otherwise she didn't feel like talking. I would then tell her homecoming stories, battle stories, stories of justice, the stories of the long-winded Winkelried at Sempach and of Mennon and Eugène. More often than not she fell asleep before the story was over. Sometimes she had back pain, and I massaged her.

She talked about her husband too, of course, but I did not find out what I wanted to know. I did not want to know the dangers he might be in or the dangers he had been in and how he had got out of them; I did not want to discuss the ways they attempted to maintain hope and patience and fidelity in light of the arrangement they had set up; what I wanted to know was what she saw in him, loved in him. And whether she still loved him. She could not write to him that they were through, because she could not write to him. But what would she write if she could?

19

ELUSIVE AS HE WAS, he was ever present. Perhaps his very elusiveness made his presence all the more palpable. When she was quiet, absent, pensive, sad, I thought: She's thinking about him; when she leafed through a newspaper looking for something, I thought: She's looking for a report about him; when she jumped up to answer the telephone, I thought: She's hoping it's him.

I would give her an occasional ultimatum: "I can't take any more of this, Barbara. If you can't commit to me, I've got to reconsider my own commitment."

"But I *am* committed to you, every day and every hour we're together."

"No, you aren't, and you won't be until you give up your commitment to him."

She gave me a sad look. "What do you want me to do? Write him a farewell letter, prop it against the mirror, and hand it to him without a word if he comes? I can make all the inner commitments you like; they don't mean a thing in the outside world until I tell him."

When I stayed over at her place, I sometimes awoke at night. Had I heard something? A car door slam? A car take off? Had he rung the bell? Thrown a stone at the window? Then I would lie there listening to the sounds of the night—the Church of Jesus chimes, a train passing if the wind was from the west, the patter of the rain in the trees outside the window—waiting for him, if it was him, to ring again, call again, throw another stone.

"Does he know where you're living now?" I asked, after waking up the first time and listening in the night.

"Yes. Mother had died by the time he left for Sudan, and I had decided to move into her apartment."

So it was not completely crazy of me to listen in the night. Sometimes, while falling back to sleep, I thought of looking up the late evening and early morning arrival times of planes from Africa and calculating how long it would take him to get from Frankfurt to Barbara's apartment, but I never did.

He came in broad daylight. A Saturday. We had been shopping and were emptying the bags. Our wine merchant had offered to deliver the four cases we ordered, and when the doorbell rang, Barbara said, "That must be the wine" and went to the door. But she did not say, "It goes in the basement. I'll show you," or "Just leave it there. We'll take it down ourselves." She did not call out cheerily, as was her wont, to either the delivery man or the parcel post man or the landlord; she just stood there and, as far as I could tell, listened to the footsteps coming up the stairs.

I reached her just as he appeared on the staircase. She let out a cry and ran down the stairs, flung her arms around his neck, and burst into tears; he dropped his bag, which bumped down the stairs, and took her in his arms. I grabbed my coat off the coatrack and walked down the stairs. His eyes were closed. As I passed them, she threw a teary glance at me and whispered, "No." I stopped for a moment, but as she said nothing more I went on. I waited another moment before letting the entrance door go, but she did not run after me or call down.

Part Three

I

I LATER LEARNED to give an ironic account of having tried to reconstruct the end of a story of a man who returns home after a long absence, climbs the stairs, and sees his wife in the doorway standing next to another man and of my having stood next to a woman in a doorway as her husband climbs the stairs, returning home after a long absence. I would get questions like "Had you known anything about the man beforehand?" and I would tell the truth: "I'd hoped she loved me more than him. But she ran up to him and flung her arms around his neck." Then I would laugh and say, "At least I had the ending to my story."

It always went down well, especially with women. Women find sad, sensitive, valiantly laughing losers interesting.

But that was later. That Saturday I drove into the woods thinking a walk would do me good, but I soon saw that with every step, every movement, every breath, things in fact got worse. I asked a doctor friend of mine to prescribe some powerful sleeping pills and switched off the telephone. I had read somewhere that one mourns a love for as long as it lasted, and hoped I would recover by spring. When a letter came from Barbara—the envelope so slim it could have been no more than a single sheet—I carried it around with me for a while but eventually tore it up, unread, and threw it away.

I was also on the point of throwing away the file containing Karl's story. I was sick and tired of homecoming stories. Many soldiers came back, many did not. So what. So what if Karl came home or moved on. Augie came home like Odysseus, and Barbara had waited for him like Penelope, a modern Penelope who did not weave by day and undo what she had woven by night; no, she had fallen in love, but she too knew when to tear apart the fabric of love. That was all that counted. But in the end I kept the file.

I bought a dining table, four chairs, and a leather couch. I saw a lot of Max and occasionally went out with friends. Yes, I did feel better by the spring, and in the autumn I slept with a journalist who invited me home after a reception my publishing house gave at the Frankfurt Book Fair. The morning after, she accused me of having forced her into it: she hadn't wanted to, I'd followed her home against her will, insisted on coming in, then all but raped her. I was furious and defended myself, and though I apologized in case I had misconstrued something or other, I had not misconstrued a thing: I remembered her invitation to come up for a drink word for word. It was all terribly disconcerting, so much so that I made a note to ask a colleague whether I had had too much to drink at the reception. Then I forgot about it, and when the journalist phoned me at home a few days later and bawled me out again I was completely indifferent.

That same autumn I received an offer from another publisher in another city. It meant a fresh start in a city where *she* did not live, a release from hoping and fearing to meet her. Of course she might have moved away. She and Augie. I was still tempted to dial her number and see whether she answered.

My employers did everything they could to keep me, and Max's "That means no more movies together" was so plaintive that I felt terrible. I stayed. What good was a fresh start that smacked of retreat?

2

NO, THAT'S NOT what happened. I wish it had; I wish I had been so ironic, removed, in charge. Instead I was childish.

I did not treat the staircase scene with irony; I ridiculed it. Once I started going out again, I made fun of women for running from man to man, and men for believing in the love of a woman. It was embarrassing: the men laughed only to be polite, and the women were either pitying or put off. But I could not let the wound be. A friend once sat me down with a drink after a party and tried as diplomatically as possible to convince me I was making a fool of myself. He talked about renegades intent on showing how much they scorn what they have outgrown: the atheist his faith, the communist his bourgeois upbringing, the social climber his modest origins. I refused to understand him.

The sleeping pills did their job: a combination of pills and alcohol put me out of commission for days. Because the telephone kept jangling, I ripped the wire out of the wall. I did not let Barbara in when she stood downstairs ringing the bell or when someone else let her in and she came upstairs and knocked on my door shouting. I was drunk at the time, though I remembered it well enough to know that I had to destroy the follow-up letter when it came.

But that was not all. If Barbara had really been in earnest, wouldn't she have written another letter? Would she have left off after one ringing, knocking, and shouting session? After all, she could not have known whether I was even there to hear it all. That she had come and written but did not come or write again was proof she did not love me enough. Yet not even a second coming or a second letter would have sufficed, because true love requires a third and fourth attempt, an unlimited number.

Table, chairs, and couch, Max and friends—life went on, and after a few months things were going better. What I feared most about the night with the journalist was not that I had raped her: I had not. But she had been right in feeling that during the act I had been absent in a way that was insulting to her. She had found nothing in the way I treated her of what usually brings two people together for a night: the need for intimacy and tenderness, the fear of loneliness or demons of the past. She saw through me, and my conduct had so outraged her that she identified it with rape.

I began to wonder if I had lost the ability to feel. In fact, I seemed to lack the ability not only to feel engagement in the act but also to feign feeling; it had been torn off like a wig, a mask. Was I having blackouts? Did I need to keep an eye on myself? How could I ask a colleague about that!

I should also mention that though I never waited long enough for Barbara to pick up the phone I repeatedly gave in to my temptation to dial her number. I would let it ring two or three times, then hang up. I did it not to wake or annoy her or even to dare myself to let it keep ringing; I did it to be part of her life.

3

ONE NEED NOT BE TOLD by a psychotherapist that it is bad to repress pain, to bury oneself in one's work, to sleep with journalists one does not love, to move in with the first woman who comes along. That one must let the mourning process take its course. These are the psychotherapist's stock-in-trade.

But how was I to mourn? How to meditate? And on what? How long was I to stay at home listening to records and reading? How often was I to tell my friends about my pain? Embarrassed but not wanting to hurt me, they heard me out, ready to do anything to hasten our return to normal, friendly relations. I knew that the mourning process meant one did not throw oneself at somebody else, but I had no desire to do so anyway.

Nor did I find that friends and colleagues who had taken up with sweet young things soon after their marriage or relationship went sour suffered inordinately from failing to work through their past or that those who had retreated into themselves eventually made hale and hearty comebacks. Sometimes I thought of the work-through and let-be alternatives as analogous to the baby-on-the-back versus baby-on-the-tummy wars that raged from generation to generation. I remember the long talks on the subject we had had with doctors and nurses after Max was born.

Yes, once I was able to work, I worked more than ever. Then again, the situation demanded it: the publisher had acquired some other scholarly presses and was scaling ours down, which made me the only legal expert on the staff and increased my responsibilities. Our legal list was smaller than our medical or science list, smaller too than our fishing, sailing, skin diving, and other hobby lists. Presumably the executive board, whose members all came from those fields, would not even notice if my little niche failed to hold its own. But I needed either to write off the line of textbooks I had initiated or put them out immediately so they could make a place for themselves. The same held for the journal: either I gave it up or went all out for quality and visibility. And I had invested too much thought and hard work to be able to give the projects up.

During those early months of reshuffling I had no time to look at a woman. I left the house early, came back late, and traveled a lot. Even my mother noticed I was working hard. Not too hard, because that was impossible for her, but hard. When my efforts met with success—several of the textbooks became bestsellers, and the circulation of the journal grew monthly—I became a worka-holic as a way of handling the ever-increasing workload. After the success of the textbook series the old textbooks and reference man-uals had to be updated in both content and design, so that the stu-dents who had grown accustomed to buying our books would find the material they needed in them once they began practicing. So I got the executive board to hire two students to assist me.

I did not hire Bettina because of her velvetlike beauty. I did not really notice her unintimidating, low-pressure, calming looks until she started work. I cannot quite put my finger on what made her so pleasing to the eye and heart. The brown hair, the brown eyes, a mouth that was always slightly open, a characteristic thoughtful-ness in the gestures, which led me to interpret them as a promise of kindness, acceptance, and indulgence?

In any case, kind she was. And she accepted and indulged me as no one had ever done. Sometimes I had the feeling she let me do as I pleased because she did not care what I did. Not that that would have bothered me: nothing wrong with a relationship based on well-meaning mutual indifference. Then I noticed I could not allow myself to be indulged: I did not want to be in her debt, and I saw the price she would extract from me or at least had the right to extract. Indulgence has an ulterior motive, and that ulterior motive is love. But not even if I had loved Bettina would I have felt I could repay her for so much indulgence.

4

I HAD TOO MUCH WORK to be able to do much reading, but *The Odyssey* lay by my bed. When I was too keyed up to fall asleep or when I awoke in the middle of the night, a few lines of my tried-and-true *Odyssey* hit the spot.

In books nine and ten Odysseus reports on the first part of his wanderings. He and his men sail from Troy to the Cicones; they sack the city, kill off the male population, ravish the women, and distribute the spoils among themselves. From the Cicones they move on to the Lotus Eaters, who so indulge Odysseus' men with their honey-sweet lotus fruit that they lose all thought of departure and homecoming. Odysseus and his band have a hard time of it with the one-eyed, man-hating and man-eating Cyclops, but Aeolus, who hosts a daily feast with his wife and six strapping sons and six comely daughters, regales them with food and shelter for an entire month. The Laestrygonians have it in for Odysseus and his company; like the Cyclops, they are giants (though two-eyed) and hate and eat men. With only one ship and few men Odysseus lands on Circe's shores only to have the men turned into swine. Circe would have done the same to Odysseus had he not, forewarned by an emissary from the gods, stood up to her with sword in hand—whereby he wins her love and his men's return to human form. During the rest of his wanderings, in books eleven and twelve, Odysseus meets the shades of his mother and other great women in the realm of the dead; the Sirens, who try to lure him to death with their haunting songs; Scylla, a monster with six heads, countless teeth, and twelve feet; Charybdis, who thrice daily gulps down the dark sea's waters and thrice daily regurgitates them; and the glossy-plaited, fragrantly arrayed Calypso, with whom he takes his ease. The last women Odysseus encounters before returning home to Penelope are Nausicaa and Arete, the chaste daughter and understanding wife of the king of Phaeacia.

If the ravished journalist was my Ciconian woman and the indulgent Bettina my Lotus Eater, a one-eyed female Cyclops was waiting in the wings. But I wanted none of a giant with one eye in the middle of her forehead or of a monster named Scylla, with all those heads, teeth, and feet, or her sea-slurping-and-spewing companion, Charybdis; and finding a family with six sisters and six brothers was out of the question. One of the popular novels my mother read in the fifties was called *Cheaper by the Dozen,* but a family with six sons and six daughters was a media story, and if there were any such families in my vicinity I would not know of them. Should I settle for fewer siblings? Should I substitute a group for a family and look for a soprano in a chorus, a harpist in an orchestra, a member of a mixed-doubles team? I already had a candidate for the female giant in mind: a woman at the checkout of the local supermarket. She may not have been a match for the queen of the Laestrygonians, whom Homer compares to a mountaintop, but she was certainly up to her daughter, whom Homer describes as merely sprightly. When one day she arose from her cash register throne to extricate a packet of cigarettes for a customer, her colossal womanhood towered over me by half a head.

I decided in favor of the chorus. I had enjoyed singing in the school chorus and thought that if I could manage the rehearsal schedule it would provide a good counterbalance to all the work I was doing. I actually chose a choir, the choir of the Church of Peace, which in addition to singing for church services gave highly praised concerts. If the chorus of the secular Bach Society had not had such a long waiting list, I would have chosen it instead: looking for a daughter of Aeolus in a church choir must surely be blasphemous. Not that my project was particularly grandiose: I merely wanted to put a little structure into the eternal game of seeking and signing up and finding and letting go; besides, a church chorister was nothing compared with the classic challenge: a nun.

My worries were for naught. At the first rehearsal I realized the "choir" could not have been more secular: the two much-courted beauties, the blond soprano and the alto brunette, the young tenor adored by the middle-aged women, the old-timer clique constantly evoking tradition, the elderly basses looking at everything with suspicion—the same as in any chorus. I set my sights on neither the beauties nor the cheerful anesthesiologist and the caustic legal secretary, both altos, whom I liked: the way I saw it, Odysseus, given his status as guest in Aeolus' household, would have been friendly with all the daughters and waited until one chose him.

The one who chose me was not one I would have chosen. She was an instructor at her father's driving school and consumed by a passion for cars that I knew and despised in men. But the project had taken such a hold on me that as soon as she invited me home I went and bedded her.

5

THINGS WERE MORE complicated with the checkout woman. She was suspicious by nature, and I had to modify my courting ritual: I had to buy her but not with money, no; with gifts, gifts that so appealed to her that she no longer cared about the false grounds on which I gave them to her. I went on giving her gifts after we had slept together, and she began to forget her suspicions. It was then I should have left her. But if women do not do what they should—Barbara had not—then why should I?

Besides, she was such a wild, overwhelming, all-consuming lover that I felt liberated by her. Yes, she was a giant, but instead of tearing me to pieces she tore me free from what had been holding me down and gave me such a shaking that nothing of the old me remained. Until she thought I was in earnest, at which point she turned earnest—and tender.

Next on my list was a sorceress. I had developed a collector's

passion not so much for accumulating individual objects as for filling in the blanks. A plastic surgeon who instead of turning men
into swine—not willingly, at least—was adept at making swinish
faces look more human? A palm reader and fortune-teller who
dealt in prediction rather than transmogrification? An artist, the
creator and destroyer of illusions?

I decided in favor of a cosmetician. The art of cosmetics is to
turn ugly ducklings into beauties, not vice versa, but like plastic
surgeons, cosmeticians should in theory be able make people ugly
if they so desired. There was a cosmetics shop around the corner. It
had two cosmeticians: the elder was the owner, the younger, her
assistant. I made an appointment with the elder one, but she was
out when I got there and the younger one took care of me. She was
from Persia and had skin like an apricot and a voice like a shawm,
and she massaged my face with such fervor and enthusiasm that I
was on the brink of tears. That was the beginning of my problems.
I may have gone only to the brink of tears, but nothing remotely
like that had happened to me since childhood, and it baffled me.
Then the dreams began and baffled me even more.

I would awake and know I had dreamed of Barbara. I knew it
before I remembered the content of the dream: a banal nothing of
a scene in which we were riding in a car or making the bed or
cooking. I knew it because I awoke with the blissful feeling of intimacy I would have on good days with Barbara. As I grew more
awake, the feeling would turn into desire, a desire that at first I
thought I could satisfy simply by reaching out for her. Then, in the
next stage of wakefulness, I realized I could not satisfy it but kept
feeling it for a moment until it turned into disappointment. By
then I was totally awake and started searching my memory for the
dream.

I did not desire Barbara by day. My diurnal intimations of desire
had long since given way to irony and objectivity. How did the

desire in my dream avoid being tainted by them and live its own life?

I began to dream more than I had dreamed since childhood. I dreamed of chases, flights, and falls, of exam anxiety or day-to-day situations with my mother, and, once, of a train trip with Grandfather during which we unpacked one picnic basket after the other without eating anything. I also dreamed a very different kind of dream. I come back one night from a trip; I get out of the taxi and look up at the house: it has burned down. It must have burned down that day, because there is still smoke coming out of the rubble. I am not upset. I am surprised at first, then filled with a feeling of freedom and bliss. Phew! I am finally rid of the casing I had to fit into, of its furniture surrounding me, eyeing me, of all the things I have to put away, keep clean, and in good repair. I am finally rid of my life and free to live a new one.

Each time I came back from one of the many business trips I had to take for the publishing house I would remember that dream. Sitting in the taxi, I would picture smoke rising out of the rubble and feel both hope and despair, because I wanted a new life and did not know what it should be like. But each time, the house was there, and my life went on as it was.

6

COMING BACK ONE summer night from a trip, I found Max standing in front of the house looking lost and forlorn. His shirt was half out of his trousers, his hair unkempt.

"What are you doing here?"

"I . . . Mom . . ."

He pointed to a suitcase standing next to the cement alcove where the trash cans were stored. "Mom says I should stay with you for a while."

"Has she got a new friend?" I shook my head. "Sorry, Max. No go. Come on, I'll drive you home."

He said nothing when I took his hand and picked up the suitcase, walked over to the car, and got in with him. "She's crazy," I said as we drove off. "I could have been away much longer."

"She tried to get you at work, and they told her you'd be back tonight."

"They couldn't have told her that. They didn't know when I'd be back. All they knew was that I'd be at work tomorrow morning."

We were on the Autobahn. The sun had sunk behind the Rhineland hills, but the sky was still luminescent. I was tired from my trip: I had been looking forward to sitting out on my balcony and going to bed early. I felt sorry for Max, but I felt sorry for myself as well.

"Mom's gone."

"What do you mean?"

"She went to Florida with her new friend. That's where he's from. She said that if you didn't want me to stay with you, you could take me to Inge's on Sunday. Inge's away till then."

It was Tuesday. On Wednesday and Thursday I had my hands full at work; on Friday I had to be in Munich, and I had planned to take advantage of it by spending the weekend at Lake Chiemsee. "What about school?"

"What about it?"

"How will you get there?"

"Mom didn't say."

I took the next exit, turned around, and got on again in the opposite direction. I was going home for the second time that day.

Max sat silent next to me. "How long had you been waiting in front of the house?"

"They dropped me off at two. Their plane was leaving at five. I found some kids, and we played together."

"Have you had anything to eat?"

"No. Mom said—"

"I don't want to hear what Mom said and didn't say."

Max fell silent again. I was used to a Max who fidgeted at the movies and whined until the pizza came. I stopped at McDonald's and bought some hamburgers. We ate them at the kitchen table not knowing what to say to each other.

"We've got to get up early tomorrow. I need to be at work at eight and take you to school first."

He nodded.

"I'll make up a bed for you. Have you got everything you need? Toothbrush, pajamas, clean underwear, schoolbooks?"

"Mom said—" But then he remembered I did not want to hear what Veronika had said and failed to say. I opened the suitcase, laid out his pajamas and clothes for the next day, and gave him a toothbrush.

While he brushed his teeth, I put fresh sheets on my bed for him and pulled the old ones over the couch for myself. He made a fast job of it but was not eager to go to bed, and after he had climbed in he asked, "Will you tell me a story?"

Can you still tell a ten-year-old fairy tales? I tried the saga of the knight Hildebrandt, who comes home after many, many years and meets the young knight Hadubrandt. Hadubrandt is unaware that he is Hildebrandt's son, Hildebrandt that he is Hadubrandt's father. Hadubrandt, now ruler of the land, is furious that the stranger fails to greet him with the deference that he, as his sovereign, deserves. The two duel until they can duel no more. Then Hildebrandt asks Hadubrandt for his name and lineage and reveals himself as his father. But Hadubrandt does not believe him: he believes his father dead and Hildebrandt an imposter. He resumes the duel.

"And?"

Well, well, the old saga had won over the comics- and cartoon-jaded Max: he wanted to know how it all ended.

"The only way Hildebrandt could ward off a fatal blow was to strike Hadubrandt dead himself."

"No!"

"Well, that's what the singers who handed down the saga to us thought one day too. And from that day on they sang that the two men finally recognized each other, threw down their swords, and embraced."

7

THUS BEGAN MY life with Max. I canceled the trip to Munich. On Wednesday, Thursday, and Friday I drove him to and picked him up from school. Over the weekend we practiced the trip in the half-streetcar, half-train that connected the cities plus the ten-minute walk from the last stop. We also practiced the route to the publishing house, where Max reported after school from Monday on, eating with me in the canteen and doing his homework next to me in the office. On Monday evening I found a letter from Veronika announcing her return in seven weeks. I hoped that Max would not start taking my surrogate parent role for granted and that he would remain on his best behavior.

No such luck. Day by day he grew more lively, headstrong, demanding. First he found an empty office to do his homework in;

then, rather than doing his homework, he wanted to play with the children he had found while waiting for me. When it was time to go home, he wanted me to take him to the swimming pool or the movies or to a hotel: he took an odd pleasure in sitting in hotel lobbies and ordering a Coke.

But as Max grew more restless, my life settled down. I wanted less, I worked less, yet things seemed to get done. I abandoned Odysseus' women and searched no more: no shades of great ladies, no temptresses unto death, no plaited tresses and fragrant raiments, no chaste daughter and understanding mother. I went out less often and began feeling more at home in my apartment and kitchen. Max was in bed by nine and would fall asleep once I had told him a story. I did not waste my time waiting for food or the bill in a restaurant: I ate and did the dishes and had two or three hours to do whatever I pleased.

So I went back to Karl. I wrote to the register office and learned that in the thirties and forties the ground-floor flat of Kleinmeyerstrasse 38 had been inhabited by a couple named Karl and Gerda Wolf, the flats on the next floor by the Lampe and Bindinger families and the flat on the floor up from that by a Rudolf Hagert. Karl Wolf died in 1945; Gerda Wolf moved to Wiesbaden in 1952. Rudolf Hagert moved into an old people's home in 1955 and died there two years later. I found Gerda Wolf's name in the Wiesbaden phone book and wrote her a letter explaining my interest in the former inhabitants of Kleinmeyerstrasse 38 and asking whether she would be willing to see me. Three days later I had her response: Yes, do come.

On Sunday morning Max and I drove to Wiesbaden. We took a ride on the funicular—whose upper car fills its tank with water and uses the weight of the water to descend into the valley and pull the lower car up—and a walk in the vineyards. Shortly before three I sat Max down on a bench with a book and made him promise not to budge from the spot. I was at Gerda Wolf's at three on the dot. She looked to be in her midseventies. Her place was small and full of books and paintings and of medals that hung in small frames like pictures.

"The medals are my father's," she said, pointing to a picture of a man with a chest full of them.

"Karl Wolf was your father?"

"Yes. He shot himself when he read the report of the Führer's demise. He was at home because he had lost his leg."

We were sitting at the dining table, and she served me tea and homemade marble cake. I told her once more what I had written in the letter: Karl's story, his return to Kleinmeyerstrasse 38, my conjecture that the author had lived in the building before or during the war or had gone in and out.

"You have no real evidence?"

I shook my head. "I suspect he had a decent education and had never been to Siberia or even in the war. But I can't be sure."

She gave me a questioning look.

"I think when you've experienced something," I said, "you want to write what actually happened. You don't make your Siberian rivers run south rather than north; you don't make your soldiers speak a slang no soldier ever spoke except in novels or on the screen. Or do you? Maybe the author was trying to humor his audience with clichés."

"Rudolf Hagert was a research chemist for BASF. He was also mad about cars. I can't imagine him reading a novel much less writing one. He never took in lodgers, nor did we. Frau Lampe let out rooms to students; she wanted to find a husband for her daughter—and did. Her daughter married a man by the name of Bindinger, one of the students, though"—she wrinkled her nose—"anyone who was a student at the time was either a cripple or a mental case."

"Did you meet any of the lodgers?"

"In all the years I lived there only one had the decency to ring our doorbell and introduce himself. Only one."

"A cripple? A mental case?"

"A nice young man who sorely regretted that his bad heart kept him from being conscripted. He so wanted to be part of the fray that I had a word with Freda and she with Karl, and Karl took him under his wing."

"Freda? Karl?"

"The Baroness von Fircks, my old friend, and her husband, Karl Hanke, the gauleiter of Silesia."

"Do you know what became of the young man? Do you know his name? Did he—"

"—write? I have no idea. He was a student, so he must have done some writing. But so did the other lodgers. I don't remember his name. Frau Bindinger must have known it. They were friends."

"She died last year."

Frau Wolf nodded, as if her death were painful but only just.

"Are Freda von Fircks and Karl Hanke still alive?"

"Freda remarried and lives with her husband, a man named Rössler, in Bielefeld. As for Karl Hanke—can you young people be so ignorant of your own history? There were rumors he fled via Spain to Argentina or ended up in an American POW camp or was hanged by German soldiers or executed or beaten to death by the Czechs. In any case, Freda needed to have him declared dead in 1950, but I believe he is still with us. He was the best of them all."

She pulled herself up and beamed at me. "His chivalrous treatment of Magda, his commitment to the panzers—he volunteered, you know—his defense of Breslau: little wonder the Führer loved him so."

8

SHE WAS RIGHT. Hitler did love Hanke, so much so that shortly before his death he appointed him SS Reichsführer to replace Himmler. The people of Breslau have never forgiven him—the man in charge of turning the city into a fortress, of defending it and destroying it, of holding it to the last man—for having taken off on May 2, 1945, from a runway that had cost the Breslauers many lives to construct and on which no plane had ever landed and no plane taken off other than the Fiseler Storch that Hanke had hidden and used for his escape. Though perhaps it was not an act of cowardice; perhaps he had wanted to meet up with Schörner, whom Hitler, also shortly before his death, promoted to commander in chief of the armed forces.

There was no reason to believe him a coward: he volunteered in 1939, when he could easily have sat out the war in Berlin as Goebbels' undersecretary, but he had had it out with Goebbels over the latter's affair with Lída Baarová and the hard time he was giving his wife, Magda, and before that he had jeopardized his position as teacher and eventually lost it because of his work for the Party. He was a gifted organizer and full of ideas: it was he who came up with the plan of using the Berlin indoor tennis centers as the scenes for Goebbels' extravaganzas, when no one wanted to rent the Party assembly rooms; it was he who organized the press coverage of the war, to which he personally contributed. At the same time he dipped deeply into the Party's coffers and set himself up in luxury in his Breslau fortress; he was hard-nosed, high and mighty, and hotheaded; he would stop at nothing. Yes, Gerda Wolf was right: Karl Hanke was pretty much the best National Socialism had to offer.

When I told Max about Hanke's career, he clicked his tongue.

The long phone conversations about Hanke I had had with a historian friend had piqued his curiosity.

"But I thought brave was good."

We were sitting on the balcony having dinner. I had always thought it must be nice for a father to lay out the world before a child. Perhaps I had dreamed of learning about the world from my father. I did not know that children think the hard questions they ask are easy and thus expect easy answers to them, and that they are disappointed when they get cautious, complex answers. I looked up at the sky and took a sip of wine while arming myself against Max's disappointment.

"Bravery is good when the cause is good. When the cause is bad, bravery is . . ." I paused. "Not good" was too pale, "bad" too strong.

"Bad?"

"It's like hard work. When you put a lot of work into something good, then the work is good; when you put a lot of work into digging a hole for your neighbor to fall into and get hurt, the work is bad. Because digging the hole is bad, the work you put into it is bad."

Max was concentrating so hard that a crease had formed between his brows. "Would Hanke have been better if he'd been a coward?"

"Brave or cowardly, zealous or lazy—if the cause is bad, it doesn't matter." Was that true? Couldn't cowardice and sloth be virtues if they sabotaged an evil goal?

Max had the same idea. "If I'm lazy about digging the hole, it won't be that deep and I won't hurt my neighbor that much." Then he went off on a tangent. "Isn't there an expression about falling into a pit you dig for somebody else?"

"That's something different," I said, and instead of being pleased at the turn in the conversation I tried to wind things up. "The value of being brave, working hard, saving money, keeping order depends on what it's for."

"But I don't know yet what I'm saving my money for."

For a moment I thought Max was making a joke, but then that frown came back, and he looked up at me with concern.

"Well, when the time comes, spend it on something good."

"But what if I spend it on something bad?"

I may have said what I thought I should say, but I didn't believe it. Bravery was a lesser virtue than fairness, the love of truth, or compassion, but it was a virtue all the same, and even a man like Hanke was, in my eyes, better brave than cowardly. I did not like lazy people, and I did not like it when people made a mess of their financial affairs or their lives. I was my mother's son. I did not want to argue with Max over whether the diligence I expected him to show at school or the order I expected him to maintain at home served good ends. My answer to his first question should have been: Yes, bravery is good, but bravery is not enough. It was too late for that now. All I could say was, "Spend it on something bad? Just don't, that's all."

9

I GOT THE PHONE NUMBER of Barbara's sister Margarete from information. When I phoned, she interrupted me the moment I gave her my name. "I thought you'd forgotten about me."

"You . . ."

"You were going to call ages ago. When was it you were in touch with my sister?"

"As you say, ages ago."

"Barbara told me then you wanted to know who might have written about us and whether there were any clues in Mother's papers. Is that what you're calling about?"

"It is."

"You can come on Saturday at eleven. If you want copies, though, you'll have to bring your own photocopier." She hung up.

I got hold of a photocopier and arrived at the designated hour. Just to be sure, I was early and waited around the corner in the car. Margarete Bindinger lived in a fifties housing development of semidetached houses with gardens. I would have been glad to grow up in a place like that. Mother and I would take an occasional Sunday walk through one, and everything looked so nice and friendly: each house with a basement and attic, a balcony, and a bathroom with its own little window right next to the entrance; a garden with a terrace and swings and a stand for beating carpets, with fruit trees and ornamental trees and a vegetable patch; places for children to roller-skate and play hopscotch and dodgeball and soccer. Now the trees were tall; the gardens were all grass, bushes, and flowers; and the streets were lined with cars.

The garden door had a knob that did not turn, but there was a bolt on the inside. Since I felt squeamish about reaching over to push it open, I rang the bell. The house door opened, and Margarete Bindinger said, "You don't need me to come out, do you?" and waited for me to make my way to her. There she stood, short and gaunt, with a gray face and a look that made me feel less than welcome. Instead of responding to my greeting, she pointed to the photocopier and asked, "Does it take a lot of electricity?"

"I don't know. I just want—"

She put up her hand. "I don't want to charge you for the electricity you use. It looks like a handy machine, and I was wondering whether I should get one." She let me in and closed the door. It was only then that I noticed that her right leg was shorter than her left and that she walked with a cane. She led me into the room facing the street and sat me at a table with six chairs. There was a folder on the table. She sat down opposite me.

"I—"

But she put up her hand again. Instead of letting me speak, she posed a series of brief questions to which she expected brief answers, and grew impatient when they went on too long. Once I had finished telling her about Karl and my search for his creator, she asked, "Why are you interested in him?"

"He knew my grandparents and knows the place where I grew up, and I would like to find out how the novel he wrote ends. I'm just curious, that's all."

She looked me straight in the eye. "No, you're not just curious. But that's none of my business. Barbara told me to help you, and I have no reason not to. There's not much to show you in any case." She put her hand on the folder. "Mother didn't keep a diary, but she did keep letters—letters from her parents, her best friend, my father, and us. There are also a few letters from a man who is a stranger to me. I don't know anything about their relationship." She stood up. "I'll leave you alone now. Let me know when you've finished."

I opened the folder.

10

My dear Fräulein Beate:

All is right with the world: there is a rightness about your being where life is whole and my being where it is coming apart at the seams, a rightness about our having met, a rightness about your not loving me.

It is three days since you told me. With so much grace, so much kindness, so much warmth that while I failed to find the happiness I sought I am still, after a fashion, happy. One can love and not be loved in return and feel it as an injustice. But there is also a justice to unrequited love.

I arrived here yesterday evening. Fighting began early this morning. It is splendid.

I thank you for allowing me to make you the witness of my thoughts while I was in your midst. May I continue to write?

Yours,

Volker Vonlanden

17 January 1942

The next letters, written several weeks apart, were similar: a few sentences about the world, a few about the war, and a few about Beate. Volker Vonlanden compared Beate to the dawn, to the evening and morning stars, to warm rain, the air after a storm, a drink of water after a day in the sun, and the warmth of an oven after a night in the snow. I found the dawn passage particularly fetching:

No, Beate, you do not remind me of the gentle dawn that slowly bathes the world in ever more radiant light. There is another dawn, brief in duration and great in strength, which frightens off the night, drives away the mist, and ushers in the day. This is the dawn you remind me of. Once there was a revolution initiated and won by a single shot from a warship. That ship bore the name of Aurora, dawn. *You know, do you not, that you can revolutionize my life with a single word?*

After summer there is a break in the letters. A Christmas letter explains why. The letter also makes it clear that his spring and summer letters have touched Beate's heart and brought her around.

Dear Beate,

Last winter I wrote to you that you had opened my eyes to the justice of unrequited love. What did you think I meant by that?

Unrequited love does not rest until it can reject the love that rejected it. Either it thereby creates its own justice or it deserves none.

We enjoyed our summer days together, but what is past is past.
Farewell! On my way back to the front I met a girl I like. You know how
it is.
   Volker
   Christmas 1942

The next letter dates from a year and a half later. There is a newspaper article enclosed.

   Dearest and much esteemed Beate:
   You must not take offense at the portrait. I know you do not make a
great fuss about yourself or wish that others should do so, but that is not
why I undertook to write the piece. I wrote it not so much for you as for the
men in the field. That you were there before my eyes and are now before
theirs—does this not make you ever so slightly proud?
   I feel it should.
   Yours,
   Volker
   12 June 1944

The article, which covers half a page, is entitled "Yet Another Cause" and signed by Volker Vonlanden:

She loves me not. She told me so during my last leave. She is fond of me,
but I am not the one, and she is certain he will come one day; she is wait-
ing for him. Sometimes I wonder where he is fighting: in Italy, in France,
in Russia? Or here at my side perhaps.
   She is a girl with blond hair, blue eyes, and a smiling mouth. She loves
to laugh out loud. You can tell by her forehead that she has many thoughts
and by her chin that she will give in to no one. When bombs fall, she
laughs defiantly and gets to work. She has strong arms and can pitch
in. She is tall and straight, and when you see her walk you want to dance
with her.

She loves me not. One day she will love someone, the one. And one day someone, the one, will love me. She, too, laughs defiantly when the bombs fall; she, too, pitches in clearing rubble, turning lathes, bringing in the crops; she, too, is waiting for me. She just does not know it.

Many of us are fighting for our wives and children. We know that every shot which finds its man, every attack which makes its mark, every defense which holds the line saves German lives. You say you have no wife? You say you have no child? You say you have no girl or had one and she loves another? You love a girl who loves you not? Even though you do not know her, somewhere there is a fine German girl who is the one for you, a girl who is laughing defiantly and pitching in while she waits for you, who needs your protection as much as your comrades' wives and children.

Yet another cause to fight for: the joys to come. We may not know when and how they will come, but that they will come we know.

The next and last letter also mentioned an enclosed article, but I was unable to find it.

Dear Beate,

You may be interested in my latest article. Much around us is falling apart, and many people are following suit. As if men were buildings.

What are the ruins, the ashes of buildings to us! Let us celebrate what cannot be destroyed and what will protect and restore us wherever we go.

I hope to see you again.

Yours,

Volker

16 March 1945

But there was more in the folder after the last letter. I found a twenty-page undated typescript, "The Iron Rule," under Volker Vonlanden's name. Were these the thoughts Volker had made Beate witness to?

It began with three great epochs of world history, the first recognizing the law of nature—brute force, combat, and victory—and calling for the annihilation of the weak, the alien, and all enemies; the second following the Judeo-Christian commandment to love one's neighbor; the third returning to the priorities of the first. The third epoch was now beginning; the second had begun with the fall of Rome. The next part dealt with the ban on killing and the killing of prisoners by the Aztecs, of wounded Spartans by the Spartans, and of diseased Roman children by the Romans. Then came the passage that gave the text its title:

The golden rule in its various formulations forbids one from doing to another what one would not oneself wish to suffer. At times the prohibition is complemented by an exhortation, encouraging one to do for the other what one would oneself wish to experience. In either case the golden rule is a rule of submission. What is its relationship to the law? It goes against the very first of all legal rights: the right to defend oneself against attack. It tells us that since we do not wish to meet with defense when we attack, we should offer none when we are attacked.

The law rests not on this golden rule but on an iron rule: whatever you are willing to take upon yourself you have the right to inflict upon others. The iron rule too comes in various formulations. If you are willing to subject yourself to something, you have the right to subject others to it; what you demand of yourself, you may demand of others, and so on. It is the rule that supplies the foundation for all authority and leadership. The hardships the leader imposes upon himself he has the right to impose upon those whom he leads; indeed, it is because he imposes them upon himself and them that they recognize him as their leader.

After appending a number of examples, the author returned to the ban on killing. A ban on killing would not make the law more right or people more righteous. The iron rule applied to killing as well:

If I am prepared to be killed, I have the right to kill. I am prepared to be killed when I enter into a life-and-death struggle, be it declared or not and no matter who declares it. The Jews do not attack us? All they want is to make deals, jack up prices, and charge high interest? The Slavs do not attack us? They care only about plowing the land, baking bread, and making moonshine? Neither Jews nor Slavs will be saved thereby. Germany has entered into a life-and-death struggle with them.

II

AS IF SHE had been spying on my reading, Margarete Bindinger turned up in the doorway the moment I was through. "I have no way of answering your questions. I don't know if he came to the house after the war. I have no idea if my mother was pregnant when she met my father and if the marriage was a rush job. Is Vonlanden my father? I was born five months after the wedding and am told by my relatives that I look like my father. Those *were* your questions, weren't they?"

I nodded. "When did the wedding take place?"

"October 1942."

So Beate had realized that Volker Vonlanden was not the one soon after the summer they had spent together; it did not take her until Christmas.

"Did your mother ever speak about him?"

"No."

"I don't imagine she gave him much thought. He was . . ."

". . . an unpleasant character? Well, he definitely was not pleasant. But Mother had a way of dumping people, and if that's what she did to him I can see why he wanted to get back at her." She was looking straight ahead, frowning, pursing her lips, as if recalling all the times her mother had fobbed her off onto somebody.

"I'm less interested in his need to get back at your mother than in what he has to say about justice and—"

She gave a derisive snort. "She never loved me back, much as I would have liked her to, but where's the injustice in that?" She looked at me for a moment as if expecting an answer but then lost interest in her question. "Whatever. It's the kind of thing you keep to yourself."

"Why did your mother preserve all this?"

"Another question I can't answer. She wasn't one for reminiscing. You know what I mean: making picture albums, collecting souvenirs, keepsakes, memorabilia, passing them around at family reunions—there was none of that. The letters she kept she kept for herself."

I unwound the cord I had wound around the copier, plugged the machine in, and said, "I'd like to make copies of everything, if you don't mind."

"You know the rules: One copy of anything published on the basis of archival materials must be submitted to the archive. So we agree you'll let me know what else you find out?"

"It's a deal."

She stood there in the doorway while I copied page after page. I could not tell whether she was trying to make sure I did the materials no harm or took any away with me, or whether it was simply a diversion for her to have somebody around the house. It was quiet, the hum of the machine being the only noise. I knew Margarete Bindinger had no husband or children, but the quiet was such that it gave me the feeling she not only lived alone but didn't even live there. When I was through, I rolled up the cord and placed the copies on the copier and the cord on the copies. Then I tucked it all under my arm and stood up.

"Why don't you ask? Don't you dare?"

I did not understand.

"Don't you want to know about Barbara?"

"I . . . I don't know," I said, feeling as I said it that it was not true. Of course I wanted to know what Barbara was up to. That was why I had been so elated on the drive here and while preparing my route the day before.

"You don't know if you want to know about Barbara?" She shook her head and laughed a scornful laugh. "Then I won't tell you anything." She went up to the front door.

"I . . ." I was going to thank her.

"So you do want to know."

I was unable to nod or shake my head or repeat that I didn't know. I just stood there. She looked at me expectantly, and what I saw was not so much scorn as cruelty: she was playing a nasty little game with me and enjoying every minute of it. By then I would rather have bitten my tongue off than ask about Barbara. But when she noticed the defiance in my eyes, she lost interest in the game and said, "She spent a few years in New York with her husband but has been living here since the divorce."

12

I TOOK A DETOUR and drove past Barbara's house. The Friedrichsplatz market was packing up, the stands coming down. The few apples and potatoes I got I bought for a song: the woman had no desire to take out her cash register and scales again. The ground was so full of rejects I had to watch my step.

Barbara's house looked just as I had remembered it. After a few minutes of trying to make myself believe I was not waiting for the door to open and Barbara to come out, I drove off.

The weekend after next Veronika would be coming home and taking back Max. I had grown used to him. I had been unaware how much the need satisfied by living with a woman can be satisfied by living with a child: the need for daily, undemanding togetherness, for exchanges about what one is involved in, for the input and output of sympathy, for minor rituals. Instead of ingesting a cup of instant coffee while dressing and a banana while driving, I would sit down to a real breakfast with Max. When we went to the pool or a hotel in the evening and I was quiet, he would say, "I bet you worked hard today" or "We're lucky. The day is over and we can do what we like."

Every day I looked forward to telling him his bedtime story. After the first homecoming story he kept wanting to hear more. The story of the man who, when his wife fails to recognize him, puts her to the test by courting her, and rejoices when she rejects him—out of fidelity to himself. Or the one in which the man confirms his wife's devotion by telling her about her husband's supposed family happiness abroad and watching her sad but ungrudging, loving reaction. The story of the man who finds his wife with another man and moves on without identifying himself because he had been declared fallen in action and does not wish to trouble the happiness his wife has found after her long mourning. In one story a man spreads the false rumor that the man who has now come home died in the war, and the latter takes his revenge on the former by killing him, while in another the man who returns reveals his identity and, having thus exposed and won out over the man who spread the rumor, saves his wife from a bogus happiness. Max was especially partial to the variation in which the man happens to arrive on the wedding day and must decide what to do when he sees them on their way to the ceremony. He also liked the one in which the two men become friends and try to find a way out of the impossible situation together.

Then there were the stories about the man who comes home

with another wife, because he had been mistakenly informed about his first wife's death or because the other woman had helped him to flee or had saved his life in one way or another. There were stories of a returning son with and without an evil brother, with and without an evil stepmother, with a good or hard-hearted father. There were stories about a returning man—father or son—who after his long absence feels so alien, so out of place, and is so cold or downright ornery and unjust that he drives his family to despair and out of the house. Only as Max clamored for more did I realize how many homecoming stories I now knew. And I kept finding and reading new ones.

What would I do once Max was gone? Would I work more, travel more? Resume my search for Odysseus' last women? See more of my friends? Take up tennis or golf? None of the above, I decided as I drove home after dropping him off. But what?

It must be my midlife crisis, I thought. By giving my problem a name, I felt a sense of reprieve. But it was soon over, and I took a good look at myself: a man in his midforties, a somewhat successful and accomplished editor with a boring car and a tidy flat. Family—none. Love—none. No change for better or worse in the offing. I began to take pity on myself but then thought of the dead Achilles, who tells Odysseus he would rather be a hired hand on Earth than a monarch in Hades.

13

I WROTE TO THE Institute for Military History in Freiburg and inquired about Volker Vonlanden. The answer came after two weeks: they had three articles appearing under his name, but they knew nothing about his person; the name might be a pseudonym, pseudonyms and altered names having been common among war correspondents.

They enclosed copies of the pages, complete with heading and date. "Yet Another Cause," the article I was acquainted with, had appeared on June 10, 1944, in the *Deutsche Allgemeine Zeitung,* "The Battle" and "Indestructible" on August 16, 1942, and February 4, 1945, in *Das Reich.* Both papers—the former a daily, the latter a weekly—were published in Berlin, but since neither was a Berlin paper they established no relation between Vonlanden and the city. I knew that *Das Reich* had been Goebbels' organ and had a certain intellectual and programmatic cachet. Vonlanden could not have got published there without connections.

I presumed "Indestructible" to be the article Vonlanden had enclosed in his last letter: both date and topic tallied.

We need not go into the hardships of the current situation: we are all expe-riencing them. Nor need we point out that many are growing weak, wavering in their faith or losing it completely. Such is always the case when the going gets rough. As long as they carry out their duty, how-ever, we must not condemn them; we must help them to regain their strength.

We must remind them of what is indestructible, remind them what endures in all our hardships, through all our hardships. We were a people divided, a people in which the poor were pitted against the rich, the fac-tory workers against the factory owners, the commoners against the nobles, mammon against intellect. In the past twelve years these rifts have been mended. We have become united. We were a people diseased—our culture degenerate, our society jewified, our heritage contaminated. In the past twelve years we have rooted out and obliterated everything that had so pol-luted our minds and bodies. We are cured. We were an indecisive people: we could not decide what sort of future to envision, what sort of path to follow, whom to regard as friend and whom to fight as foe. In the past twelve years we have become secure in our mission: the thousand-year

Reich exists in our hearts. Yet in the world the thousand-year struggle has only begun.

There are those who wish to abandon us and betray us, who will try to take what is rightfully ours. They shall not succeed.

The article entitled "The Battle" was about the siege of Leningrad. All I knew about the siege was that it had been particularly hard on the population and had failed in the end, so I did some research and learned that on July 8, 1941, Hitler had proclaimed he would raze Leningrad; on September 8, 1941, he had ordered the city to be besieged and starved into submission instead; and on September 14, 1941, he once more ordered its destruction. By then it was too late: the Wehrmacht had other, more urgent tasks, and on January 18, 1943, the siege was broken and on January 14, 1944, the besiegers expelled.

Vonlanden's article examines the relationship between the chivalric tradition and modern warfare. The siege of Leningrad, with its goal of starving the population as a means of conquering and destroying the city, serves as his exemplary material. He concedes that he is perhaps overcomplicating the issue: chivalry vis-à-vis Bolshevism? But he does not want to oversimplify either; one should not make the use of chivalry contingent upon the quality of the enemy. One is chivalrous for one's own sake, not to please or spite another.

Vonlanden derives chivalry from his iron rule: to be chivalrous is to demand nothing of others that one is not ready to demand of oneself. Germany was engaged in a life-and-death struggle and had demanded the ultimate of every man, woman, and child. It was thus chivalrous to meet the fray no holds barred.

Then he stops and asks, Does not the usual definition of chivalry mean quite the opposite, consideration on the part of the strong for the weak, for women, children, the elderly? How does that tally with the "iron rule" brand of chivalry?

I expected the answer would have to do with the third world-epoch, its rejection of the Judeo-Christian commandment to love one's neighbor, and its return to the law of nature: brute force, combat, and victory. But he transforms that return into progress, a movement toward greater equality: chivalrous behavior now includes regarding and treating the weak as equals. In peacetime this means recognizing they have a capacity and need, equal to those of the strong, to be happy. Thus, whereas in peacetime the usual definition of chivalry is valid, in wartime it is false. In wartime too the weak are to be regarded as equals of the strong because they are equally capable and ready to kill. Kill? Yes, the weakest of the weak is strong enough to kill.

The article points out that partisan women are fighting side by side with partisan men, that they are aided by child and gray-beard alike, no one being too old or too young to pull a trigger, throw a grenade, plant a mine. And as they are our equals in their capacity and need to kill us, so we treat them as our equals when we besiege, starve, conquer, and destroy them. The article concludes as follows:

Thus unfolds before our eyes a battle for a city the likes of which has not been seen since the battle for Troy. This is no ordinary battle: it may be as quiet before the gates of Leningrad as it was for much of the time during the ten-year siege before the gates of Troy. Unlike the Leningraders, the Trojans did not undergo starvation, but they were so worn down and made so blind and mindless that they themselves let the enemy in. The Trojans were not bombarded or even fired upon, but the fighting outside the gates was merciless. The final clash was of a violence so appalling and sublime that it could end only with the razing of the city. The final clash over Leningrad will likewise be appalling and sublimely violent and likewise end with the razing of the city—the chivalrous end of a chivalrous battle.

14

IF THAT WERE NOT ENOUGH, I had a call from my historian friend, who had found out how Hanke met his death.

Whether he never made it to Schörner or had a falling-out with him, or whether it was too late to agree or disagree about anything, on May 4, he fled with others of his kind. They spent the night in Komotau, at the house of a German farmer, but the farmer's Czech stable boy reported them to the local partisans, and they were captured and taken to a prison in Gorkau. There they stayed a few weeks, officers and civilians both, during which time neither the partisans nor the guards recognized Hanke for who he was. Next they were sent with another group of prisoners to Seestadtl.

It was a sunny spring day. There were many people out, and the guards had the prisoners walk along the railway embankment, which ran parallel to the street. At first they walked on the tracks, but when a train made its appearance they stepped to one side. As the train approached, Hanke scrambled across the tracks. Others followed. They scurried down the slope toward a stream, bushes, and thicket, but the train was short and soon passed, and the guards fired at the fleeing figures from the embankment. Other prisoners ran off in the opposite direction with other armed Czechs in close pursuit. Two men who had been hit by the locomotive while running across the tracks bled to death. A prisoner who later made a statement about the incident spoke of chaotic running, shooting, and shouting. Hanke and two others were brought down by the guards' bullets and then beaten to death. The others got away.

Including Volker Vonlanden? Had he fled Breslau with Hanke, been captured by the partisans, run across the tracks, made it down the slope?

Be that as it may, I had the author of my homecoming story. In 1940–41 he had studied in the city I was living in, lodging with the Lampe family at Kleinmeyerstrasse 38 and making an unsuccessful play for Beate Lampe. During the winter of 1941–42 Hanke took him under his wing and sponsored or appointed him as a war correspondent. During the summer of 1942 he saw Beate again and had greater success. It is highly likely that he was in Hanke's orbit during the latter's last few weeks or months. It is also highly likely that he went back to Kleinmeyerstrasse 38 after the war. He would have written the novel sometime between this second visit and the midfifties, when my grandparents gave me the bound galleys.

I liked him because he liked *The Odyssey* and had played with it; because his lively novel was my first encounter with light fiction; because its open ending, which was not of course his ending, made me wonder. Besides, it is impossible to spend so much time with a person without coming to like him.

Or hate him. And while I can't say I actually hated him, the playful quality I found attractive in the novel seemed repellent in his letters and articles. With the same levity he had employed to make Hades a dream, the sea a desert, and the glossy-plaited Calypso the full-breasted Kalinka, he had made ruthlessness an ethical principle, the siege of Leningrad an act of chivalry, and the seduction of Beate a tribute to justice.

Did I want to know any more about him? I still wondered how the novel ended. I had imagined so many sequels to the encounter at Kleinmeyerstrasse 38 that I wanted to see how he would wind it up. It might be a homecoming that had never before been told, never before been imagined. It might be the archetypal homecoming.

15

MAX WAS LOATH TO BELIEVE that an evil person could come up with the homecoming of all homecomings. Children always hope against hope that what is good is true and beautiful and what is evil is false and ugly. I too bore remnants of that hope in my breast and would not have been disappointed had the novel fallen flat at the end. I just wanted to know what the ending was.

Not that there was much I could do about it. I put classified ads in the major dailies and weeklies characterizing Volker Vonlanden with the data I had at my disposal and posed as a historian look-ing for more. Two detectives offered their services, a genealogist offered to draw up his family tree, and a "former friend" asked for an advance of five hundred marks for "important information."

I wrote to Freda von Fircks, who answered that she did not recall having met a Volker Vonlanden. The prisoner who had been with Hanke and perhaps Vonlanden and had made the statement about the embankment incident had given it to a reporter with the *Norddeutsche Zeitung* in 1949. I would have to find the reporter to find the prisoner, who would be old and feeble and most likely unwilling to say any more than he had told the reporter. So I gave up on that front.

I switched my attention to Hanke. My historian friend had come up with some articles Hanke had written for the *Schlesische Tageszeitung* and speeches he had given, and sent them to me. They were all of a piece and sounded familiar. Could Volker Vonlanden have been his ghost writer?

Hanke took the threat of defeat seriously. He wrote nothing about miracle weapons and sudden turnabouts; he wrote of past glory rather than imminent victory:

Only twelve years ago Bolshevism was on the point of annexing the Reich to Asia. Just as then it attempted to achieve its goal by political means, so now it is trying to overrun the Reich and Europe by straining its last military reserves. We thank Fate for having sent us these twelve years and granted us the possibility to resist the foe gun in hand. Had Bolshevism prevailed in the Reich twelve years ago, those of us who survived would have regarded the current situation as manna from heaven.

In an article in which he took on what had apparently become a flood of enemy leaflets, he found time for a brief etymological study:

Our Führer's name is his program. Genealogical research has shown that his grandfather spelled his name Hüttler. *It thus derives from* Hütte, *hut. And in fact Hitler tells us in* Mein Kampf *that his father was the son of a poor villager with nothing but a hut to his name. Hitler's ancestors came from a rugged countryside on the Danube much like our mountain regions. When we say* Heil Hitler! *we are saying* Hail Hut Dweller! *and are thus greeting ourselves, born as we were in mountain huts. The Hitler flag is thus a hut-dweller's flag, and we can only agree with the enemy propaganda that labels this war Hitler's war: it is the war of us hut dwellers.*

In his last speech, which was broadcast over the radio and printed in the *Völkischer Beobachter*, Hanke abandoned all pretense at making military sense of the defense of the Breslau Fortress, taking instead an existentialist stance:

The reason for it is that we have jettisoned all the ballast we have been dragging through our lives and falsely calling culture when it was in fact nothing but cheap civilization. We often believed that by destroying this external backdrop to our day-to-day existence we would be destroying ourselves. That is not true. Tens of thousands of men and women in the Bres-

lau Fortress have learned that they can take leave of everything they regarded as an integral part of their existence—their homes, their heirlooms, their goods and chattels, a thousand trifles they have always clung to—and hold up perfectly well.

When we spoke earlier of total war, we meant what we said, but only now do we know what waging total war truly involves.

My historian friend also included an eyewitness report describing Hanke's bunker: a broad carpet protected by runners led down into a broad passageway—it too covered with runners—flanked by functional offices and with a narrow passageway leading to a modern kitchen, showers and toilets, bedrooms, and another, more modest kitchen for the personnel. Hanke's room stood at the very end; it was large, brightly lit by concealed lights, and furnished with heavy furniture and valuable paintings and rugs. Here the Hanke who enjoyed surrounding himself with beautiful women by day would hold "boisterous parties attended again by beautiful women, elegantly dressed, women as charming and enticing as the models in peacetime fashion magazines. Where did they come from in this chaos? Nobody knows: the ones who did know went down with Breslau."

16

MY MOTHER RETIRED in the summer of 1989, and I gave her a week in the canton of Ticino as a retirement gift. When I was a child, she told me of a trip she had taken there, of the slow, quiet funicular that runs from Locarno to the pilgrimage church with its view of the blue lake, of the tables and chairs along the Ascona shore and the piano music wafting out of the hotels, of a boat trip around islands with enchanted gardens and heavily wooded valleys where wolves still howled. I would not have been surprised if she had turned the offer down, but she accepted.

The relationship between single mothers and only sons has a bit of the married couple to it. This does not make it a happy one: it can be just as loveless and aggressive, just as much of a power struggle as a marriage. As in marriage, though in its own way, there is no third party or parties—no father, no siblings—to drain off the tension that inevitably arises in so intimate an association. The tension does not truly dissipate until the son leaves the mother, and often the dissipation takes the form of a nonrelationship much like that of a divorced couple. It may also turn into a lively, intimate, tension-free relationship, and after years of going through the motions with my mother—seldom making trouble and always a bit bored—I was looking forward to our week together as a promise of better things to come. And in fact we enjoyed what we did and saw. Mother was so involved that there were times when I could have sworn the dismissive, derisive look on her face had disappeared. We talked over her plans for the years ahead and my dream of starting a publishing venture of my own—she with unfeigned interest in my questions and I with unfeigned interest in hers. I was surprised at how clearly she saw the possibilities and problems of my dream from the vantage point of her years in the business world.

As everything was going so well, I asked her one evening in Ascona, "You've never told me how you got through the war. How about it?"

"What makes you think there's something to tell?" she countered.

"You're from Silesia. You knew Breslau, Gauleiter Hanke. You were there when the Russians surrounded the city; you were there for the Allied victory, the expulsion of the German population. I'd like to hear what it was like."

"Why?"

I filled her in on my progress with the Karl story. "He's the one who led me to your neck of the woods."

"My neck of the woods? I come from Upper Silesia. Breslau and Hanke are Lower Silesia."

"There, you see? You have to tell me. I don't even know the difference between Upper and Lower Silesia."

She laughed. "I don't 'see' anything. There's absolutely nothing to tell about the difference between Upper and Lower Silesia." She paused, hoping I too would laugh and move on to something else. But at last she shrugged, a sign she had given up, and went on. "We moved from Neurade to Breslau in the autumn of 1944. Father was asked to take over a job he had done before at the Department of Public Works, but don't ask me what it was exactly. They needed engineers, and although he had retired by then they recalled him. But when they declared the city Breslau Fortress, he and Mother had to leave. They were strafed by a low-flying plane as they fled."

"What about you?"

"Me?" She gave me a look that seemed to ask what made me want to know. "I . . . I stayed in Breslau until the war was over. Then I came here."

"Were you there for the entire 'Fortress' period? What was it like? Did you ever meet Hanke? Or his people? Were you ever in his bunker? Did you—"

She laughed and held up her hands. "Not so many questions at once!" But she showed no indication of answering even one. We were looking out at the lake. The hotels no longer had pianists, but there were some young people in a rowboat singing the latest Italian hits, their voices first soft, then louder, mixed with laughter and shouting, and finally soft again and distant.

"The worst part was building the landing strip through the city. The lifting and dragging and pushing; the endless commands, shouts, curses. I'll never forget the buzzing, sawing, roaring, clattering sound of the planes and machine guns, the bullets smacking into the stone. We had to run into buildings for shelter, but the wider the strip got the farther we had to run, and as we ran the planes would hunt us down. It wasn't so bad for the young people like me, but if you were old . . . One night I came home to find half the house gone. Long before I got there, I could see the curtains blowing in the wind, red roses on a yellow background, and I thought to myself, Funny, they look like mine. That night there was a firebomb attack, and by the next morning the curtains and everything else in the flat had burned to a crisp. Standing outside, I could look up at the sky through the window openings."

Mother turned and looked me in the eye. "Or do you want to hear about our soldiers breaking into houses and looting? Or their basement orgies and their whores? Or the bomb that hit the post office and ripped a woman into so many pieces—here the head, there a leg, there the guts—that they could fit them all into a small box. Or the bomb that hit a cart, killing the horse and hurling the soldier across the road and into a garden, and just as he got to his feet—smiling at me, amazed he was still whole—the house behind him collapsed and buried him? Or do you want to hear about the poorest of the poor, the workers brought in from conquered territories who were done for the moment they were wounded?"

She talked louder and louder, faster and faster. The people at the table next to ours were staring at us. She turned her head and looked back at the water. "But spring did come. When I woke up on my birthday, I could hear a blackbird singing, and there were snowdrops blooming in the garden, lilacs budding. It was a beautiful morning, though rubble and ruins were everywhere. The rain was beautiful too. It had rained during Holy Week, the first rain in a long time. It began at night. I was sleeping in an open basement facing a garden and woke up to the patter of rain. I lay there listening, trying not to fall asleep again it was so beautiful. It was a gentle spring rain; I could smell the dust growing wet . . ." She shrugged her shoulders after a pause and said, "Well, that's how it was."

"Thanks. Is that it for today or is that it for good?"

She gave me a look of relief mixed with coquetry. "For good? How do I know?"

17

WE COULD HAVE MADE the trip home in a day, but I wanted to stop off in the village where my grandparents had lived. I wanted to see their house again, see the pine trees, the apple tree, the bushes, the field, the garden; I wanted to sit on the shore, gaze out at the water and feed the swans and ducks; I wanted to hear whether the stations still signaled the departure of a train to each other by ringing a bell; I wanted to show Mother the world Father had grown up in. I may also have wanted to use the occasion to shake her up a little, open her up, break down her reserve. In any case, I refrained from telling her where we were until we had unpacked and showered and were walking along the lake before dinner.

"Do you think I didn't notice the route you'd taken?" Her eyes were all scorn and provocation.

I did not reply. We came to a small park at the confluence of the village pond and the lake. I went to the water's edge and took out a bag of stale bread I had collected, and just as in the old days the birds paddled up before I could throw out the first crumbs, before I had even broken the crusts into crumbs; just as in the old days there was a great to-do when I did toss them in, the faster, stronger birds snapping them up before the slower, weaker ones could get at them, and I did my best to restore justice by aiming carefully.

Mother laughed when she caught on to what I was doing. "So you want to teach the ducks justice, do you?"

"Grandfather made fun of me too. 'That's the way nature is,' he would say. 'The strong get more than the weak, the fast more than the slow.' But I'm not nature."

Mother held out her hand, I gave her a piece of dry bread, and she crumbled it up and threw it in the direction of the swans, two white parents and five light-brown offspring. "Only because I prefer swans to ducks."

"Weren't you ever curious about where Father grew up?"

She held out her open hand again and threw the swans more crumbs. "I know what's coming now. What was Father like anyway? How did you meet, fall in love, get married? When did he leave? How did he die?" She shook her head. "Why do you think I haven't told you? I don't like to talk about it. I hate to talk about it."

By the end she was in such a frenzy I couldn't say a word. I knew her frenzies: I had to be prepared for the worst: insults, shouts, even violence. Only the disciplinary structure of the words and sentences kept her from going off the deep end. As a child I was sometimes spanked, not so hard it really hurt but enough to throw me off balance. She hit me as if she wanted to push me away, get rid of me. Whenever she threw herself into a frenzy, I would panic. But now I could see that she could turn the frenzy on and off at will: it was all a game. And I was not in the mood for games.

I gave her a few more scraps of bread, and we fed the ducks and swans until the bag was empty. "Shall we go back to the hotel?"

After dinner she asked, "What do you know about your father?"

"I know he grew up here, that he had a hobbyhorse and a tri-cornered paper hat as a child and got a suit and tie and bicycle

when he went to the Gymnasium, that he later wore tweed knickerbockers, collected stamps, played handball, drew, painted, read a
lot, liked poetry, was nearsighted, was exempted from military service, studied law, went to Germany, and died in the war."

She laughed. "You know more than I do!" She waited again,
waited for me to laugh and thereby close the issue. But then she
took a deep breath. "He was an adventurer. A Swiss law student
who one day says to himself he must be crazy spending all his time
in lecture halls and libraries tracking life and the law secondhand,
when right next door, lives, laws, everything, was going up in
smoke. How he got to Silesia I don't know.

"We met in September 1944 in Neurade. It was a warm, sunny
day. I went to a garden restaurant for dinner and, sitting alone at a
table waiting for a friend, I must have kept looking over at him: I
had forgotten how good a young man can look when he's not in
uniform, when he's wearing a suit, a well-cut three-piece tweed
suit, a blue shirt, and a red tie with blue polka dots. All of a sudden
he stood and came over to my table and asked me with a smile if he
could join me or take me for a walk and have dinner with me afterward. I . . ." She stopped.

"Well . . . ?"

"We spent the evening together and the night. We had another
two days and nights together and got married on the last morning.
Then he had to leave, and I didn't see him again until April 1945 in
Breslau. One morning there he was in my basement ruins with a
Swiss passport for me. His Swiss accent made everything sound so
simple. Even the ruins, the misery and death didn't seem so bad.
When he saw my stomach, he said, 'Take good care of yourself, of
the two of you.' A few days later he was in the wrong place at the
wrong time and got shot."

"You . . ."

"I saw it. He'd just said goodbye and was walking down the

street when he was shot to death. That kind of thing happened all the time: you'd be walking along and suddenly the Germans and Russians would start shooting at one another."

Again she clammed up, but when I tried to ask a question she just looked up at me. Until then she had been looking down at her hands. "He was the same height as you, and you have his slant green eyes and his hands." That was an encore. Her face made it clear that the performance was over and the curtain had fallen.

Part Four

I

WHILE THE BERLIN WALL was falling, I was in bed with a fever. I had gone to bed early: no news, no images of the boys and girls straddling the wall at the Brandenburg Gate, of jubilant East and West Berliners crossing the transit points, of the East German police surprised, even embarrassed, by their own ability to be friendly. The next morning the pictures in the papers were history. Did they document an error soon to be rectified or the start of a new world? The editorials had not a clue.

I recalled the workers' uprising in East Berlin on June 17, 1953, the Hungarian uprising, the erection of the Wall on August 13, 1961, the Cuban missle crisis, Kennedy's assassination, the moon landing, the Americans' retreat from Saigon, Pinochet's putsch, Nixon's departure from the White House, the Chernobyl nuclear disaster. Each came with its image: workers waving the German flag at the Brandenburg Gate; masons piling up cement slabs under armed surveillance; an aerial view of a rocket site, Jack and Jackie in an open limousine; a man all bundled up posing next to an oddly fluttering American flag in the midst of a wasteland; people crowding into a helicopter on the roof of the American Embassy; Allende ready to defend the presidential palace with machine gun in hand, though the straps hanging from his helmet presage disaster; Nixon on the White House lawn; an aerial shot of the Chernobyl reactor, which bears no outward signs of danger yet looks deadly. Instead of a pictorial image for the Hungarian uprising I had an aural one:

my mother and I happened to have tuned in to Budapest Radio as the events drew to a close and it was appealing to the world in English, French, and German for help.

In addition to watching history from a distance, I could have watched it up close. I could have had more than images; I could have had experiences. But I let it pass me by. When the students took to the streets, I went to my job; instead of mingling with the last hippies and flower children, I studied massage. I did not demonstrate in Bonn against rearmament or in Brokdorf against the stockpiling of fuel rods or in Frankfurt against the expansion of the airport.

This time I did not want to let history pass me by. I had woken up free of fever. I drove to work, arranged to take some time off, and flew to Berlin that very day. I took a room in a street off the Kurfürstendamm. The pension occupied the third and fourth floor of a once majestic, now shabby apartment house. My room was all plush and kitsch and plastic shower stall. The gloomy breakfast room boasted a jungle of artificial plants. Looking down into the courtyard, you could not tell whether it was day or night.

I took the S-Bahn to East Berlin and roamed the streets. It was noon. The crowded snack bars, the pedestrians scurrying to get through as much shopping as possible during lunch hour, the flow of Trabants, Wartburgs, and humpbacked vans on the broad streets, the stench of brown coal fumes, here and there a pile of coal waiting on the sidewalk to be shoveled into the basement through the ground-level window, here and there a red banner celebrating the fortieth anniversary of the German Democratic Republic— common, everyday socialism.

East Berlin had the same grayness about it I had seen on class trips before the Wall was built and afterward as part of a seminar I took on Marxist legal theory. Now as then I found it touching. The outdated lack of efficiency in all aspects of life and the futile attempts at trying to demonstrate up-to-dateness with superfluous traffic lights, dull advertisements, and mirrored glass in the windows of new buildings reminded me of the futile solemnity with which children construct their version of the grown-up world and play at being grown-ups. I found it touching, though I knew that the world they had constructed was disturbingly narrow and that their games could be sordid and cruel.

I went into the Alexanderplatz department store in which Christmas angels were already on sale under that strange communist alias of "winged end-of-the-year figures." I let myself be carried by the crowds past counters with little to see and nothing to buy. I wanted to do something with the money I had exchanged and decided on stationery: pads, envelopes, folders, which always come in handy. But the pads and even the envelopes were ruled, and the folders looked as if they would come apart as soon as you opened them, so in an Unter den Linden bookshop I bought some chess books I knew I would never read.

The university no longer boasted the guards it had had when our seminar visited. I went in, inhaled the sharp smell of disinfectant, and found the notice board containing announcements of events and Free German Youth meetings. I slipped unnoticed through an open door and found myself listening to a lecture on contemporary East German literature. I stayed to the end, enthralled by the charmed atmosphere of the nearly empty hall, lit only by a small lamp on the lectern. By the time I was outside again, the lowering gray sky was nearly dark and the streetlamps had gone on. What had I expected from my encounter with history? Demonstrations? Street-corner debates? The occupation of ministries and radio stations? Police intervention? The destruction of the Wall?

History is clearly in no hurry. It respects daily activities like work, shopping, cooking, and eating; it understands that bureaucratic processes, sporting events, and get-togethers with family and friends must go on. Presumably the same rules applied to the French Revolution: it is all very well to storm the Bastille on July 14, but on July 15 the cobbler must return to his last, the tailor to his needle; they must make up for lost time. After a morning at the guillotine, back to nailing and sewing. What is there to do all day at a Bastille already stormed? Or a Wall already scaled?

2

PART OF THE TIME ALLOTTED to East Berliners by daily life they now spent in West Berlin, shopping. They had a lot to learn: how to compare goods, brands, and prices; how to sniff out sales; how to tell imitation schnapps from the real thing; how to ask, bargain, and demand without shame. It took practice.

I walked through the Kurfürstendamm and Tauentzienstrasse shopping districts, went into department stores, clothes and shoe shops, supermarkets, household appliance shops, and do-it-yourself centers and watched people shopping. Was this the West? Did it show its true face in the behavior of these shoppers, who had not assimilated it gradually but had to swallow it whole from one day to the next? Its face of greed? But then I saw a young couple gazing so tenderly at the display of bras, panties, and slips, handling the articles so reverently, walking away with their purchase so blissfully that it made my anti-consumer-society bias feel arrogant. In Wittenbergplatz, the man hawking bananas, a rarity in the East, could scarcely cope with tearing open the cartons, pulling apart the clusters, handing them over to the customers, and giving change. He would not sell me one banana; I would have had to take at least ten. An East Berliner gave me one of his.

The next day too I spent hours roaming through East Berlin, but this time I left the center for the residential districts: streets full of potholes, sidewalks whose flagstone paving had been constantly repaired with gravel and tar, fences of gray, crumbling wood, façades with plaster peeling in sheets to reveal the bricks beneath. At first I was puzzled by how homey I found the decay, but then I realized I was passing through the streets of my past, the streets of my hometown in the late forties and early fifties, the streets of my childhood. I was able to crumble a gray, rotten fence slat with my bare hand the way I used to as a child.

All day the sky had hung low and heavy over the city, and when darkness came it too seemed to weigh heavy on the houses, parks, squares, and streets. I looked longingly at the bright windows with their false promise of security. I felt another rush of longing when, sitting in the U-Bahn, I watched the passengers on their way home, though I did not envy them their homes or families or the evening they were about to spend.

In the pension I met an American journalist who had just arrived. He tried to debrief me over dinner. Where would things go from here? Did the East Germans want to live in a free German state of their own or did they want reunification? What did the West Germans want? Would there be reprisals against the Communists in East Germany? Would the Russians stay on in East Germany or would they pull out? Would Gorbachev last? Would the military stage a putsch? He was not at all put off by the fact that I had no answers to his questions. Could I tell him what I personally hoped to see happen?

I went on about the two halves of Germany: the Catholic, Rhinelandish, Bavarian, opulent, life-affirming, extroverted western half versus the Protestant, Prussian, frugal, hard-boiled, introverted eastern half. The eastern half was as much a part of my spiritual world as the western half, and I wanted free access to it, the right to work, live, and love there. Maybe a free East Germany, like an Austria or a Switzerland, would be enough for me. But wouldn't it be more natural for two halves to make a whole?

He let me have my say, and what I said I did not know I would say until it came out. Yet it sounded perfectly reasonable, as if I had thought about it long and hard. Or as if while making my way through East Berlin I had come across the world of Luther and Bach, Frederick the Great and the Prussian reformers instead of a bunch of tumbledown houses.

I also told him why there would be no reprisals. "The only reason Odysseus could kill the suitors and string up the women who had reveled with them was that he did not stay on. He kept moving. When you stay on, you have to get along with people, not get back at them. There were no reprisals in America after the Civil War, were there? Because the country had to heal the split if it was going to stick together. Well, Germany too will have to heal the split if it's going to stick together."

Was his smile a smile of goodwill or of derision? We had emptied two bottles of wine. But I was just as intoxicated by the two days. Past and present, indulgence and sobriety, joy and rigidity, the outer life and the inner life—everything coming together, the world growing round and full—and I sat nursing my wine in the midst of it all.

3

BEFORE FLYING HOME, I went back to the university. This time I climbed the broad red-marble steps past Marx's thesis "Philosophers interpret this world in various ways; what matters is to change it." The broad corridors were empty; nor did I meet anyone on the stairs or in the corridors on the next floor. The sharp disinfectant smell was everywhere.

Next to one door I noticed the announcement of a seminar on constitutional law in capitalist countries. As I was reading through the topics under consideration, the door opened and a man came up to me and offered me his hand.

"Dr. Römer?"

I shook his hand and said, "Debauer."

"Professor Pfister told us to expect a Dr. Römer. Are you here to replace him?"

"He may still be coming."

"In any case, do come in."

He made a welcoming gesture and introduced himself as Dr. Fach. He took my coat and led me through another door into a room with lockers along the walls and a long table in the middle. Sitting at the table were several men and women—some young, some old, some in ties and jackets, some in sweaters. Dr. Fach showed me to a place at the narrow end. Additional participants filed in while he spoke.

I learned that Professor Pfister from the Faculty of Law in Hanover had been one of the few German-German contacts Professor Lummer of Humboldt University had been able to maintain over the years and that the two of them had agreed they should take immediate advantage of the fall of the Wall to organize an exchange whereby a few instructors from Hanover would teach at Humboldt and vice versa. They had been expecting Dr. Römer, and here I was. "Are you at the university?"

"I haven't quite finished my dissertation actually. I'm not from Hanover and have had no personal contact with Professor Pfister, but . . ."—here goes!—". . . it was thought that constitutional law was in special need of attention." My master's thesis had dealt with basic constitutional rights.

I was not asked who thought I should teach constitutional law at Humboldt University; I was asked only about the thesis, the dissertation, other publications, future projects, teaching experience, extracurricular and political activities. I tried not to lie, but in the end I had studied comparative constitutional law in America rather than massage, published articles there, directed research here, and all but completed my dissertation.

An open window notwithstanding, the room was overheated and I was sweating. The lockers, the long table with all those people around it—I felt like a schoolboy called on the carpet. Perhaps that was what had made it increasingly easy for me to lie. When I hinted that I had been a consultant for local governments with Social Democrat majorities in cases before the Federal Constitutional Court, I noticed several heads nodding. I elicited the same reaction by promoting myself from editor to editorial board member at my publishing house and promising to provide their library with scholarly literature free of charge. Dr. Fach thanked me in the name of his department and said, "We hope you can return in December to give a lecture course and conduct a seminar in the constitutional law of the Federal Republic."

4

AND SO IN DECEMBER I started a new regime: I would teach on Mondays and Tuesdays and work at the publishing house during the rest of the week. For one of my days in East Berlin I took the day off; for the other I was given the day off—the house's contribution to German unity. At first I would prepare my lectures at home and fly to Berlin on Monday morning, but before long I took to packing the books I needed and flying in on Friday evening. I stayed at the University Guesthouse, a brick building from the turn of the century, and the courtyard my windows faced was so quiet day and night that the people living and working behind the other windows might as well have been bewitched into a deep sleep. In what looked like a laboratory across the quadrangle I pictured a chemist snoring away before a sizzling Bunsen burner; in the office a floor above the lab, a row of bureaucrats, their heads down on their desks; in the flat to the left, the husband sprawled out in his armchair, a beer bottle at his feet, the wife prostrate on the floor next to the stove.

I took breakfast at a hotel two blocks away. I would walk along the buffet, plate in hand, picking up a roll here, a piece of sausage there, a slice of cheese, some butter and jam. Then I showed the plate to the cashier, who told me how much it came to: seventy-three or ninety-seven pfennigs or, if I had felt like splurging, one D-mark thirty-six.

Dr. Römer came with me on the first Tuesday morning. He had knocked on my door the evening before, introduced himself, and launched into a conversation that grew ever more embarrassing. When I stemmed the tide by saying I still had some preparation to do, he suggested we meet for breakfast.

He found it demeaning to have to show his plate and be charged for every bite. It was all so petty; it put him under the outrageous suspicion of taking more than his share; it made him feel someone was peering over his shoulder. The cashier was clearly working for the State Security, the Stasi. And, he added sardonically, hadn't Marx promised, "From each according to his abilities, to each according to his needs"?

When I defended the buffet, he took it as a defense of the Stasi. He had written his dissertation on the Nazi interpretation of the Civil Code and saw parallels with the socialist interpretation. He maintained that the cowardice of the judges and law professors in the Third Reich willing to twist the law for their careers' sake was the same as the cowardice of the judges and law professors in East Germany, that it had been possible to show courage and put up resistance under both systems. "We must never make the mistake our parents made," he said, laying his hand on my arm. "If history hasn't taught us the lesson of resistance, then history is nothing but one long aimless, senseless bloodbath." He squeezed my arm. "That is our historical mission. That is why we are here."

For the first time I took a good look at his round, friendly, self-satisfied face, his pudgy hands, his ample body. I could not say what got to me in what he said; I only knew I did not like the way he looked, the way he sat there with his hand on my arm. "Resistance? Do you propose to stand up to the cashier?" I did not say it to get rid of him, but when he rose and left the room without a word, I was only too happy to see him go.

In the beginning I had thirty or forty students in my lecture class, but the number increased from week to week. They did not come because I was such a good speaker but because from week to week it became clearer that the German Democratic Republic was on its way out and that entry into the Federal Republic, reunification with it, was imminent. All male students were officers in the National People's Army, all female students skilled workers; they were mature young people, many with families, for whom the future had meant lives as lawyers and judges in the GDR. Reluctant but determined, they set about adapting: they studied the new legal system as if it were a foreign language, the language of a country where one finds oneself out of professional necessity rather than preference. In neither the lectures nor the seminar did they ask questions or express opinions, and they treated my questions as annoying interruptions. When I asked them to write critical accounts of decisions or articles, they gave me only the briefest, barest plot summary. Once hearing a student mutter to himself, "He can't believe that," I engaged him in a conversation about it. I soon realized that what threw him off was not that I was saying something I did not believe but that I wanted to make him believe I believed what I was saying.

My relationship to my colleagues in the department also changed from week to week. When we were introduced, they saw me as a suppliant seeking their acceptance, but with time I became the messenger of a world making ever greater inroads into theirs, a world that would radically alter, even destroy theirs. But as often as I met with open disapproval, cool formality, and sarcastic jibes, I also experienced genuine interest in an exchange of views over our differences, enthusiasm for a common future, and a combination of courage and anxiety vis-à-vis the coming challenges.

One colleague took me to a meeting of departmental Party members. They were discussing a recent Gorbachev speech. The man chairing the meeting of twenty to thirty people started with a few sentences about the occasion and topic of the speech and then opened the floor for comments.

It was a gray Berlin winter day. By four it would be dark, and the meeting room, which doubled as the dean's office, was lit only by a small desk lamp. Like all rooms in East Berlin it was over-heated, and in the long silence following the man's introduction I could sense eyelids growing heavy and feel myself battling to keep awake. Then somebody I did not know took the floor. At first I listened with only half an ear, but in the end I was fascinated: he spoke without saying anything. The sentences followed one another logically enough, and each one had a beginning, middle, and end; the Marx and Lenin quotations had a certain ring to them, and the references he made, the issues he brought up seemed substantive. But there was no thesis, no idea behind what he said: it was neither approving nor critical. He assiduously avoided any statement, any pronouncement he might later be called to task for, he might later have to recant. It was a brand of speech that, obeying its own strict laws, had evolved into an art form. A theater of the absurd. I would not have shed a tear to see it go under with the world that gave it birth, yet I was sorry that art can go under like that.

5

ONE DAY I CAME HOME to find a letter from East Berlin. Was I still interested in Volker Vonlanden? A woman named Rosa Habe had only now seen my request: some West German friends had crumpled up some newsprint as padding for a package they were sending her, and it included the page with the ad.

I phoned her immediately, and she invited me to come and see her in Pankow that Sunday morning. I brought her flowers, the finest bouquet I could muster in the East Berlin flower shop. Although it looked for all the world like the feathers of an ailing brood hen, she accepted it all smiles. She was a sprightly old soul who spoke in a soft, clear voice and moved with grace. She served me tea on her glassed-in balcony.

"Your ad mentions places and articles in connection with Volker Vonlanden, but you don't say what makes him historically interesting."

"I myself don't know. Sometimes the clues I find seem to lead somewhere; sometimes they don't."

She gave me a skeptical but not unfriendly look. "All that expense for clues?"

I laughed and told her the story of my grandparents, the homecoming novel, the Kleinmeyerstrasse house, the war articles, and the Hanke connection. "I'm no historian. I posed as one because I wanted people to take the ad seriously. But yours was the first serious response I received."

"You could have had it without such elaborate lies." She shook her head. "Oh, those skeletons. Still in the closet. For us he was Walter Scholler, and when a man once went up to him and addressed him as Volker Vonlanden he dismissed him with such amiability and aplomb that those of us who were with him then were not the least bit taken aback and the man who had spoken to him was no longer sure of himself. Then one day he vanished, poof, without saying goodbye."

"And yet you remember his Volker Vonlanden identity. Was it because you suspected something behind it?"

"Suspected something? No, I didn't suspect anything." But she did not go on to tell me what had caused her to remember him, and I did not pursue the matter. "Without saying goodbye." That could mean they were close.

"What did he do, this Walter Scholler?"

"Up to the autumn of forty-six he edited the art section of a minor popular daily called the *Nacht-Express*. He did some writing too: theater and book reviews, essays, stories. We had the impression he was in with the major from the Soviet military administration who was the power behind the throne, a round, clever little Jew from Leningrad. He really ran things, while Scholler was the nominal editor in chief of what was nominally a politically independent tabloid."

"Not a bad career for a nobody from nowhere."

"What are you talking about. He was a Viennese Jew who'd hidden in his parents' house in the Alps until a neighbor turned him in during the winter of 1944–45. He knew names and faces, by which I mean the names and faces of the Communists the Nazis murdered at the last minute in Auschwitz. And he had a number tattooed on his arm."

"Impossible!"

"I knew the number by heart until"—she blushed—"until I had my stroke two years ago. You see, I had taken him under my wing. Like the others of his kind he was homeless: they could never be at home again in their former world and despite our best intentions never quite fit into ours. That's why our wonderful poet Becher took a fancy to him: they shared similar fates."

"What did he say became of his parents?"

"They were rounded up right after Anschluss. His father was a politically active lawyer, his mother a psychoanalyst. He never saw them again."

"Do you know whether there actually was a lawyer by the name of Scholler in Vienna? Or by the name of Vonlanden?"

She sat there, tense, her hands in her lap, her eyes on the floor. "I didn't snoop. He was here one day and gone the next. He wasn't the only one. It was the times."

"But now that you know . . ."

She gave me a hostile look. "I don't know a thing. You're not trying to tell me that Walter Scholler deceived me like the awful man who addressed him as Volker Vonlanden."

"Do you know who that awful man was?"

"No, I don't. Maybe he wasn't an awful man; maybe he just made a mistake; maybe he'd been looking for Vonlanden for so long that he started seeing him in everything and everybody. You of all people should understand that." The look was now defiant.

"And I do," I said, nodding.

She stood. "How nice of you to have come to see me. My son lives in Rostock, my daughter in Dresden, and now that my job at the ministry—" She broke off. "Why am I going on like this? What do you care about my children and my career?" She looked down at the floor again. "I liked his Viennese accent. It was only the hint of an accent, but it was a greeting from another world, the world of the waltz, of balls and coffeehouses, of stone steps leading from one street to the next, like Paris . . ." She looked up at me again. "Do you know Vienna?" But she expected no answer. She was on her way to the door to see me out.

Within a few days I had ascertained that the Viennese telephone books of the thirties listed no lawyer-psychiatrist couple by the name Scholler and no couple at all by the name of Vonlanden.

6

THE SEMESTER CAME TO AN END. Although I had been invited back, I would not be returning for the following semester: Dr. Römer bore me a grudge and would work out who I was sooner or later, and that would be embarrassing not only for me but also for my colleagues, who were trying to turn the department into a reputable facsimile of its Western counterparts. To say nothing of the fact that keeping track of the myriad petty lies I was forced to spin to keep the big lie plausible was more than debilitating; it was humiliating. It made me think of a man with a mistress whom his wife knew nothing about and who might not even know about his wife, of unofficial Stasi collaborators who spied on their colleagues and friends, of bookkeepers who amassed a fortune by stealing petty sums through the years. I did not particularly condemn them; I just didn't see how anyone could live like that, constantly in fear, constantly on the lookout, constantly playing someone one is not. Perhaps it helped to have a major objective in mind. I had none.

And so the party a colleague invited most of the department to turned into my farewell party. I cannot recall what it started out as: his sixtieth birthday, an anniversary of his employment at the university, the finally successful purchase of a house on a lake just outside the city, a move by the administration to grant the department greater independence. I was glad Dr. Römer had not been invited.

It was not until later that I realized that the colleague who threw the party was also celebrating his own farewell. I could never tell how much truth there was in the stories of Stasi collaboration circulating at the time about him and other colleagues. I could easily picture an internationally known, mundane-looking copyright lawyer like him getting involved in the Stasis' games, thinking he could play them by his own rules. Whether he feared the outcome of the investigations or simply didn't want to expose himself to them, he had decided not to return to the university. He later went into private practice and was soon much sought after. He was the first to go off on his own.

The party took place in his Karl-Marx-Allee apartment. Desolate as the much-too-broad and windy thoroughfare was and depressing as the once ornamentally tiled and now hideously pock-marked façades of its buildings were, the apartment itself was a haven of comfort and hospitality. Beaming all the while, the man's wife greeted me at the door with the following: "You weren't hit by a tile, were you? Good. Here in the East we've learned how and when to duck. You'll have to learn now too." As my stay had progressed, I felt my colleagues were treating me more and more like an officer in an occupying army; here a beautiful hostess was simply trying to put a younger, somewhat flustered guest at his ease. She took me into two large rooms connected by a sliding door and furnished Biedermeier-style and handed me a glass of Red Riding Hood Sekt, the East German excuse for champagne. "I don't need to introduce you to anybody. You know most of the people, and the others will take care of themselves."

I made the rounds. Dr. Fach was there, Berlin accent and all, carelessly dressed as always and as always reeking of alcohol and cigarettes. My first impression of him back in November had been of a hidebound bureaucrat, but later I heard that he had sheltered students from the niggling infantilizations of the Party. His combination of learning, simplicity, melancholy, and magnanimity made him the model of a proletarian gentleman. Dr. Weil, the woman who had invited me to take part in the meeting of the department's Party members, was there too. I had since learned that just before the Wall started coming down she had had the courage to publish an article in which she more or less reinvented the idea of the rule of law and called upon her country to institute it, an act heroic and futile, as if an Inca had invented the wheel only months before his entire culture was overrun by Spanish wheels. The speaker who had delivered the empty, long-winded oration was there. I had later come to know him as Dr. Kunkel, friend and aficionado of the arts and elegant opportunist. Dr. Blöhmer, a legal historian, gave a witty, rough-and-tumble account of his early life as a boxer and made eyes at the women. Dr. Flemm, a legal philosopher, recounted the "bourgeois aberration" that he had committed at a conference in the fifties and for which he had been banished to a tiny provincial town, the distance in time having transformed a tragic event into a comic adventure.

The older I am the more I have to strain to understand party conversations. The ear doctor I went to gave the ailment a name: social deafness. Since it has no medical cure, I must treat it on my own, and the way I do it is to stop listening when the listening gets too hard, and put on a friendly, attentive face. I laugh when the others laugh, but think my own thoughts. I thought back to the morning after the Wall came down, my first trip to Frankfurt, my first flight to Berlin and the many trips and flights since, the days at the university and nights at the University Guesthouse. I had not gone to meetings of the civil-society movement or of the church opposition or of the new political parties, nor had I sought contact with the "social niches" or the Stasi victims—that is, I had not done what I could easily have done to get some idea of the historical situation. Instead I had let myself be dragged through an alien academic world that would soon be defunct, blissfully registering my impressions, condemning no one, exonerating no one, and thoroughly enjoying the foreign, last-gasp nature of it all.

I likewise enjoyed the melancholy nature of the farewell party. I had a seat in history's waiting room: one train had just been shunted to an abandoned platform; the other was due in at any moment and would set off again after a brief halt. Not everyone who alighted from the first train would find a place in the second; many would remain in the waiting room, watching the snack bar close, the heating and lights go off. But as long as the old train was still out there and the new one still on its way, the snack bar was still open and everything was warm and brightly lit.

7

THE PLANES WERE ALWAYS FULL. I often took the first morning flight or last evening flight and was surrounded by tense, exhausted passengers. Once, because all the overhead compartments were full, the man next to me stuffed his bags into my legroom. Then there was the time the man next to me tried to prevent the stewardess from giving me her last bottle of wine, insisting she divide it between the two of us, and the time the man next to me explained that a passenger in a row with four seats has a right to one-and-a-quarter armrests and a passenger in a row with three seats a right to one and a third, and proceeded to show me what this meant in practice. Most of the passengers were men.

Then on one of my last flights from Berlin to Frankfurt I saw Barbara. All the rest of the passengers had taken their seats when she ran on and opened and closed the jam-packed overhead compartment about ten rows ahead of me, handed her bag to the stewardess, and sat down. We both had aisle seats, and I could see a bit of her arm and, when she shifted position, a bit of her head, shoulder, and back.

I stopped looking and opened the novel I had recently bought now that I did not need every free minute to prepare my lectures. I began reading as the plane started down the runway and lifted into the air, but I was unable to retain anything and kept reading the same sentences over and over.

I was suddenly terribly tired. Was it from the many trips and the two jobs? The prospect of going back to the publishing house, where since my encounter with history—if only in the waiting room—the work had lost its luster? The fight I had fought for Barbara years ago? Suddenly the hope and despair came back to life as if the years had been mere days.

The plane had reached its cruising altitude, and the stewardesses were serving drinks. The navigation lights at the tips of the wings were blinking on and off, and now and then the lights of a city twinkled between the clouds. Why do lights on the ground always seem to be twinkling? Why can't they just shine? I closed my eyes. I pictured Barbara making herself comfortable in the seat ten rows up, exchanging a few words with the person next to her perhaps, then opening a book and taking a sip of wine. I saw her face before me: the pale skin, the tiny scar on the upper lip, the dimple at the inner end of the left eyebrow. I had noticed she was wearing black slacks and a pink sweater and was neither fatter nor thinner than she had been, and I conjured up her body so vividly that I felt I could touch it if I held out my hand. It made me jealous of that person next to her: I envied him her closeness and the easy, natural contact between the two of them, superficial though it was.

Jealousy only made me more tired. But even as I drove it away with thoughts of the joys of those early days—the weekend shopping expeditions, the intimacy of our nights together, and the discovery of tenderness and passion, Barbara dripping wet in the doorway, then sitting in the armchair in my jeans and sweater with her hands around the cup of hot chocolate—I could not shake the fatigue. In fact, the happy memories seemed to be exacerbating it. That frightened me, and I retrieved one icon after the other from my memory: Grandfather picking me up at the station, Lucia holding my head and kissing me, my thoughts on justice in the first years of my work on the dissertation, the California paradise, my successes at work, Barbara sitting up in bed and pulling off her nightgown, the weeks with Max, the trip to Ticino with Mother, the farewell party in East Berlin. I was not disturbed by the fact that the memories made me nostalgic, because I could never bring back the events, or that they made me sad, because they reflected only the positive side of experiences that had their negative side as well. Such is always the case with happy memories. What disturbed me was that they made me more than nostalgic and sad: they made me tired. Deeply, dumbly, blackly tired.

The strain of preparing regular lectures, the tedium of the work awaiting me, the frustrations of my fight for Barbara—none of this could explain my state. Not the latter, at least, as I had put up virtually no fight: she hurt my feelings; I crawled away. As for my job at the publishing house, I had capitulated without even trying to come up with a better configuration. Nor had I really put much effort into my teaching in the last few months; I had kept my distance, observing the others play out their roles while I kept mine quiet and took my leave before its irregularities came into the open. How could I put real effort into something I was not really involved in?

I polished off both the small bottles of wine the stewardess had given me. It did not bother me that I did not get involved with Lucia: I had been too young. But I had played the Parsifal with my grandparents when I was old enough to pose questions that would confront them. As for the dissertation, I was too much in love with the play of my ideas to impose a structure on them. I could have made more out of the California experience and had a greater impact on Max's life, and with my mother I gave in early: evasion not involvement was the name of that game. I was not being unfair to her—she deserved it—but it did not do me any good.

Is existential fatigue then the result of too little commitment rather than too much? Is it taking things too lightly that wears one out or taking them too seriously? Or is the whole thing nothing but hogwash? Is it nothing but my mother's work ethic in another guise? Was I simply more tired than usual because there are times when one is more tired than usual?

As soon as the plane landed and pulled up to the gate, I jumped up and elbowed my way forward, a terribly boorish thing to do and deeply repellent to me. But I did manage to stand behind Barbara at passport control and ask, "Got any plans for the weekend?"

8

THAT WEEKEND ON OUR WAY home I asked her to marry me.

We had set off on Friday at two, as in the old days. "Where to?" she had responded to my question in the airport without missing a beat or giving a hint of surprise, and nodded when I suggested Konstanz: on our last weekend excursion, the trip to Basel, we had designated Konstanz as our next destination.

We took the Autobahn then the Black Forest scenic highway. The Black Forest was covered with snow, the slopes with skiers and tobogganers; the pines, otherwise a somber dark green, were resplendent in their white burden. The sky was blue, and at times we could look up over the mist covering the Rhineland plains all the way to the Vosges.

We talked about what had brought us to Berlin. Shortly after the Wall came down, Barbara's school had formed a partnership with a school in East Berlin. It included a pupil and teacher exchange, and Barbara had taught there for two weeks. She liked the quiet, well-behaved children and most of the teachers, who were more confident of their roles than were Barbara and her fellow teachers. But things were changing: the children were growing wilder and the teachers less sure of themselves and hence more authoritarian. The old principal, a control freak suspected of having collaborated with the Stasi, had just been replaced by a man who favored reform, and he had asked Barbara whether she could come for longer periods, the rest of this school year and all of the next.

"And what did you say?"

"I'd be only too glad to, but I've got to see what my school says. And the school board."

"You're not one of those adventurer types I'm sure you've met, and you feel no sense of duty, so it must be for the pleasure. What do you get out of it?"

"It's the combination of the familiar and the strange. I can be somebody else when I'm in Africa or America, but I have to cut myself off from my home; here I can be somebody else in my own country, with my own people, in my own language."

"How do you picture it?"

"A life as a teacher in the German Democratic Republic: the endless rules, the scant freedoms, the contact with other teachers and the children and their parents, keeping an eye out for unofficial Stasi informers, spending summer holidays in Bulgaria, Romania, or at the dacha, making quality time for family and friends, tracking down things in short supply, and experiencing the joy of a book or record from the West."

"Isn't that just the kind of life you said you hated?"

"It would be exotic in the East. It's worth a try."

"In a few months—a few weeks, even—that life will lose its exoticism and be just like the local variety, only uglier. It will have all the same chains, and your kids will be wearing Gap clothes and eating Big Macs."

She shrugged. Was she listening with only one ear? Was she as unsure as I was, afraid that our meeting on the plane had been a prank of fate and our weekend jaunt a mistake? Would we feel what strangers we were once we embraced and tried to make love? Not the kind of strangers you are at first, when you meet and are curious; no, the kind of strangers you are at the end, when it's over. Could something that had worked before work again? Could we again be the miracle we had once been for each other? Had we betrayed each other by taking pleasure in the arms of others? Would putting our arms around each other again prove an embarrassment?

We took a room at the Insel-Hotel in Konstanz. I was standing on the balcony looking out over the lake when Barbara came up behind me, wrapped her arms around my stomach, and laid her head on my back. After a while she slid into my arms and we simply stood there holding each other, not kissing, not talking, just gazing out over the lake, the shore, the sky, or closing our eyes. It was a mild evening; spring was in the air. We did not go back inside until it got dark. We turned on the light, unpacked, and changed for dinner, bustling about in high spirits. We might still have issues, but at least our bodies had recognized each other. I had touched Barbara's shoulders, arms, back, and thighs; I had felt her breasts and stomach; I had smelled her skin and hair, heard her breath.

That first night and the night following we only held each other. On Sunday we had planned to circle the lake and then set off for home, but there was rain coming down in thin gray strings, the way it does in Chinese pen-and-ink drawings, and after breakfast we went back to the room, pulled the balcony door open wide, and made love to the accompaniment of the rain. We had ordered food and champagne from room service and asked to be awoken at three thirty on Monday morning. At five we were on the Autobahn, at six thirty we got caught in the Stuttgart morning rush hour. It was then I popped the question.

9

SILENCE. I looked at her from the side, waiting for her to turn to me and answer, but she looked straight ahead at the cars. Hadn't she heard? I was about to ask when she did turn and say, "Is it important to you that we be married? It makes no difference to me."

"Well, it does to me."

"Are you afraid we'd lose each other the way we did the last time?"

"Let's say I learned then how strong the bonds of matrimony can be. I think you really loved me, yet you stood by your husband."

"Not because he was my husband. He fought for me; you sulked." The dimple over her left eyebrow had come out, and her voice was hard. "Have you forgotten? Have you forgotten that I called you, called you again and again? That I stood in front of your door and knocked and shouted? That I wrote to you? But you preferred to make a victim of yourself, the poor man ill used by the evil woman."

"I'm afraid . . ."

" 'I'm afraid . . . ,' " she said, imitating me. "Afraid of what? What are you trying to put over on me? You know what the Americans would call you? A 'sweet-talker.' No, I don't want to hear about your fears. I don't want to hear what a fearful, sensitive guy you are. I—"

"Stop it, Barbara, please," I pleaded, but that just made it worse. The only way I could get her to listen to me was to yell. "You're right. I did sulk, I did play the victim and turn you into the victimizer. I'm sorry I didn't fight, I'm sorry I hurt you, sorry we wasted years. I'm sorry, Barbara."

She shook her head. "You're only now catching on, aren't you. And only because I flew off the handle. If we hadn't taken the same plane, I'd never have seen you again. Did you expect me to take the first step and go back to knocking on your door and shouting?" She had lowered her voice, but her soft, tired delivery frightened me even more. "No, you didn't expect a thing from me—or for us. I don't get you, Peter Debauer. I don't get why you never called. I don't get why you want to be married."

The cars had finally started moving again. I turned the engine back on and drove slowly out from under the bridge we'd been stuck at.

"It wasn't till I saw you on the plane that I realized what a false life I was living, refusing to get involved, either standing off to the side or, when the going got rough, beating a quick retreat. Just seeing you made it suddenly clear. I want you. If you don't want me, I'll fight for you. I don't yet know how, but I'll learn."

She smiled her crooked smile at me, looked back at the cars, and said nothing. We got back just in time for her to get to school and me to work. When I dropped her off in front of her house, she said, "Yes. Let's get married."

But no sooner did I get to the office than the phone rang and she said, "It won't work. Or, rather, it will work only if you and I don't make the mistake the Germans are making."

"What do you mean?"

"In both East and West people think that the other side has made the same changes they have or that the other side is the same as it was before the breakup or that they are the only ones who can comprehend what they remember and think. Know what I mean?"

I did not answer immediately: I was thinking it over.

"Are you still with me?"

"Yes, yes. I am. And I know what you mean."

She sighed. "If so, would you like to come to dinner this evening?"

10

THUS BEGAN OUR fourth phase. The others had lasted only a few weeks: the weeks of the furniture search, the weeks of tenderness, and the weeks of apprehension that followed the announcement that she was married. I hoped it would take only a few weeks until we entered our next and final phase, the period of a common place of residence, of a life shared, and of marriage, possibly in East Berlin, if the school and school board allowed Barbara to go and I could find a publishing house—because my new idea was to take over a publishing house that had been privatized.

We went back to the office and set things in motion. I thought the young official a bit overzealous in his perusal of my documents.

"I see your parents married in Neurade and you were born in Breslau," he said, "and that your mother did not gather the necessary documentation until September 1961." He gave me a questioning look. "She couldn't have chosen a worse time. Do you happen to know why she did it then?"

I shrugged.

"Could she have been thinking of remarrying? Was there an inheritance?"

"I have no idea."

The official reached for the telephone, dialed a number, asked for some information from my mother's file, and acknowledged receipt of same with a mumble and a nod. Then he turned to us proudly. "Just as I thought. Your mother lost the original documents during her flight from Breslau. When she applied for replacements, we contacted the central register office in East Berlin since it had taken over the records from areas ceded to Poland and Russia after the war. The office failed to respond, either because it did not have the documents in question or because once the Wall was up it simply left inquiries from West Germany unanswered. Then your mother showed us a copy of a letter your father had written to his parents mentioning the marriage. She brought along a friend who stated under oath that what your mother claimed corresponded to the truth."

"What was her name?"

"That is not important at this point. What is important is that we have developed good relations with Poland in the interim and have access to documents we could not possibly have dreamed of seeing a few years ago. We are writing to Neurade and Breslau, so before long you will finally have a valid marriage certificate and birth certificate." He was beaming.

"But I don't want a birth certificate. I want to get married."

"I understand, but you must understand our position. We set great store by good relations with Poland and our partnership with the Polish authorities, and it is our duty to reestablish normal bureaucratic relations now that the end of the Cold War has finally made them possible. It will only take a few weeks."

"If there is no evidence to impugn the veracity of the 1961 document, it should be sufficient." I knew nothing of the relevant branch of law, but it could hardly be otherwise.

He gave me a look that seemed to say, I've been kind to you until now, but I can change. "You are free to take legal action if you feel it will expedite matters."

Barbara looked from me to him and back to me. "What's he saying?"

"That Mother's documents aren't enough and he wants to have more sent from Poland. He says we can't do anything—"

"No, I didn't say that. I said—"

". . . we can't do anything to get married in a timely fashion. The court will need more than the time it takes the mail to get to Poland and back."

Barbara, who could not understand the legal error the man had committed with such self-assurance, gave him a big smile and said, "Would you be so kind as to do everything in your power to speed things up? And could you give us a ring when documents arrive from Poland?"

It was five weeks before he phoned to give me an appointment. They felt longer to me than to Barbara, who told me with her smile, "The difference between being married and being single is not so big as you think. Take it from one who knows."

I knew I would not love Barbara the more for being married to her, but I was constantly waking up next to her at night with the anxiety that had kept me awake before her husband returned. I wanted to be rid of that anxiety.

The official greeted me with a patronizing smile. "Take a seat. Take a seat. Your fiancée isn't with you? Well, no matter. In fact, it's a good thing." He reached for a file. "You weren't too optimistic about our relations with the Poles"—he was reveling in his triumph—"but our Polish friends have done a good job, a good job indeed. We now know that no couple by the name of Debauer was married in Neurade in September 1944 and that no child by the name of Peter Debauer was born in Breslau in April 1945. But there was a child by the name of Peter Graf born there and then to a woman by the name of Ella Graf. Graf is your mother's maiden name, is it not?" He did not wait for me to answer. "There can be little doubt that your real name is Peter Graf, not Peter Debauer. If you wish to marry, you must naturally do so under your real name."

"My real name? I'm not about to change names at my age."

The official gave me another patronizing smile. "That is not within my jurisdiction, but allow me to suggest that you consider having your name officially changed to the one you have been using up to now. I can give you an idea of what the procedure would—"

"Change my name to my name?"

"If that is how you wish to look at it. I see it as changing your real name to the name you have been using mistakenly." He shut the file and ended the conversation by saying, "It was just a suggestion. After all, most women change the names they've had all their lives."

II

I STOOD OUTSIDE, unable to remember where I had parked the car. I couldn't even remember whether I had planned to go back to work or meet an author or take Max to the movies. It was three o'clock.

I found the car and drove to my mother's. She was working in the garden. By the time I was standing next to her, she had straightened up and brushed the hair out of her eyes with the back of her hand. "Hello." She was wearing the jeans and yellow sweater that since childhood she put on whenever she cleaned house, moved furniture, or painted. She looked good—calm and relaxed—and if I was not so well acquainted with the bitter streak in her face I might even have failed to notice it. I could see in her eyes that she had registered the disappointment, frustration, and hurt in mine.

"I've just come from the register office."

"What's wrong? Has Barbara changed her mind?" I had had the two of them to dinner, and they had liked each other, or so they assured me later. They had both been determined to make the encounter a success with the hardness that I knew to be part and parcel of my mother's character and that I learned that evening was part of Barbara's as well.

"They wrote to Poland. There was no Debauer/Graf wedding celebrated in Neurade in 1944 and no Peter Debauer born in Breslau in April 1945. But there was a Peter Graf. They want me to go by the name of Peter Graf from now on."

My mother stuck her trowel in her wicker basket and pulled off her gloves. "Tea?"

"All these years. What have you been telling me all these years?"

She gave a derisive laugh. "So now I've been talking too much, is that it? A few weeks ago it was too little." She preceded me into the house and put some water on to boil. "Tea? Or do you want hot chocolate? Or don't you know what you want? Then I'll make lapsang souchong." She took the canister out of the cupboard, shook the leaves into the large strainer in the glass teapot, waited for the water to boil, and poured it over the leaves. I could tell she was thinking over what to tell me.

"Stop thinking. Just tell me."

But she said nothing until she had removed the strainer from the teapot, placed the teapot, teacups, and rock sugar on the table, poured out the tea, and sat down. She shook her head. "You act as though I owed you something. If not your father himself, then his memory, a portrait, a life story. But I don't owe you a thing. I did you no harm by telling you your father and I were married; I just made both our lives easier and gave you grandparents who had no problem seeing you as their grandson and loving you. Would you rather have grown up without them? Would you rather have been known as an illegitimate child, a bastard, by your schoolmates? Nobody cares about that kind of thing nowadays, but back then it would have ruined your life. So just be glad it hasn't come out till now." There was hostility, even contempt in her eyes. "The name thing is annoying, but I don't think they'll hold you to anything. They're not going to initiate legal proceedings to make you use it. If you don't ask anything of them, they won't ask anything of you. Just give your silly bureaucrat a wide berth and take your business elsewhere. You can get married anywhere in Germany, by the sea, in the Alps; you can get married in Las Vegas for all I care!"

"When women come up with a way of having children without fathers, what you say will be right. But as it is, I don't think it's asking too much to want to know everything you know about my father."

"But I've told you: you seem to know more than I do. Cut the part about the wedding out of what I told you and you have it."

"How did he get you the Swiss passport with that false married name?"

"How should I know? I didn't pry into who forged it and how; I was just happy to have it. Not that it helped in the hospital: they wanted to see the marriage certificate. But it impressed the Poles and the Russians. I don't know what I would have done without it. Or you for that matter. No offense meant, but the more I talk about it the angrier I get. I'm not asking you to forgive me; I'm asking you to recognize what I did for you. I brought you out of Breslau, I brought you together with your grandparents, I brought you up. And I always had a net ready for you in case you fell."

"What took Johann Debauer, a citizen of Switzerland, to Neurade and Breslau?"

"I have no idea. I wasn't interested. I was lonely; he was good-looking, charming, and witty, and he had money. I was in love. He must have told me something, but I don't remember. People ended up in all sorts of places back then."

"Did you hope he would marry you?"

"That's the last asinine question I'm going to answer," she snapped, her eyes narrowing to slits. "I hoped everything and nothing. Yes, I did dream of going through life with a rich 'citizen of Switzerland' who adored me and maybe even let me study medicine in Zurich. No, on Friday I did not expect to wake up with him next to me on Saturday and on Saturday that we would spend all of Sunday together. That's how it is when the times are crazy. You don't know today what tomorrow will be like and would probably be happier to forget what yesterday was like."

She topped up our cups. Then she sat again and went on with her musings.

"On the Thursday before the Friday when I met your father I had gone to Neurade to visit Uncle Wilhelm and Aunt Herta. Uncle Wilhelm wasn't a real uncle; he was my godfather, a friend of Mother's since childhood, and a Nazi, yes, but a lot of fun, and I liked him. He's the one who showed me the finger game you always wanted to see. Remember?" She laid her palms one on top of the other, bent the middle fingers, twisted the palms in opposite directions until they and the fingertips touched, then squiggled the middle fingers back and forth. I could not help laughing. I always thought it a miracle that the two fingers ended up swinging together like a single-finger pendulum. "I never stopped laughing when I was with them. Their children were older than me: the son was killed in Poland; the daughter had married and moved to East Prussia. On the day before I went to visit they learned that their daughter and her husband and two children had been murdered by the Russians: raped, beaten, mutilated, burned. When I got to their place, I found Uncle Wilhelm and Aunt Herta in the bedroom. He had shot her and then himself."

She looked at me as if she needed to marshal a special resolve to proceed. "It was horrible to find them like that, but it was just as horrible to have to deal with it all: the police, the doctor, the neighbors, the funeral. Father had always been the one to organize things. That night was the worst. Even though the bodies had been removed and I slept in the guest room, I had the feeling they were lying next to me. But the next morning I felt an overwhelming joy at being alive. As I woke up, I thought, I've got the whole day ahead of me and I want to enjoy every minute of it. That evening I met your father."

12

A FEW WEEKS EARLIER I had found a book about the Swiss Red Cross in the Second World War. At that point I was in no hurry to read it, but I went straight to it the moment I got home. It was not so much the survey I expected as a report by a Swiss physician who had worked for the Red Cross with other Swiss nationals in German field hospitals in Russia in 1941, the year my father finished school. But there were other such missions later as well, the physician said. Could my father have entered the fray between the Russians and Germans under the aegis of the Red Cross? True, nearly all the Swiss in the physician's report were either doctors or nurses, and my father had studied law, but perhaps he had been one of the few ambulance drivers. I wrote to the Swiss Red Cross and asked whether a Johann Debauer had worked for them between 1941 and 1945.

The physician also told about a train carrying Swiss SS volunteers—he had encountered it on his way home—but if the Swiss Army had rejected my father the SS would not have taken him.

It was evening by then. I put the book down, stood up, opened a bottle of wine, poured myself a glass, put on some Schumann, and sat down again. I suddenly realized I had missed an appointment with an author in Mainz and forgotten to phone my secretary. Nor had I phoned Max, who was looking forward to a movie and pizza. No one answered when I called to apologize, and I couldn't get through to Barbara, who was back in East Berlin and staying with a friend.

I calmed down. Peter Graf. Why not? Why not Peter Bindinger for that matter? Because I liked my name. It represented the bond between my grandparents and me, and that meant a lot. The bond between my father and me was weaker and less important, but if it broke what would happen to the other one? Then I reconsidered: the bond between my father and me may have been weaker, but it was not less important. My father was a stranger to me, but whether as a child riding a hobbyhorse and wearing a paper hat or as an unsettled young man in knickerbockers or as an adventurer loath to sit out the war at home or as the charmer who turned my mother's head, he was of great interest to me, and I liked seeing myself as his son and him as my father, in the open, not behind closed doors. He was part of me, and our having the same name proved it.

I suddenly thought of the man whose son had been my playmate for a short time one summer and who had told me I had my father's eyes. I wanted to find out as much about my father as I could, and since I was already neglecting my work I decided to leave the next day for Switzerland.

It was late morning by the time I arrived. I no longer remembered the man's name, but I remembered the house. There was another family living there, but the neighbors helped. When I reached him on the phone, he said hesitantly that he was willing to meet, but he wanted to make it clear from the start that he hadn't much to tell me.

Late that afternoon I was sitting on his terrace looking out at the lake and the Alps. He had clearly struck it rich. He was by himself: his wife was running some errands in town, and his son, who would have been only too glad to see me again, was in America. He would have to be off soon too. It all sounded perfectly plausible, though I had the feeling he was glad we could talk without intrusion.

"In 1940 my father had to give up his job in France because of the war, and when we moved back to Switzerland I entered my final year at school without knowing a soul. The school year had begun and everybody knew everybody else and had their own cliques. You can imagine what it was like. Your father had a clique of his own and was not interested in me, but we shared part of the way home, and even if we didn't always ride together we had interesting talks when we did. At least, I found them interesting. I mostly listened: I didn't have much to contribute. He was way ahead of me, though whether the direction he had taken was right or not is another question.

"He was a real charmer, your father. Well, maybe 'charm' isn't quite the word for his ability to make whoever he was talking to feel he was important, special, and enjoying the privilege of his undivided attention. He would create an atmosphere of trust and intimacy that was terribly seductive, but the next time you saw him all you got was a friendly but formal nod. I don't think he was playacting; I think that when he was with you he was fully there, all of him. It was no façade: he was trying you out. That's a serious business, but one that few people take seriously. Not him. He went at it heart and soul. And if you failed, that was it."

He looked at me with a sad, friendly smile I seemed to recall. "You can tell that your father seduced and abandoned me. We got caught in a terrible downpour when we were riding home one day, and took shelter under the eaves of a church. I could show it to you. I still drive by it sometimes. Your father put me through the third degree: what my life had been like in France, what my interests were, what I planned to do with my life. I don't know what I said that made him respond, 'We're a lost generation; ten years ago there was a spirit of rebellion in Switzerland, an awareness of crisis, a struggle for community, and the willingness to turn the staid, mechanical world of the Enlightenment into an organic, creative world of excitement, to overcome untrammeled egoism and individualism by working together, to bridge the gap between social antitheses, to replace the democracy of acquisitiveness with an aristocracy of achievement and build a new spiritual empire, a Reich of the sons of Switzerland.' He went on and on about the free-thinking, democratic conferences in the years 1928–31, about Julius Schmidhauser, Othmar Spann, Carl Schmitt, and more of the same. He spoke so passionately about events that had taken place ten years before—how much in reality and how much in his imagination, I can't be sure—that he infected even me"—here he laughed—"the most sedate, the most prudent, the most pedantic adolescent there ever was. He had even me dreaming of unqualified commitment, of a life totally dedicated to the cause. But then he said we had been born too late. 'Ten years ago they'd had their chance and they'd muffed it. What had begun as the dawn of a new day had degenerated into petty squabbling over organizational details and who would get what post, into aping what the Germans were doing, what the Italians were doing, into a caricature of the mechanistic, egoistic mediocrity they'd banded together to bring down.' "

He paused. I waited awhile, then asked, "Then what did he propose?"

"That's just what I asked. He said we had to forget about movements, parties, organizations. Total commitment, yes, but only for the individual daring enough to seek it out. Or wait for a miracle. He said it as if it were a foregone conclusion, and I didn't dare question it: I didn't want to disturb the intimacy that had grown up between us or that I at least felt. And anyway the storm had passed."

"So you just got back on your bikes and rode home."

"Right, and when the next day, after a night of tossing and soul-searching, I went up to him, burning to pour out my excitement and doubts, he gave me a friendly nod and turned away." He smiled that smile of his again. "I never had another serious conversation with your father. He began to study law, but soon left, left for Germany, and when I thought of his call for total commitment and Goebbels' call for total war I had a funny feeling. But it was no more than a feeling, and I'd learned to mistrust my feelings from that talk with your father." He smiled again. "I still mistrust them."

"Could he have been with the Red Cross in Germany or Russia?"

He looked up at me. I saw a successful businessman: relaxed, well-groomed, gray hair, clear eyes, strong chin. He had the looks of the bankers and magnates in newspaper photographs, men as far removed from the normal lives of normal people as heads of state or cardinals or movie stars. Suddenly I realized how unusual this conversation had been for him, what a favor he had done me to grant it, and also what an impression my father must have made on him. I suddenly saw too that it was not only his smiles that were friendly or sad; his entire face expressed his sympathy. As if embarrassed by this show of emotion, he turned away. "The Red Cross? It's not out of the question, I suppose. Your father wasn't a doctor, but they had use for others, and he . . . Didn't he have a heart defect that exempted him from military service?"

He stood. "Good luck."

13

BARBARA TOOK THE NEWS from the register office in her stride. "Give it some time. You may come to like the idea of Peter Graf or Peter Bindinger. And if you don't, there's always Vegas. In the meantime, you can move in with me."

"Here?"

"Augie and I never lived together here, if that's what's bothering you. We can change everything; nothing need stay as it is. And the student who's been renting the maid's room has just moved out, so we can use that room too."

I was not so sure. A friend of mine had convinced me that a reunified Germany needed a new constitution. Didn't two people who love each other and intend to live together need a new place to live? Neither should move into the other's place.

"I'll stow all my things in the basement and we'll bring in some carpenters, and when they're done it will be a completely new space with everything just the way we want it." She could see I was still hesitant. "I love this place. It's a good place. I love its big, bright rooms, I love the balcony I used to take my nap on, even when it rained. You can hear the rain in the trees, hear the birds singing, and the air is cool, but you've got a roof over your head and you pull the warm blanket up over your ears and you feel safe. Try it sometime."

I thought of the daily nap I took during the first few summers I spent with my grandparents. If it was warm enough, I could take it on the balcony, and when it rained they covered me with a blanket, just as Barbara had described. How could I have forgotten?

The remodeling took two months. Finally all the furniture we had shopped for and chosen for each other was in one place: her art nouveau dining room and my cherrywood bedroom, her leather couch and my leather armchair with matching table, the mirror from her entrance hall and the lamp from mine.

Barbara's school and school board were willing to send her to Thüringen but not Berlin. Our region was in charge of reconstruction in Thüringen; East Berlin was under the care of West Berlin. So I looked at publishing houses in Thüringen as well, and for a few weeks I was making progress with both the Berliner Verlagssozietät and the Thüringischer Verlag. Then a large Hamburg house grabbed them from under my nose.

So I was stuck with the daily round of legal handbooks and textbooks, commentaries, and journals. From time to time I received doctoral dissertations from at home and abroad, and I was thinking of turning the best of them into a series. I also wanted to start a new journal, a quarterly instead of a monthly, for longer, more theoretical essays, but the publishing house was against it: they feared that the more demanding material would jeopardize the sales of the current practical list, which all but sold itself. The new, improved work situation I had fantasized about on the plane from Berlin to Frankfurt was now dead and buried.

Not that I cared at first. I was too happy with Barbara, happy to wake up with her, shower with her, happy that we would brush our teeth and hair together, that she would put on her makeup while I shaved. I loved our breakfast conversations about the shopping to be done, the errands to be run, the plans for the evening; I loved coming home to her, seeing her get up from her desk, feeling her arms around my neck or, if I came home first, looking forward to seeing her and spending the evening with her, whether at home or on the town, and then preparing for bed together and knowing that if I happened to wake up in the night I would hear her breathing and it would take nothing at all to touch her or snuggle up to her or wake her. Sometimes she teased me, saying, "What a bourgeois match I've made. You'd be happy just to stay at home and read, listen to music, watch television, and chat, plus an occasional promenade along the river." But she would laugh as she said it. "What do you mean?" I would say, laughing along with her. "I like walking up the hill too."

Had she wanted me to, I would have taken her every night to a movie or play or concert or to see friends. But it wasn't staying home that I enjoyed; it was the routine of love. The life I had led with my mother had had its perfectly orchestrated and functioning routine, but it was cold. Routine had also been part and parcel of the life I had led on my own: if a bulb burnt out, there was one to replace it; supplies were renewed before they ran out; broken appliances went immediately to the repair shop; no suit I might want to wear was unpressed, no shirt unwashed. I was so efficient that even when I seemed to be biting off more than I could chew I managed to fill my self-imposed quota by the end of the day. But much as I needed routine, much as I suffered from the years of chaos with Veronika and Max, I was never content at the end of those super-efficient days: there was a coldness about them. Only the weeks with Max and the summers with my grandparents had combined the two: routine and warmth. And now I had found a routine of love. What could be better!

After a time, however, the happiness of my routine with Barbara put the unhappiness of my routine at work into stark relief. I had to force myself to go in each morning, to sit at my desk, to read and answer my mail, to edit my manuscripts. And even worse than the doing of it all was the knowledge that there was no change in sight.

Yet change did come. It took a different form from the one I had fantasized about: I did not move from one publishing house to another; I went off on a different tangent altogether. My whole life changed.

It began with the most everyday of everyday occurrences in the life of an editor: a book proposal. The fact that it was accompanied by the book itself rather than a manuscript did not make it any the less ordinary: it was in English, and the publisher was interested in its appearing in German. Since my idea of starting a series of monographs had died on the vine, I did not pay much attention to the letter. My secretary sent out our standard reply but put the book on my desk.

There it lay, a Cambridge University Press hardcover complete with pale-blue dust jacket featuring a blurry picture of an ancient ship, its oars in the water, its sails billowing. The author, title, and publisher were in dark blue. The title was *The Odyssey of Law,* the author John de Baur.

14

THE PUBLISHER HAD inserted a copy of *The New York Times* review of the book, which provided biographical information. The author had been trained as a lawyer and while too iconoclastic to be teaching at one of the major law schools, he was important enough to have landed a position in the Political Science Department at Columbia. He had studied under Leo Strauss and Paul de Man and was the founder of the deconstructionist school of legal theory. For some time now he had exerted his influence more through his teaching than through his publications: his Tuesday seminars were legendary. *The Odyssey of Law* was his first book since *With Rousseau at the Opera,* an innovative reinterpretation of Rousseau's philosophical oeuvre on the basis of the structure of his early operas. I had no idea what deconstructionist legal theory might be, had never heard of Strauss or de Man, and did not know that Rousseau had composed operas. I opened the book.

The introduction was about *The Odyssey,* not the law. It described it as the prototype of all homecoming stories. Throughout all his adventures and misadventures Odysseus remained true to himself. Home at last, he found a combination of brazen opposition and true love; he also found the weapon to overcome the opposition and bring the love to fruition.

Leafing through the book, I found bits and pieces of a history of law. It concentrated on mythical and epic, magic and rational law, on punitive and compensatory justice, and on legitimate rule, collective utility, and the happiness of the individual as the goals of law.

There was a chapter dealing with "cycles" of the law: the major cycle, in which the law serves one goal after another over the centuries only to come back to the original goal and start again, and the minor cycle, in which the fabric of the law is constantly being woven yet also unwoven, like Penelope's shroud. Societies that failed to unweave the fabric of law, that wove it ever thicker, were destined to suffocate in it.

There was also a chapter dealing with the role of truth and lies. Truths are often lies and lies truths; erudition means nothing more than shattering one ideological view of the world to make way for another. We make our own truths and lies and are responsible for deciding what is true and what is false. We are likewise responsible for deciding what is good and what is evil and whether evil should be given free rein or forced to serve the good. But something more than and different from making decent decisions is involved. The demand for intellectual decency earns nothing but scorn from de Baur: what matters to him is not a person's decent intentions but the consequences of that person's act. The decision to use evil for the sake of good requires that the decision-maker be willing to bear the brunt of evil.

There was much I could not grasp, but what I grasped immediately was that this was the iron rule all over again. The willingness to bear the brunt of evil as a prerequisite for the use of evil—it could be nothing else.

In one chapter I came upon a story from book twenty-four of *The Iliad*. After Achilles kills Hector, old man Priam, king of the Trojans and Hector's father, enters the Greeks' camp and asks Achilles for his son's body. Achilles, who is nothing if not rash and merciless, takes pity on the old man: he gives him the body and even tries to console him, telling him that at Zeus' door there are two urns, an urn of good and an urn of evil, and if Zeus gives a man only evil he totally destroys him; if, however, he sends him a mixture of good and evil, then he will have good luck and ill by turns. De Baur points out that the image of the two urns reappears in Plato: when speaking of good and evil in the *Politics,* Socrates discusses whether Zeus really has two urns at his door or only one, and he quotes the *Iliad* passage word for word. But he makes one slip: he does not say that the man who is totally destroyed receives his share only from the urn of evil; he says he receives it from only one urn. In other words, if Zeus does not give him a mixture of good and evil, if he draws from only one, either the urn of evil or the urn of good, then the recipient will suffer untold affliction all his days on this earth. That is philosophy's fulcrum for de Baur: unlike religion, philosophy rests on the equal status of good and evil; good without evil is as unsuited to mankind as evil without good.

15

I AM SLOW TO REACT. I neither rejoice when something wonderful comes my way nor despair when I meet a setback. It is not that I have self-control; it simply takes time for things to register. At first it is only an intellectual fact, and I can go on with my work or go home as usual or go to the movies as promised.

So I made my final run-through of the journal, checking the proofs and the mock-ups and entering page numbers in the table of contents. But my heart wasn't in it. Nor was I good company for Max at the pizzeria after the movie. I got away as soon as I could and went back to the book, reading with the same haste and lack of concentration that had plagued me earlier in the day. It was late, I was tired, I could barely keep my eyes open, but I had to get through the book even if I was missing half of it. I simply had to.

Once we have set aside such ancillary issues as premeditation, duplicity, and the gruesome nature of the act, murder amounts to ending a person's life without his will. Without, not against: outsmarting a person or break-

ing his will introduces ancillary issues of its duplicitous or gruesome nature. In its pure form murder is the ending of a person's life in his sleep.

A person loses his life. A person commits a mad, desperate, or courageous act which costs him his life. A murderer "steals" a person's life. We speak of it as if afterward the person were standing before us without his life—still standing, only without his life—as if he were rubbing his eyes in bewilderment over having mislaid it, as if he could make a fuss about having it stolen, as if he could mourn for it.

But the person is no more. He is not bewildered, he can make no fuss, nor can he mourn. He no longer suffers from what he suffered while alive: loneliness, illness, poverty, stupidity. A person never suffers from his death: he does not suffer before his death, because he is alive, or after his death, because he is no more. By the same token, a person does not suffer from being murdered. Death and murder are the transition from a condition perfectly natural for a person to another condition equally natural for him. After all, what could be unnatural for him if he is no more? Predicates sans subjects are homeless and senseless.

We do not punish a murderer because he has ended a person's life without his will. There is nothing punishable in that. No, we punish the duplicitous, gruesome nature of the act, that is, the disappointment and pain he has caused the victim before his death. Then why do we punish murder when these ancillary issues do not obtain, that is, why do we punish murder in its pure state? Not for the victim's sake, no, but for the sake of the wife who has lost her husband, the husband his wife, the child his father, the friend his friend, that is, for the sake of all those who depended upon the victim and are now deprived of him, for the sake of the order of things, on which we all depend and which tells us that life and death have their natural times.

That is why suicide was regarded as a sin and attempted suicide as a punishable offense: it deprives these same people in nearly the same manner of the perpetrator. That is why murder was punished according to the value the victim's life had for others: the life of the son or daughter for the father, the life of the slave for the master. That is why the white man who killed a black man received a milder punishment than the black man who killed a white man: it was not that the perpetrator deserved greater mercy; it was that the victim had a lower value. That was why genocide could so often be committed with a clear conscience: it left no one behind to feel robbed of the victims. The prerequisites are the following: that the people in question be isolated, that it not be involved with other peoples in the ordering of a world, and that the methods employed be radical.

How many peoples, how many people go to make up a world? The way we cut up the worlds in which we live and the order we impose on them is our doing, not the murderer's. He does not commit the murder; we do.

16

I WOKE UP because Barbara was shaking my arm. She was sitting next to me on the couch, the book in her lap, staring at me in amazement. "This is evil."

I looked at my watch. It was one thirty. "Where have you been?" I asked.

"After the rehearsal we went to the Sole d'Oro and had a bite. Then we tore the whole production apart and redid it from scratch." She was still high from the evening with her amateur theater group, so alive and glowing that I couldn't get it into my head that she was mine. "You've never stayed up with a book so long that you fell asleep over it. What is it anyway?" She looked down at the pages she had just read.

I stood up. "How about some tea? Mint, peppermint, chamomile?" She nodded. I went into the kitchen, put the water on, poured the leaves into the strainer, and placed it in the teapot.

Barbara followed me in with the book in her hand. "Do you know him, this John de Baur?"

"I think he's my father. He changed his name from Debauer to de Baur when he got to America. Or somehow got a passport with that name before he left. He was good at that kind of thing: he got my mother a Swiss passport in Breslau from the gauleiter or the Reich security officials or for money. He called himself Vonlanden for a while and Scholler for a while. Before the war he wrote for the Nazis, after the war for the Communists. He's also the one who wrote the novel that brought us together."

"Didn't your mother say your father was dead? Didn't she see him get killed?"

"She was wrong. Or she lied. It wouldn't be the first time."

Barbara put her hand on my back. "Wow!"

The kettle began to whistle, and I poured the water into the teapot. Barbara gave me a questioning look. "When I was a little girl, I would dream of being a foundling and learning that my real parents were a king and queen or, later, famous movie stars or artists or millionaires. Did you ever have dreams like that about your father?"

"No, never. Maybe I should try." Should I try to see de Baur as a king who will save me from a pitiable fate? My fate was far from pitiable.

She turned the book over. "Too bad there's no picture of him."

"Read the testimonials. Apparently he's an important figure in America. Famous even."

Barbara read one aloud. "I don't understand a word, but it sounds good, doesn't it?"

"Your first reaction was, 'This is evil.'" I was annoyed by her interest in John de Baur and by how easily she had changed her mind about the book. I was even annoyed she had read out the testimonial.

"Yes, what I read of it was bad." She poured herself some tea, added honey, and stirred. "Shall we take the tea into the bedroom?"

But once in bed I was unable to sleep. Barbara had snuggled up to me, her head on my shoulder, her right breast and arm on my chest, her right leg over my stomach. How many nights had I savored the weight of her body on and against mine, grounding me almost. But this time it bothered me: there was too much of it, it was too heavy, too close. Besides, there she was, sleeping away. Didn't she care about my state of mind? Couldn't she have kept me company until I fell asleep? I wished I had my own bed so I could be alone with my anger. I was not hurt by my father's having cleared off and taken no interest in me, not disappointed by a lie of a conceivably much greater magnitude than my mother's lies; I was not depressed. I was angry; I felt a frustrated, defiant anger that I could not turn against the people who had caused it. Taking a few days off, flying to New York, and accosting an elderly gentleman who had apparently found a way to forget his past, accosting him with my anger—ridiculous. Confronting my mother and squeezing a bit more of the truth out of her, though no more than she felt it absolutely necessary to reveal given what I now knew—a waste of time. Nor did I want to vent my anger on Barbara or let it poison our relationship or direct it against myself. But what should I do with it?

17

I HAD A HARD TIME sleeping the next few nights too. The anger of that first night was joined by hurt and disappointment and a tenacious aggressivity that would not be soothed. I did not believe that I would have been a happier child had I known that my father was alive but wanted to have nothing to do with me. Or that I would have been happier later on had I had the chance to decide whether to confront him. Or that I would have led my life any differently had I known about his activities—except that I would not have wasted so much time looking for the author of Karl's story. Or that I would have written to him or visited him or asked him about how the story ends. But that did nothing to appease my anger.

I took out books on deconstruction and deconstructionist legal theory from the university library. I learned that deconstruction is the separation of a text from what the author meant it to say and its transformation into what the reader makes of it; I learned that it went even further to reject the notion of reality in favor of the texts we write and read about reality. This does not tally well with the binding nature of legal and moral rules of civility. If one wanted to insist that the only possible model was the existentialist one, an article I read predicted that de Baur and deconstructionist legal theory would lead to a renaissance of existentialism. Perhaps I should have read up on existentialism as well, but I had had enough. As far as I could make out, if texts are not about what the author meant to say but what the reader makes of them, then the reader, not the author, is responsible for the text; if reality is not the world out there but the text we write and read about it, then the responsibility for murder falls on neither the real murderers nor their victims—they having lost their existence—but on their contemporaries who lodge the complaints and prosecute the plaintiffs. Exactly how to get from there via existentialism to a demand for the willingness to expose oneself to what one exposes others to I could not yet see. But if the others are probably going to die and one is relatively safe oneself, what was the point of it all?

He had remained true to himself. With the playful levity I had found so enjoyable in the novel and so abominable in the letters to Beate and the war essays, he kept several balls in the air: reality and its representation, responsibility, and the roles of author and reader, of perpetrator and victim. I could imagine what the articles he wrote for *Nacht-Express* looked like: they would follow the line set forth by the Soviet major, yet in the de Baur style, now praising what was supposed to be reviled, now reviling what deserved to be praised, and occasionally transfiguring the power he was serving into an ethical principle. What was left? What was left at the end of his life and the end of *The Odyssey of Law*?

I did not like my father, and I did not like his theory: it freed him of all responsibility, the responsibility for what he had written and for what he had done. At the same time, I was fascinated by how he had made his way through life, getting involved in whatever came his way, then moving on, and in the end creating a theory to justify it all. Yes, his playful levity fascinated me, so much so that I found it hard to condemn it out of hand. After all, I had been only too happy to sit playfully, frivolously in the waiting room of history.

No, I did not like my father. But that did not diminish my aggressive feelings: I was not comforted by the idea that I had missed nothing by losing a father I did not like. That a person who had given no thought to me had thought of no one but himself made me feel even more aggressive.

My talk with Mother did not last long. "As far as I'm concerned," she said, "he's dead."

"Did you ever see him again after Breslau? Did he tell you to come here? Did he promise to come here? Did he get in touch with his parents after the war? Did he write to you from America?"

"As far as I'm concerned, he's dead."

Barbara waited a week and a half. Then at Sunday breakfast she asked, "Where do we go from here?"

"What do you mean?"

"We're not making love anymore."

"There have been times when—"

"No, we've never gone more than two or three nights."

She made it sound as though I had purposely, willfully made her unhappy. Yet she must have known how unhappy I was myself. It made me furious. "We went years without making love."

"You're out of your mind," she said, staring at me.

"I . . ."

She stood up. "You have the nerve to blame me for the years we spent apart? You want me to apologize so you can forgive me? You're out of your mind." She marched out of the kitchen but turned back at the door. I could see she was trying to regain her composure. I also saw the dimple over her left eyebrow. "You don't make love, you don't cuddle, you don't talk; you just lie there like a stick. When I wake up in the middle of the night you're sitting at your desk, and when I ask you what's wrong all I get is a pained look. I've been waiting for an explanation for two weeks now. How much longer am I going to have to wait?"

"It's only been one and a . . ."

She was about to say something but gave up and left the room with a wave of dismissal. She also left the flat, but instead of slamming the door she left it open as if wishing to let the wind in, let the rain, snow, dust, and leaves in, let our nice, cozy life together go to rack and ruin.

I listened to her footsteps fading into the distance, then shut the door and cleared the table. I knew I was in the wrong. It would not be the last time. But I could not get rid of my aggression and vented it on the only people I could: Barbara and myself. I was incapable of a major explosion, so I was simply petty and nasty a lot of the time. Even so, I eventually caused irreparable damage.

I was at a loss what to do: with Barbara, with myself, with the rest of that Sunday. I had fallen into a trap and saw no way to extricate myself from it. I sat on the balcony, listening to the bells toll the beginning of the service and, an hour later, its end. I fell asleep, woke up stiff after a few hours, and started making dinner, though it was much too early. I wanted it to be dinnertime, for Barbara to come into the dining room and for us to have dinner together.

She did come back, but late, and she was distant. Still, when I spoke about my hurt, my disappointment, my aggression, and the trap I had fallen into, she heard me out, and when we got into bed and I put my arms around her she did not push me away. True, she was aloof in her lovemaking, but as we were drifting off she put her arms around me. That made me happy. At the same time I knew I was still trapped and had to free myself if we were to get back to normal.

18

WE STOPPED ARGUING. I was still seething and fumed at my shoelace when it broke, at the windshield wipers when they did not do their job, at the passengers when they clogged the stairway to the train platform, at my secretary when she forgot to write a letter, at my clumsy hands when they refused to put a new strap on a watch. There were times I was ready to explode over the nasty, malicious minutiae of daily life, yet I never fumed at Barbara. We made love, we cuddled, we talked.

One day my mother came to see me at work. She had never done so before, and she asked me what such and such a thing was used for and oohed and aahed over something else so as to put off the moment of truth. Finally we were having coffee in my office.

"Yes, he told me to come here after the war. He said he would come too. Otherwise I would have moved to the country, to a village or farm." There was a long pause. I did not push her. She had come to fulfill a duty, and fulfill it she would. "He was true to his word: he showed up in the autumn of 1946. How he found me I don't know, but he'd found me in Breslau too. He was good at that sort of thing. Anyway, he offered me a deal: if I confirmed that he was dead, he would leave everything he had to me as his wife and to you as his son and you would get Swiss grandparents. For both your sake and mine I accepted. I wrote to his parents that I had seen him get shot and had found a letter on him. The letter, which I enclosed, said that we had married." She looked away, trying to preclude any emotional reaction I might have, and to keep her own distance. But I could see the trace of a smile. "Now you see why I didn't want to meet your grandparents."

"Why did Father want to get away?"

"He said he was in danger, he couldn't afford to be caught, he had to hide, he needed to emigrate. I didn't believe him: a man who can parade around in a jacket, blue shirt, and polka-dot tie during the last months of the war knows how to keep out of danger, though he was still wearing bits and pieces of a uniform." She shrugged. "He stayed three months—ten weeks, to be exact. Then one day I came home from work to find him gone."

"So he knew me."

"He was the one who took care of you while I was at work. He didn't go out much. He was waiting for false papers, a visa, a ticket, who knows what. He stayed home, looked after you, and wrote novels for me to sell, to provide me with a little extra money."

"So he knew me!" I was furious, beside myself.

"You mean you might have forgiven him for abandoning a pregnant woman, but a son . . ."

I knew her scorn was justified, but that did not change matters: being abandoned after he had seen me, talked to me, played with me, cared for me, was much more hurtful than being abandoned before birth. Surely I was no less lovable than Max. What I had been unable to do even to a friend's son he had done to his own: deny him a place in his life and his heart.

I never again made the mistake of directing my rage at Barbara. I controlled myself. Only when a shoelace broke or a letter did not go out or my hands failed to obey me did I realize how much energy it cost me, but I had no idea what I could do, other than control myself.

That summer another publishing house turned up, but again I lost my chance. It was a good house, an old house, and I liked its list—it ranged from philosophy to poetry—and its Potsdam location, but it too fell to a large chain. The way it happened was similar: negotiations went smoothly at first but hit a snag, after which the man I had been dealing with failed to return my calls, and in the end the secretary was surprised to hear from me because the house had been sold the week before.

Not that the summer did not have its brighter moments. Barbara still pushed for her weekend excursions, this time to points east, and we went as far as the Ostsee, to Wismar, Rostock, and Greifswald, to the Darss and the Oderbruch, to Görlitz on the Neisse, and up the Elbe. We found much that was monotonous and shabby but also enchanted gardens and strings of houses, even whole streets, that bore the scars of history with dignity. Time had stood still on the tree-lined cobblestone roads, where we met only an occasional tractor, Trabant, or truck, and when we stopped and got out we heard nothing but the birds and the wind. Storks trailed the combines as they moved through the fields.

For Barbara and me it was also as if time had stood still years before. At first we merely tried out the old rituals, willing to abandon them if they no longer felt right, but they felt just fine. The playful jostling when we used the bathroom together, the dancing on the way there and back, the Gernhardt poems, the long periods of shared silence—they felt right in the way they had felt right then and seemed never to have stopped feeling right.

19

ONE NIGHT I BEGAN TO TALK. I had not prepared anything or planned it beforehand. I just did not seem to be able to keep it to myself any longer.

"It's usually okay when we're off on a trip, but even then there are times when it takes everything I can muster to keep from flying off the handle. Remember the time we got stuck for a half hour behind a tractor that wouldn't let us pass? Or yesterday, when we couldn't sit at one of the free tables because the waiter was serving only reserved tables? Or just this morning when you opened and closed your bag three times because you forgot something? That kind of thing drives me crazy, and bringing those crazy impulses under control wears me out." I took her hand. "It began when I found out about my father. I know I'm taking out my rage for him on you. I'm really sorry. Ever since I learned about him, I'm hypersensitive about anything that goes wrong. The publishing house deal would have been a real breakthrough. I could finally have been involved with the world, with the risks of life. I have the feeling I've always lived on the sidelines."

I sat up. The moon was shining into our room, and I could see Barbara's face, a bright spot looking over at me.

"The smartest thing I ever did in my life was to talk to you on that plane. And the most stupid thing I could do now is to leave you and go to America. But I have to go. On the first of September I'm going to resign, move to New York, and confront my father. And I mean not just mumble a few words and let him push me aside; I mean confront him head-on. I'm going to pose as a scholar from Humboldt University who is doing research on some topic or other and who would consider it a great honor to attend his seminar. We'll see what happens then."

"And you want me to wait for you here."

"Come with me. You resign too and come along."

"You know I can't do that." She sat up. "What am I supposed to do with my desire to come home to a cuddle, a desire you awoke in me? You promised to satisfy that desire."

"I'm sorry, Barbara, but I'll be back."

"I don't want to wait for my husband. I've had enough of that."

"I'll come back as quickly as possible."

She shook her head. A while later she started crying, but she let me take her in my arms. If I could cry, I would have cried with her.

Part Five

I

IT WAS DRIZZLING IN NEW YORK. The wipers made streaks on the yellow cab's windshield, and the drops on the side windows wandered into streaks only to peter out or merge with others. The cars had switched their headlights on early, and the light was refracted in the streaks and drops. For a while I could not see much, but then we rode over a bridge and the city suddenly towered sparkling into the rain- and evening-dark sky.

Barbara had made a few calls and found a cheap Riverside Drive room for me. Even though she told me the room was in the back of the building, I kept fantasizing about a river view until I stood in the door and looked through the window at a wall across a ventilation shaft. I unpacked and put my things away. In Germany it was past midnight, and I was both tired and awake. I walked to the university. It had stopped raining. People were rushing along the street as if trying to make up for the time they had lost because of the rain. The entrance to the campus was bustling as well: students and professors going in and out, people passing out leaflets, selling umbrellas. The campus itself was dark and quiet, the buildings sheltering it from the traffic noise. There was no one on the grass and only a few souls on the paths and steps leading up to a building with columns and a dome. I looked at one of them as he passed under a light coming in my direction. Could it be him?

I knew that political science was located in a modern high-rise behind the main campus. I found it and found the floor with faculty offices. John de Baur. Why did it hurt me to read his name on the door? Hadn't I come because I would find his name on the door and him behind it? Suddenly another door opened and I bolted. I did not wait for the elevator or the person whose steps I heard coming down the corridor. I took the stairs.

On the way home I had dinner at a Chinese restaurant and went into a supermarket to stock up. All at once I was so tired that everything seemed unreal: the endless aisles and shelves, the mounds of food, the loud conversations of the customers at the checkout counter, the warm, heavy, humid air outside enveloping me like a cape, the unfamiliar advertisements, the crowded streets, the gigantic trucks, the howling sirens of the police cars and ambulances. Just before entering my building, I gazed up at the sky. It was clear: I could see the stars, I could see the planes blinking red and white, practically on one another's tails. Even the planes seemed unreal to me. Where did all those people want to go? What was I doing here? What ghost was I after?

2

THE NEXT DAY HE WAS sitting opposite me. A man in an open-necked blue shirt and rumpled light linen suit ensconced in an armchair next to his desk, his feet on a chair, a book in his lap. The door to his office had been open, so I had had a moment to observe him before he looked up and spoke to me. Tall, slim, white hair, blue eyes, a big nose and mouth, and a headstrong though relaxed expression on his face.

I saw no similarity. Either with the child in the paper hat on the hobbyhorse, the boy on the bicycle, or the young man in knickerbockers or with myself: my eyes are a greenish-brownish gray, my nose and mouth are inconspicuous, and I am anything but head-strong, much as I would like to be. My mother claimed to see his slant eyes in mine, but I did not find his eyes particularly slant.

Though not struck by any similarity, I was overwhelmed by his physicality. Till then he had been an idea, a construct made of the stories I had heard about him and the thoughts he had put down on paper. He had been both all-powerful and powerless: he had stamped my life without my having a chance to react, and I had created an image of him without his having any input into it. Now he was a body—tangible, vulnerable, visibly older and presumably weaker than I was. But the physicality gave him a palpable presence, a dominance that I had yet to come to grips with.

"Come in!" he said, taking his feet off a chair and nodding invitingly to another. I went into action, telling him, as I had planned, about my teaching at Humboldt University, about the book I wanted to turn my dissertation into after ten years as an editor, and about the role deconstructionist legal theory would play in the revision. Then came the bait: "In addition, my publishing house is thinking of buying your book, and I have been asked to translate it. So the dissertation is only part of my reason for coming. I feel I could do a better job on the translation if I spent a semester attending your lectures and seminar. Would that be possible? I know that tuition in American universities is not free, far from it, and—"

He stopped me with a wave of the hand. He could arrange for me to become a visiting scholar. I wouldn't have my own office or desk, but I would have library privileges and the right to audit any courses I wished. He would be only too happy to have me in his seminar—I might even give a talk to the students—and he would consider it an honor for me to translate his book. Moreover, it made sense for us to be in touch during the process. "I speak your

language, and I will be the one to authorize the translation. I want
to make sure that the misunderstandings that inevitably creep into
a translation are nipped in the bud."

He spoke with animation, using his hands, looking straight at
me. His slight accent did not make his words sound wooden as
it did in other Americans of German origin and in myself; no,
his English was soft, ingratiating, seductive. I remembered Rosa
Habe, who had taken his Swiss accent for Viennese and been literally seduced by it. I remembered my one-time playmate's father,
who had let himself be taken in by his charm. He too had compared my eyes to my father's.

"If you are familiar with my book, my lectures will not hold
many surprises, but I will go a bit deeper here and there. In the
seminar we are reading the classics of modernity. They have a lot to
say—to one another and to us." He stood up, pointed me in the
direction of the departmental office, and said he would phone the
secretary and let her know I was coming.

The secretary took my picture and gave me a laminated plastic
card identifying me as Dr. Fürst. Such was the name I had used
when introducing myself to de Baur and the name he had passed
on to the secretary, who did not ask me to prove it was mine, only
to spell it.

I stepped through the door with a feeling of triumph. I had
done more than gain access to his lectures and seminar; I felt that I
had him in my power, that I, who knew him inside out, could do
as I pleased with him, who did not know me from Adam, that I
had finally come into my own.

3

THE SENSE OF TRIUMPH lived on even after life assumed a daily routine. At times I felt intoxicated though I hadn't drunk a drop; at times I walked with such zest that I might have been crossing a meadow instead of asphalt streets. I bought a pair of running shoes, and my daily jogging sessions down by the river left me invigorated. I got on more easily with the people I happened to meet.

For the first time I believed Odysseus when he said he both desired Penelope and enjoyed his peregrinations, if not for all ten of the years—not for the years with Calypso, and not for the year with Circe—then at least for the weeks of adventures and discoveries. I spoke to Barbara every few days. We talked about school, the department, friends, films, a doctor's appointment, a mishap, a dream—a telephonic wrap-up of our daily news. I was occasionally afraid that although she did not show it she would hold my New York stay against me. But while I was convinced that the two of us belonged together, while I loved and desired her, the desire was for her as part of a life that would once again be mine but was not now mine: I was in New York.

De Baur opened his lectures, like his book, with *The Odyssey*, but he did not treat it as the prototype for all homecoming stories, as I had thought he would when I first read his book. What he meant to do, in fact, was to *deconstruct* the idea that *The Odyssey* is the prototype for all homecoming stories. He claimed that it was readers who desired to view the homecoming as the goal of *The Odyssey*. Take away that desire and you got a different picture. Odysseus was in no hurry to get home: he was perfectly happy with one woman, then the other, and if he did go home it was not because he himself willed it but because the gods did, not because his situation abroad required it but because his wife's situation at home did. The suitors had seen through Penelope's ruse of unweaving by night what she wove by day and insisted that she complete the shroud and do as she had promised, namely, marry one of them once the shroud was ready. Odysseus did not even truly come home: he had to set off again immediately, and although this departure was meant to augur well for a permanent return, that return was by no means certain.

The reader's hopes and desires played other tricks on him as well, de Baur argued. Readers liked to believe that Odysseus covered the whole of the known world on his journeys, that he faced all the horrors known to man at the time, and that the totality of his experience was what gives the journeys their meaning. But the text said that Odysseus was a liar. All we knew about his journey was what he tells the Phaeacians, and he had every reason to ingratiate himself with them by lying. Sometimes lies and wiles played an instructional role in the narrative: they overcame the magic power of Polyphemus, Circe, and the Sirens. But later Odysseus lied to the goddess Athena and to his wife and son and father simply because the stories he spun around his lies were so engaging. Was he true to himself? The liar who remains true to himself as a liar embroils us in a paradox and turns fidelity to betrayal.

The reader could not even be certain what the ending meant. Was it that the insolent suitors are to be murdered, as Aristotle suggests? Was it marital bliss, as a Hellenistic commentator would have it? Was it, as for medieval readers, the re-establishment of the ruler's legitimacy? Or was it the interpretation that surfaced after the great wars, humility in the face of destiny?

The closer one looked at the ending the more bewildering it was. Were the suitors really murdered as a punishment for their sins? The sins were actually not all that outrageous in the end: they courted a woman they assumed to be a widow, and while they did live off her property they paid her back with gifts. Moreover, the threat to murder Telemachus never materialized. Was the murder of the suitors really a heroic victory in spite of being outnumbered, on the part of Odysseus and Telemachus? The spear meant for Odysseus was deflected not by him but by the goddess Athena. And look at the gods: now they were fair, now unfair; they rewarded and punished, loved and hated at whim, threw dice for men's destinies. So, everything was in flux: the work's entire intent and meaning, its portrayal of truth and lies, loyalty and betrayal. All that remained was that *The Odyssey* transformed the primordial myth of departure, adventure, and return into an epic, a story set in a specific moment and place, thereby creating the abstract quantities of space and time without which we would have no history and no stories.

Then de Baur made a wild leap: the same flux was evident in the odyssey of law—its goals, its upswings and downswings, what it saw as good and as evil, as rational and irrational, as truth or falsehood. All that remained of the odyssey of law were the abstract quantities of justice and injustice and the fact that decisions were constantly to be made.

4

RELUCTANT AS I WAS to admit it, he was a brilliant teacher. I would have much preferred to find him a good speaker but shallow, a deep thinker but vain, an inspiring flash in the pan. But no, he kindled true passion in his students: he got them to read long and arduous texts with a sensitivity that showed in their questions and answers. He spoke clearly and vividly and was always ready with an example. His body language was so spirited that one day during the seminar, rocking on his chair as he liked to do, he fell back and picked himself up laughing. Otherwise he was not one for laughing, and his students had to go elsewhere for the jokes American professors are fond of making.

The lecture course took place in an auditorium designed like an amphitheater. It could seat a hundred and twenty students and was always packed. The seminar had eighteen students. We sat in a circle, each with our own desk. If you had something to say, you just said it: de Baur did not use the roster. Two-thirds of the students were young and had entered graduate school in political science directly from college; the other third were older law students who had decided on the law after practicing another profession, and they included a doctor, a psychoanalyst, a French professor, and a former marine. They were trying to do the three-year law course in two and a half years and felt guilty about taking a seminar on political theory rather than a business law class. They liked my proposal that we older students get together for a drink, but were too busy to act on it. All but one. He and I were the only ones attending the lecture course as well as the seminar, and whoever arrived at the lecture first would save a seat for the other in the front row. Jonathan Marvin had sold a profitable business, and the returns made him independently wealthy. He had been attending de Baur's courses for several years and fancied himself more up on him than the others.

"Did you know that for years he ran a utopian commune in the Adirondacks?" he whispered to me on the day de Baur lectured on *The Odyssey* as a search for utopia. But when I pressed him for details after the lecture, all he could tell me was that it had been in the seventies and had begun well and ended badly. One of the twenty to thirty participants who stuck it out was said to have written an article. Jonathan had been on its trail for a long time. "It must have appeared in some obscure New Age rag. No library can possibly collect them all."

One day I discreetly followed de Baur home after the seminar. It turned out to be a short walk: he too lived on Riverside Drive, where, as I had learned by then, the university had bought up a number of buildings to house its faculty members in comfort. My route to the university or the subway did not lead me past his place, but I took to going out of my way to pass it. And so I met him once taking a rottweiler on a walk and once coming out of the park wearing whites and carrying a tennis racket. I also took to jogging past the tennis courts and saw him playing one day, his strokes so sure and powerful that he could afford to refrain from running after fast balls.

I still felt I had him in my power. I was stalking him, observing him, sniffing him out. Soon he would have nothing to hide behind.

But then came the last Sunday in September. It was a bright day with the first red and yellow leaves in the trees and the last warmth of summer in the air. I had rented a bicycle and ridden to the tip of Manhattan to see the Statue of Liberty, and I passed de Baur's apartment building on the ride home. I had had my eye on it since it came into view. I saw a silver Mercedes in front of the entrance, and there was de Baur, standing behind it while the rottweiler jumped into the back through the open tailgate. De Baur shut the tailgate and turned to the building. The doorman was holding the door open, and a young woman with two children came out, a boy of eleven or twelve and a slightly younger girl. I could tell at once from a gesture, a glance: the woman was his wife, the children his children.

Seeing him with wife and children, I suddenly felt him slipping through my fingers.

5

EARLY IN OCTOBER he invited the seminar to his apartment for dinner. "The whole seminar—that's a rarity," Jonathan told me. "He usually limits himself to a few. The dinner is a test, I think: if you pass, you get invited to the January seminar."

"A seminar during the break?"

"For years he's been holding a week-long retreat in the Adirondacks. You have to be personally invited. I don't know what goes on there. The students who've gone have been very secretive about it. De Baur is too. I'd finance it until his retirement if he let me come."

"You mean he pays for it himself?"

"It looks that way. It's not an official course, and the students don't fork out a penny."

I did not want to arrive too early or too late, so I was standing at his door with a bouquet of daisies—having been announced from below by the doorman and taken the elevator to the eleventh floor—at precisely the hour indicated. His wife opened the door, greeted me, thanked me for the flowers, and took me into a large room with a view of the river and the Palisades beyond. After pouring me a glass of wine, she left the room for a moment and returned with the daisies in a vase. "You're the visiting scholar from Germany, aren't you?"

My stepmother was a bit younger than me. Tall, blond, slim, fit. She had an open face, probing eyes, and a mocking smile. What did she know about her husband? What had he told her? Was she his second wife? Had she been his student? Did she admire him, despise him, love him?

"Yes. Are you in political science too?"

She shook her head. "I'm a stockbroker."

Although I had no idea what that involved and would have liked to ask her about it, I had another line of questioning to pursue, and the other guests could arrive at any minute. "I really admire you. How do you do it? Stockbroker and mother of two. I happened to see you with your son and daughter the other day."

They were my half-brother and half-sister. Did we have anything in common? Would we understand one another, accept or reject one another? I could presumably sue them for part of their inheritance, and I would presumably upset them a little by telling them about their father and my mother.

She smiled. "They're wonderful children, both of them. But they leave for school at seven thirty and more often than not aren't back till five. They don't hold my job against me."

"In Germany school is out at noon. My mother had to work when I was their age, but luckily my half-sister from my father's first marriage was able to look after me. An extended family can come in handy. Have you got anyone like that?" I could not come up with anything better.

She was taken aback. "Excuse me? You want to know whether I have any stepchildren? No, we have . . ." The doorbell rang. She was relieved to get away. Then it rang again, and the guests started arriving in rapid succession. When everyone was there, de Baur emerged from the kitchen with two large bowls, one of pasta, the other of salad. He was wearing an apron and playing a trattoria chef in broken Italian. He beamed at the applause, which Jonathan had initiated. Though I stood out like a sore thumb, I could not bring myself to join in.

Everyone helped themselves to food and wine and found a seat. The children were there too, eating away, not in the least self-conscious. They happened to be near me for a while, but I must have stared at them too intensely, because they started looking uncomfortable and wandered off before I could strike up a conversation.

My social deafness is not the only reason I feel ill at ease at large parties. I am no good at small talk: I can never quite find the tone to make the weighty sound trivial and the trivial sound weighty. Either I take my conversation partner's words too seriously and get too involved, or I take them as blather and dismiss them out of hand.

I should never have let myself in for a discussion of a play I had not seen, but I got carried away because I had not said a word all evening. And because I was furious.

Jane, the former psychoanalyst, and Anne, the former French professor, had just seen a black comedy in four scenes entitled *Mosaic* that made a deep impression on them. The play was based on an experiment by a social psychologist, Stanley Milgram, in which the subject is instructed to ask a person a number of questions and punish incorrect answers with electric shocks. The strength of the shocks increases with each incorrect answer until the person screams with pain, then begs for his life, and eventually falls silent. In fact, the shocks are bogus and the subject receives his instructions from a bogus scientist, who explains that the experiment is in the interest of science and encourages him to proceed whenever he hesitates. When the subjects can only hear the other person, about sixty-five percent of them are willing to go all the way; when they can see him as well, the percentage falls to forty; and if they are required to restrain the person physically, it goes down to thirty.

Jane was shocked by the subjects' behavior. "It shows that Hannah Arendt was right, doesn't it? That evil is banal, that normal people are willing to commit atrocities when egged on by somebody in power."

Anne disagreed. "You think thirty to sixty-five percent of the human race are Eichmanns? Well, I don't. I don't believe that Eichmann and all the others were just being obedient either. They enjoyed what they did. They were eager to be cruel. Haven't you read *Sophie's Choice*?"

"Nobody is cruel out of obedience alone," Katherine intervened. She was the one who had been a doctor. "I saw the play too, and the cruelty didn't begin with the shocks; it began with the questions. Didn't you notice? They were questions that had no answers. Anyone willing to ask that kind of question enjoys torturing people."

"That's only the way it was in the play. In Milgram's experiment the questions had to do with a topic the scientist had told them about and the subjects were supposed to keep in mind."

It made me furious that Jane, Anne, and Katherine did not seem to see that the experiment itself was an outrage irrespective of how the questions were worded or whether they were an additional torture. But before I could say anything, one of the students blurted out, "But you can't just . . . you just can't experiment on people like that!"

"Is that so?" de Baur chimed in. "Milgram's subjects did not see it that way. They regarded the experiment as an enriching experience, an opportunity to get to know themselves and"—he paused—"fear themselves." He spoke in a way that implied the matter was settled, and moved away.

I was still furious. "If everything that offers us an opportunity to get to know ourselves is positive, then everything in the world is positive."

De Baur turned around. "Well, what is wrong with that?"

I could hear the derision in his voice. Clearly the others could too: they looked curious.

"Just because we can learn from something bad doesn't make it good."

"Wouldn't you have us learn? Or are there only instant insights?"

"An insight doesn't change the thing that occasioned it. We can gain insights from good things, bad things, and things that are nei- ther good nor bad."

"These 'things' you are talking about—they are nothing but the interpretation we give them. Why shouldn't we have an insight that tells us that what at first appeared bad is actually good?"

"But the experiment itself was bad. It deceived and exploited people and drove them to do what they would rather not have done. Would you like to be treated like that?"

He raised his arms and let them fall. Then he laughed and said, "There is nothing to like or dislike. I am willing to make a demand on myself for the sake of science and progress. That is all."

"And a demand I'm willing to make on myself I can then impose on others, is that it? Is the golden rule too weak for you? Is that why you need an iron rule?" I would never have said it had I not been so worked up at the time. The muffed conversation with de Baur's wife, the failed attempt at contact with his children, the misguided discussion with Jane, Anne, and Katherine, the corner de Baur's questions had driven me into, and his mockery—I was so upset I could no longer observe; I had to attack.

De Baur nodded. "An iron rule . . ." I had the feeling he was wondering whether to ask me how I had come up with the idea of the iron rule. On the one hand he seemed gratified to have lured me out of my shell, on the other nonplussed by what he had found concealed there. Everyone waited to see how the showdown would progress. But de Baur said nothing more; he just gave me a quizzi- cal look and exclaimed, "Fill your glasses, everybody! I should like to propose a toast! Today, the third of October 1990, is a historical day, the day of German reunification. To our German friend!"

6

FROM THEN ON, our relationship was different. After the next seminar de Baur asked me whether I would walk home with him: I lived on Riverside Drive too, didn't I? I expected a question about the iron rule, but instead he inquired about how the translation was coming along, if I had any problems, if I had any suggestions for the next edition. He seemed bent on showing me that he did not need to ask that question. Even after he repeated the invitation and a certain intimacy began to arise from our walks together, he steered clear of questions about why I was interested in this or that, why I maintained this or that, and what my background was.

During the lectures and seminars he would address me directly with a mixture of complicity and disdain, as if touched by my naiveté. "The world as a community of law, isn't that what you'd like?" Before I could respond, he would explain why it was a beautiful but misguided notion: community presupposed homogeneity, not necessarily ethnic or religious homogeneity but at least a homogeneous vision like the one shared by the immigrants to America. "The nation—you don't believe in the nation anymore?" He claimed that globalization might rend the nation-states asunder but would not make all men brothers; no, it would turn them back to their families, to their ethnic or religious communities, to their gangs. Sympathy for the insulted, the humiliated, the slain in the abstract, outside one's personal experience, was mere ritual.

"The good in evil is something our friend here cannot accept. He cannot even imagine such a thing." He smiled first at me then at the rest of his audience. "What is the good in evil? That it rouses and sharpens our moral sense? That it enables us to build institutions to subdue it, the institutions that give us our culture? That it lays the foundation for the enmity between good and evil and thereby the enmity among men, without which man would have no identity and lead a life of tedium?" I could see the look of puzzlement in the faces around me. "The good in evil," he continued, "lies in the fact that it can be made to work for the good." For a moment the puzzlement turned to relief, but de Baur took pleasure in turning it back into bewilderment. "Poverty and misery make progress and culture possible; power safeguards peace; sacrifices by the innocent help to make just revolutions and wage just wars. Had it not been for the Sirens, Odysseus would not have bound himself to the mast, and by doing so, yet not plugging his ears, he gave us the concept of the Constitution: enjoy power, yes, but bind yourself lest you should fall prey to it. We are the ones to decide whether evil shall overcome good or serve it; we are the ones to decide what is good and what evil. Who if not us?"

He smiled at me again. "Our friend here is wondering what point there is in all this talk about evil. Are not the great scoundrels dead? Have not the evil empires crumbled or been destroyed? Are not freedom, democracy, and the market spreading over all the earth? Has not peace eternal supplanted the Cold War? Will not the century of good succeed the century of evil within a decade?"

The class was over. The students stood slowly, hesitantly under the burden of so many unanswered questions. De Baur waited until the first few had reached the door, then started in again. They stopped and turned. "Be suspicious. Trust neither the coming decade nor the coming century. Trust neither the good nor the normal. Truth first reveals itself in the face of evil and in the moment of crisis."

De Baur picked up his notes and books and was out of the room before the students grasped that these were his last words. It was an impressive performance, and I was certain he had staged it and taken pleasure in it. He wanted to do more than impart academic knowledge; he wanted to teach them to question and think. He wanted to change them. Into what?

7

BY EARLY NOVEMBER Barbara had begun to nag: "How long do you plan to stay? You know him now; what more do you want? Do you want to expose him? Well, go ahead! What's stopping you?"

I equivocated. I said I needed to know him better. I wanted to try and make closer contact with his wife and children. I couldn't get out of the talk I'd promised him, and it was still two weeks off. Besides, I had to complete the translation of the book. She was not at all convinced by my translation argument, and two weeks later the talk was behind me. I had even met Mrs. de Baur and the children again.

I intended to provoke him with my talk and spoke about Hannah Arendt's definition of totalitarian thought. I knew he did not care for her. I thought that her definition—namely, that totalitarian thinkers consider facts liable to arbitrary fabrication and manipulation and hence deeply disdain them—would offend him. Didn't he consider facts liable to arbitrary interpretation? Didn't he feel cornered by Arendt's definition? Didn't it make him uncomfortable?

De Baur was not easily provoked. Arendt was right, he said. But we were all totalitarian thinkers nowadays: thought had become totalitarian. Our best defense against arbitrariness lay in the responsibility we take for our thought. "The great lies propagated by totalitarian regimes—was it facts that did them in? Would the regimes have survived by destroying more proof, murdering more witnesses, falsifying more documents? No, it was thought that did them in. We refuse to think everything people want to make us think, even things the facts want to make us think."

On our way home he praised my talk and invited me to have dinner with his wife and children. His wife gave me a friendly greeting, as if our embarrassing conversation had never taken place; the children had a good time practicing their German on me (they were taking it at school); even the dog came up to me to be petted. After dinner the children made espressos for us, then went off on their own.

"What do your brothers and sisters do? The ones you started telling me about."

One lie led to another, and soon I had to be careful to keep my fabrications straight.

"Where were you brought up?"

This time I told the truth so as to be able to follow it up with the question as to whether they were familiar with the city. No, they'd never been to Germany together.

"But your trace of an accent tells me you come from Germany, don't you? Or is it Austria?"

"Switzerland. In 1950 I got a scholarship, and that one year in America has turned into a life."

"Aren't you ever homesick?"

He laughed. "After forty years?"

"Odysseus, whose story you love so much, was homesick enough after twenty years to expose himself to all sorts of dangers."

"Homesick?" his wife asked. "You call that homesick? Wasn't it more of a desire to see his wife and son again?"

"But he had Calypso, and he'd totally forgotten Telemachus. That's how I see it, but your husband knows the story better."

She looked at him. He shrugged. "Homer says he longed to see Ithaca, his home, and Penelope, his wife. As for Telemachus, I doubt Odysseus even knew he had a son."

"Because if you know you have a son you don't simply forget him?"

He was not the least bit suspicious. "We know for certain that Odysseus had no interest in Telemachus until he got to Ithaca. Penelope was a different story. The desire to see her goes back to the Calypso episode. But where does it come from? If we are to believe Homer, he longed to come home because he had simply grown tired of Calypso." He paused. "How do you think he would have behaved had Penelope been unfaithful? Would he have murdered her the way he murdered the suitors? Did he take into account that she might try to murder him the way Clytemnestra murdered Agamemnon? They played by hard rules back then. Iron rules. Wasn't that how you put it the other day?"

Now I did sense suspicion: he wanted to corner me as much as I wanted to corner him. But whereas I was still feeling my way, he knew what he was after: he wanted to know where I had found the iron rule idea, his rule, his idea. He was so obsessed with it that the allusion to the forgotten son had failed to register.

"Iron rule? It doesn't ring a bell. Can you remind me of the context?"

He waved off the question. "It doesn't matter."

If I didn't remember, my use of the term was harmless; if I was only pretending not to remember, I wouldn't tell him anything and would only play games with him. So the iron rule issue was taken care of. If I had thrown him off and he still wanted to corner me, he would have to take another tack.

Seeing me to the door, he invited me to the retreat. Was that the other tack? "The first week in January. I should be glad to have you as part of the group."

"I should like that very much."

"We are having a preliminary meeting in early December. You will be notified. But please keep it to yourself. I do not wish to hurt anybody."

I told Barbara I would be home in a few weeks, right after the preliminary meeting.

There was such a long pause that I had to ask whether she was still on the line.

"And you'll go back again in January?"

"Just for a week. Doesn't school start again on the seventh? I'll be flying back the day before, the last day of your break."

There was another pause.

"Barbara?"

"What do you expect to find out in one week that you didn't find out in three months? And if you don't find it out, how much longer will it take? Another month? Another two?"

"No, that week will be it."

"How can you be sure? If you don't know what you want, you can't know when you have it."

"I love you."

"Peter?"

"Barbara?"

"Don't come back until you really come back."

8

SHE STUCK TO HER GUNS. I was welcome to come home. Of course I was. She'd be only too happy to have me. But if it was only to go back, well, it was better not to come at all.

"But surely it's not better to—"

"It's better for me. If you can't make up your mind, you can't make up your mind. But I don't want a guy who can't make up his mind. I want a guy who knows what he wants and knows he wants me, not one who runs off after an idea he can't pin down. I want a guy here." Her voice had grown louder. "And will you please stop calling me every day and saying the same things!"

"But Barbara, we could have Christmas together and start the new year together, I'd be away only a week, Barbara, you've been away for a week, Barbara, you can't lock me out, it's my place as much as yours, Barbara—"

"Oh shit." She hung up.

She called back a few hours later. "I don't want 'Oh shit' to keep ringing in your ears. Look, I don't hate you or anything. You are what you are. Don't worry. I'm not going to run off with the first guy who comes along. Things could really work when you come back in January or February or whenever. But do stop calling me all the time. It's upsetting. And don't come until you can stay, okay?"

We tended to talk just before she went to bed. For her it was twelve or one, for me six or seven, and weather permitting I would go for a jog after the call. I would start from my place on 127th Street, go uphill past Grant's tomb, turn down into Riverside Park, take a wooded path all the way to 96th Street and then the wide, street-level promenade back. When it was over, I would stand huffing and puffing on a large terrace that had once had a station under it and gaze out at the Hudson, the ships, the houses, the rocks and wooded areas on the opposite shore, the radiant setting sun, and the evening star in the deep-blue sky. It was a spot made for longing: the ships plying the river, the occasional train roaring through the abandoned station below, and the unending succession of airplanes above were a continuous invitation to leave, to go home, to go anywhere.

During my run after that last talk with Barbara I had made up my mind to fly home in early December. My determination grew with every step, every time my foot hit the ground and pushed off again. Whether I would then stay or come back for the retreat remained to be seen. Everything remained to be seen. After Barbara and I had had some time together. But on the terrace things seemed less simple. Hadn't I resolved against halfway measures?

What could be more halfway than going home without deciding whether or not to return and how to cope with de Baur? I
would sleep on it and come up with a decision. I watched the sun
set, found the evening star, and longed for Barbara. Tomorrow. I
would settle it all tomorrow.

The semester was coming to an end. What I had read of de Baur
and heard him say in the lectures and seminar all fell into place.
What we take for reality is merely a text, what we take for texts
merely interpretations. Reality and texts are therefore what we
make of them. History has no goal: there is no progress, no promise of rise after fall, no guarantee of victory for the strong or justice
for the weak. We can interpret it as if it had a goal, and there is
nothing objectionable in that, because we must always "act as
if"—as if reality were more than text, as if the author were speaking to us in the text, as if good and evil, right and wrong, truth and
lies actually existed, and as if the institutions of law actually func-
tioned. We have the choice of either droning back what has been
droned into us or deciding for ourselves what we want to make of
the world, who we want to be in it, and what we want to do in it.
We come to our truth, which enables us to make decisions, in
extreme, existential, exceptional situations. The validity of our
decisions makes itself felt in the commitment we make to carrying
them out and the responsibility we take for carrying them out,
responsibility in the sense of the iron rule, which de Baur did not
mention by name and for which he gave rather more anodyne
examples than in the wartime pieces.

In his final lecture de Baur spoke on Saint Augustine. *Ama et fac
quod vis.* Love and do as you will. In other words, a passionate heart justifies a passionate commitment; what we love is in fact
our responsible decision; love is a matter of the will, not of
the emotions. "I have no business telling you what to love, but
I cannot hide my respect for the new generation, which sees its

mission as bringing freedom, democracy, and prosperity to the world."

The students applauded, then stood and applauded on. I remained seated until the students had filed out after de Baur. So now it was freedom, democracy, and prosperity. Times changed; missions changed with them. That was what he would tell me if I tried to confront him. And what would I respond?

I stood up and looked around. Empty rows of folding desks and folding seats, a large green board with the dates of Augustine's birth and death, a lectern de Baur never stood behind, paneling without windows. A neon light flickered off for a fraction of a second. It had started bothering me during the lecture.

No, I would never return to this room. I did not know what I wanted of him, but I did know I never wanted to hear him again. Oh, I would go to the January retreat, but I would not talk to him afterward, I would not try to confront him, I would not reveal my identity; I would simply drop the whole thing. I could see myself gradually returning to my life. For a long time I had been certain that something had to happen between us, that I at least needed to find out from him how the story ended. I was no longer certain.

9

IT WAS NOT SO EASY to dismiss de Baur and leave him behind. In early December I received a thick letter with Barbara's return address, but when I tore it open it turned out to have been forwarded from Switzerland: it was from the father of my former playmate.

Dear Peter Debauer:

In the years before his death I kept up with my German teacher. He was an inspired lecturer and an outstanding Goethe specialist. During our last year we read nothing but Faust. *The class had had the teacher before, a year or two prior to my return, and he kept a composition your father wrote for him then. He showed it to me, and I photocopied it and put it in my edition of Gottfried Keller. I am enclosing it now.*

The teacher liked your father and liked the composition. He said the ending was a bit overblown for the fifteen- or sixteen-year-old your father was at the time, but he admired his interpretation of Wenzel Strapinski— the tailor in the dark coat who, after being given a lift in a count's carriage and dropped off at a tavern, was taken for a count—as more than a plaything of circumstance and milieu, as an individual acting on his own. The only thing he missed in the composition was that Strapinski was moved to act through love.

I too like the composition.

Best wishes,

Gotthold Rank

The photocopy was new, a copy of the old copy. The handwriting was not only neat; its thin upstrokes and thick downstrokes made it pleasing to the eye. The paper was unruled, and as the space between the lines was less than uniform I could tell he had not used a ruled sheet under the paper as a guide: it was just page after page of lively, attractive script. The Swiss teacher had found no spelling or punctuation errors and written "Bravo" and a "6" after the last sentence, the highest mark.

WENZEL STRAPINSKI: A CONFIDENCE MAN IN SPITE OF HIMSELF?

The idea of a confidence man in spite of himself is a contradiction in terms. Because a confidence man wants to be more than he is, and if he wills it, it cannot at the same time be in spite of himself.

Thus Wenzel Strapinski in Gottfried Keller's story "Clothes Make the

Man" cannot be a confidence man in spite of himself. Either he was a confidence man or he was not. If he was, then one must clearly determine the kind he was. Because there are sympathetic and unsympathetic, moral and immoral, happy and sad confidence men.

Wenzel Strapinski did everything a confidence man does. His behavior is a veritable set of instructions as to how to be a confidence man.

1. *Make the most of what you have.* The dark overcoat with the black-velvet lining gave Wenzel Strapinski a noble and romantic appearance and attracted attention and curiosity. Wenzel Strapinski wore it with style.

2. *Make the most of what you know.* Wenzel Strapinski had served on an estate and with the hussars. He knew horses and knew the expressions squires and officers use. He used those expressions too, and when he was handed reins and a whip he knew what to do with them.

3. *Do not hide your weak points; turn them to your advantage.* Wenzel Strapinski was awkward and shy. He impressed the innkeeper and his cook with his manners by taking small portions of fish and wine; he said little, which gave his words weight; and he blushed in Nettchen's presence, which she found charming.

4. *Play your part in such a way that you can pursue your interests instead of hiding them.* It was in Wenzel Strapinski's interest to keep his past and his plans in the dark. By making people believe he was a fugitive and being pursued, he dodged all questions about his past and plans.

5. *Do not make unnecessary use of your false identity.* Wenzel Strapinski had it easy in this respect, because his name was exactly the same as the count he was taken for—except for the title. But he was smart enough never to call himself count and to sign his name only as Wenzel Strapinski.

6. *Do not introduce yourself under your false identity; let other people invent it for you.* The reason the people of Goldacher believed

in Count Wenzel Strapinski is that they themselves invented him as a count with their sensation-hungry interpretation of simple events.

7. *The secret of success is secrets. Secrets make you interesting and let others see you as they wish you to be.*

8. *Gain the sympathy of those who mistrust you, but do not trust them. The only person in Goldacher suspicious of Wenzel Strapinski is Melchior Böhni. Melchior Böhni was sympathetic to Wenzel Strapinski at first, but the latter forgot to keep an eye on him. Though he would have lost his sympathy anyway, because they were competing for Nettchen.*

9. *Do not try to hush up your defeats. Accept them.*

Although Wenzel Strapinski did everything a confidence man does, he did not at first want to be anything more than he was. However, he did not apprise the people of Goldacher of their error. Was he obliged to do so?

The people of Goldacher did not make him a count for his sake; they made him a count for their own sake. He did not take anything from them. Nothing of what their hospitality gave him could he take with him. No, Wenzel Strapinski did not owe the people of Goldacher a thing.

Was he obliged to reveal his true identity to Nettchen? Nettchen too had made him a count for her own sake, not for his. She fell in love with him for her sake, not for his, and became engaged to him for her sake, not for his. But the engagement jeopardized her reputation and her future, which she could not know, but Wenzel Strapinski did. So was he obliged to reveal his identity? Did not revealing his identity make him as much of a confidence man as if he had intentionally misled her?

Because Wenzel Strapinski did more than fail to reveal his identity to Nettchen. In the end he wanted her to take him for Count Wenzel Strapinski. He put it to her outright: He wanted to enjoy a few brief days of bliss with her as the count, then confess his duplicity to her and take his own life. The fact that he was "overcome by the vanity of this world" was not enough to turn him into a confidence man. But then vanity made him her "accomplice," or rather he himself chose to join her. Wenzel Strapinski did not jump at becoming a confidence man, but he became one in the end.

He remained one for a short time only. After he was unmasked, he did not move on and try his luck as a confidence man in other places. He stayed where he was and started a family with Nettchen; he became a successful tailor and cloth merchant and built up a reputation. And so his career as a confidence man had a happy ending. It helped him to discover what he was capable of, which he would not have discovered otherwise. He was smart enough to stick to it.

Wenzel Strapinski was a sympathetic confidence man—moral, modest, cheerful, and eager to learn. He is the best proof I know of that being a confidence man is not necessarily bad. It can simply be a chance to achieve the most one is capable of in life.

That evening I met de Baur on the street. "Still here?" he said. "I assumed you'd gone back to Germany and would be returning for the retreat." When I told him I was planning to stay here the whole time, he invited me to Christmas dinner. "Think it over, and give me a ring. We'd be happy to have you." He smiled the self-conscious smile a child might smile, and suddenly I saw him as a young man in a dark overcoat with the black velvet lining.

IO

AFTER THE ORIENTATION SESSION for the January retreat, where the participants introduced themselves, received their assignments, and found out about transportation arrangements, my life calmed down. I soon finished the book I was assigned to report on at the retreat. I had been spending less and less time on the translation of de Baur's book and eventually abandoned it altogether. I did occasionally see Jonathan Marvin, though, and learned that de Baur had finally invited him to the retreat.

Even as it got colder and darker, I stuck to my late-afternoon run in the park, ending up on the terrace with my longing. There were days when the run was the only thing that got me out of the house; otherwise I lay on my bed reading novels, drinking orange or grapefruit juice with vodka, and dozing until at one point in the evening I fell asleep. My room never really got bright. During the day I could distinguish the bricks in the wall opposite and even count them, at dusk they grew fuzzy, and at night the wall varied its countenance according to the light falling on it from the other windows facing the ventilation shaft.

Lying on the bed, I could see a higher window, in which I would observe a young woman when she opened and shut it and when she brushed her hair at it. She got up either very early or very late, and the rhythm with which she left her place and came back to it led me to believe she was either a doctor or a nurse. She was not pretty, but everything she did she did with such determination, economy, and efficiency that it was a pleasure to watch her. I had declined de Baur's invitation and planned to ask her to have dinner with me on Christmas Day should she be alone, but she was not there. She returned a few days later with a man. Things did not go well between them. I awoke in the middle of the night to a loud quarrel and slamming doors. The next morning I met her for the first and last time in the elevator; her hair was combed down over her face in such a way that it could only have been hiding a black eye.

I spent a whole week in December making a calendar for Barbara. The view from the terrace of longing, the building my apartment was in, the building she had lived in with Augie, and the school where she had taught at the time—I bought a camera and recorded them all on film. For the rest of the months I used *New Yorker* covers, and for December I cut a Christmas tree out of green plastic and pasted it on one side of the page, and tiny electric lights powered by a tiny battery on the other. I even found a chip that played "Jingle Bells." I spent all that time and effort on it first out of love, then out of a perfectionism that had nothing to do with Barbara, and finally out of spite: I was making her a unique gift whether she loved me or not. For Max I bought as many types and brands of chewing gum as I could find, and for Mother a leather cap she could wear while driving with the top down. In her package I enclosed the Political Science Department's brochure: it had a picture of John de Baur.

My life had calmed down, but I did not feel lonely. I would go to two or three movies one after the other and let myself be carried away by the gigantic images on the gigantic screen. I would go to a restaurant where voice students sang arias accompanied by an old woman, who stoically played whatever was put in front of her. It was not far from Lincoln Center, and when the Metropolitan let out, a real tenor might stray in and sing along. I would rent a bicycle and bike up and down the Manhattan waterfront.

When ten days before Christmas I sent the packages off to Barbara, Max, and Mother, I had the feeling the year was over. I tried to sort out what it had brought. The longing for Barbara, a feeling of helplessness, of doing what I was doing because I had to but not knowing what made me do it, a feeling of mourning for my mother, as if with her lies she had not merely withdrawn from me but died for me, the aggression against my father and the horror he inspired, though what I despised in John de Baur I had liked in Johann Debauer—it was not a pretty picture.

On Christmas Eve I bought a Christmas tree, the last to be sold at the stand around the corner, a miserable godforsaken runt. I was suddenly positive that Barbara would turn up on my doorstep, and I wanted to give her a festive reception. Barbara always flew Lufthansa; the last flight into JFK landed at seven thirty; it would take her at least two hours to get to my place. The hours between nine thirty and eleven thirty were the low point of those days in New York.

On New Year's Eve Jonathan and I made a bar tour of Greenwich Village, and I ended up in bed with a woman who told me her name was Callista. I liked the name.

II

WE MET AT nine A.M. on January 7 in front of the International Affairs building. All the older seminar participants were there: Jane and Katherine, the former psychoanalyst and former doctor, the former French professor Anne, the ex-marine Mark, and Jonathan. The others were participants from earlier seminars whom I had met for the first time at the orientation session. Meg and Pamela were young lawyers with large New York firms; Philip, Gregory, and Michael worked in Washington for congressmen or senators; and Ronald was with a think tank, where he headed a task force studying juvenile criminality. It was cold, and no one felt like talking. When Mark and Pamela took out cigarettes, Katherine told them in no uncertain terms to keep their distance, whereupon they moved away and Katherine launched into a diatribe about why what she had done was right. The rest of us looked on, embarrassed, until Ronald broke in and asked her if he could get her a coffee on the corner.

At a quarter past nine the van that was to take us to the retreat arrived. The four smokers sat in the back, Katherine next to the driver, and Ronald and Meg, Jane and I, and Philip, Gregory, and Michael in the three rows in between. I would have liked to talk to Jane about the seminar we had just finished and the retreat we were about to start, about her interest in de Baur and her impressions of him, about her switch from psychoanalysis to law, but she still had some reading to do, so I leaned back and eavesdropped on the conversation behind me. For Phil, Greg, and Mike the retreat was a big thing. Once you had been to one, you were in de Baur's inner circle, and that made you part of his informal but influential network in Washington. We had lunch at a rest area near Albany. To make sure I would get that conversation in with Jane, I went to a sushi bar with her. She was the child of two psychoanalysts and had grown up in New York. She had gone to an excellent prep school and done her undergraduate work at Harvard. In the midst of a successful career as a psychoanalyst she had felt a sudden, overpowering need to break out of a world that was all talk and thought and do something, change something, make a difference.

"Do what?"

She looked at me as if the answer were obvious. "Can't you see how the world around us is changing? I want it to be a success."

In the bus she went back to her reading and read until her eyes closed. Most of the others were asleep as well. We were passing through a hilly countryside of plowed fields, dirty-green meadows, and leafless woods dotted with an occasional farmhouse and large silos and an occasional small community. The sky was gray and hung so low that when the first few snowflakes fell I thought, This sky could snow on us for days. Then I fell asleep too.

I woke up when the bus veered off the highway onto a two-lane road. We started bumping over uneven terrain and pulled up in front of a restaurant. It had continued to snow, and the snow was sticking. The world was white, and the cars parked in front of the restaurant had thick bonnets of snow on their roofs and hoods. The sun was going down. I glanced at my watch. It was four. I had slept for two hours.

The driver got out, and Katherine, Jane, and Meg followed him into the restaurant. Katherine came back first, took her seat, turned to us, and said, "I'm afraid the driver is lost. It's getting dark, and the snow shows no sign of letting up. Maybe we should spend the night in the nearest motel and try to find our way in the morning. What do you think?"

"Let's ask the driver."

"No, we've got to tell him. If we ask him, he'll keep going, because he's getting paid for one day only."

A jeep pulled up next to us. Four men got out. They were wearing army green and camouflage fatigues, dark knit caps, and knee-high laced boots. They looked over at the van, laughed, and trudged into the restaurant.

"Isn't de Baur waiting for us? Didn't he say he'd be up there a few days early?"

"We should give him a call."

We had been given an emergency number at the orientation session, and Ronald went into the restaurant to phone. He was back in no time. "There's only an answering machine, and the message was from an emergency service, not de Baur."

"Has anyone got another number?"

It turned out that no one had de Baur's home number or the number of the place where we were going. Ronald went back into the restaurant and called Information for de Baur's number, but all he got when he dialed was a message saying the family was out of town and could not be reached until the fourteenth.

"If we don't show up, he'll know why," Katherine said. "He's smart enough to figure it out."

But then out came the driver with Jane and Meg. The women went back to their seats as if nothing had happened, and the driver said with a grin, "Everybody awake? We'll be there between seven and eight. Later than planned, but earlier than you've been thinking. Don't worry. You don't have to push. I've got four-wheel drive." And off we went.

"What's up? Katherine thought he was lost."

Jane shrugged. "I heard him talking about roads and places with the bartender, but he seems to know where he's going."

At first we saw an occasional car, a school bus, a truck with a garland of lights left over from Christmas festooning its cabin; then the streets began to narrow, the traffic coming toward us ceased altogether, and the windows shining across fields or through trees grew fewer and farther between. The bus was completely dark: no one felt like turning on the reading lights; everyone, like the driver, was concentrating on the road, which ran on and on, all white, unsullied by tire tracks, through endless woods of snow-laden pines. After two or three hours the snow we had been watching in the light of the headlamps petered out, and the driver said, "At last!" But without the veil of snowflakes the white world engulfing us felt even colder, more forbidding.

Then there we were. We had seen the light awhile before, first at the far end of a great, white expanse, then on and off around various bends in the road. Finally the van made its way up a few serpentine curves and stopped before a brightly lit old hotel.

"Chop-chop," said the driver, jumping out of the van and running back to open the tailgate. "I've got to get back."

By the time we were out of the van, knee deep in snow, he had unloaded our luggage and jumped back up into the driver's seat. He turned to us, waved, and was off. We watched as he drove down the curves, appearing on and off around the bends and finally making his way back along the broad, white surface. By then we could hear him no more.

12

THE HOTEL WAS A three-story wooden structure with balconies off the upper two stories. The parking lot where we were standing and the stairs leading up to the main entrance were well lit, and there was light shining out of the windows on the ground floor and the floor above it. We waited for a while, but when no one came out to greet us Ronald picked up his bag and climbed the steps. The rest of us followed.

We waited again in the lobby, but again nobody came—neither de Baur nor the manager nor the staff. Ronald called out, "Anybody home?" but got no response. A few of us took seats in the armchairs dotting the lobby; Ronald, Katherine, and I set out on a ground-floor reconnaissance mission. Mark said, "I'll go upstairs," and Jonathan went up with him. We walked through a dining room and into a lounge with a fireplace, then returned to the dining room, where we found the door to the staircase leading down to the basement kitchen and a dumbwaiter for bringing food up from below. We went down to the kitchen, crossed it, and walked through some empty rooms until we reached the far end of the building, where we climbed the stairs into a small room behind a bar. One door led to a library with empty bookshelves; another led back to the lobby, where the others awaited us. Everything was run-down, the walls cracked and stained, the upholstery threadbare, the wood scratched. A number of three-legged chairs were leaning against the dining room wall, the hooks for pots and pans in the kitchen were mostly empty, and the giant refrigerators were open and bare, yet everything was more or less clean.

"There's a suite upstairs where de Baur has set out some materials for us and rooms enough to accommodate us all. The top floor is dark; we couldn't see a thing."

"Hey, how about some heat?" Pamela was huddling in an arm-chair with her arms over her chest. It was cold.

"Listen to her. You'd think we turned it off," Katherine said, hands on hips. "I haven't seen a thermostat, but there must be a boiler room. Maybe you can only get to it from outside."

"Want to come along?" Jonathan asked me, and we went to have a look around. We found nothing like a boiler room or annex, but we did find a large woodpile and took as many logs as we could hold. We got back to the lobby just in time to find Greg slamming the receiver down on the pay phone. "The damn thing doesn't work."

"What's the wood for? Why didn't you turn the heat on?"

I too was irritated by Pamela's tone, and I was about to say something, but Katherine beat me to it. "Would you stop whining and go and get some wood."

"Wait a second," Ronald said, holding up his hand. "We need a little organization here. How about first laying in a supply of wood for the lounge, where the fireplace is, and then splitting into teams—four of us on this floor, four on the next—to look for food, blankets, candles, anything that might come in handy for a long, cold night."

We got to work; only Pamela remained ensconced in her arm-chair. When enough wood had accumulated next to the fireplace, Phil asked, "Does this thing work?"

"We'll soon see. Let's go on with the search as long as there's light. Have you noticed the switches don't work? There must be a master switch somewhere, but I haven't found it, and if one of those timer doodads turns the lights off at eight, nine, or ten we're in the dark."

This time I went with Greg, Phil, and Mike, and we cased the middle floor room by room. Each of the eighteen beds had a sheet and a thin woolen blanket on it, but the closets and drawers were empty and not a drop came out of the taps. The three of them made light of the whole thing, Greg cursing with wit and passion, Phil and Mike already rehearsing their versions of the Adirondack caper for the Washington crowd. We hesitated for a moment when we got to de Baur's suite, then searched it as well and came up with a box of candles and half a bottle of whiskey. "It's not enough for everybody, anyway," Greg decreed, taking a long swig and passing it on to Phil. Mike then polished it off, said "Sorry" to me, opened the window, and tossed the bottle into the night.

The other search did not turn up much either. Three cans of Campbell's tomato soup and two bottles of water in the kitchen, the remains of a few bottles of whiskey and cognac in the bar, and a box of cigars in the library. No central heating, no master switch, no access to the water main. Anne and Jane went up to the upper story with a candle and found nothing but empty rooms.

And yet the mood was good. Greg offered to cook, and Katherine, perhaps not trusting him to make the most of our scant resources, followed him into the kitchen. While Mark kindled a fire in the fireplace, we carried the armchairs from the lobby into the lounge. Once we had chased Pamela out of her chair, even she tried to make herself useful by piling the logs into a tower.

Then we sat around the fire—each taking three gulps from the soup pot followed by swigs from the whiskey and cognac bottles—and stared into the flames. At nine the lights went out. When Katherine announced she was going to bed, we drew lots for the sheets and blankets. The lucky ones got two blankets and one sheet, the unlucky ones one blanket and two sheets. I was one of the unlucky ones.

Cold as it was in my room, I fell asleep. I awoke at four, my arms and legs numb. I took my blanket and went down to the lounge, where a few others were sitting and sleeping by the fire.

Looking into the fire, which burned with a steady, yet always slightly different flame, I thought of my grandfather's love of waves rolling in with a steady, yet always slightly different motion. I thought of the pain my father had caused my grandparents and was gripped by a sudden fear that I had the same hardness, cold-ness in me.

At dawn, I unwrapped my blanket and went outside. The great, white expanse was a frozen lake topped by snow. On the far side, beyond range after range of hills, sky and land merged in the mist. The sun was rising, announcing its presence with a white light. I pictured it climbing up the hills, yellow, until it hung, red, in the misty sky.

Jonathan came up to me and said, "This must be the 'farm' where de Baur had his commune. He kept it under strict control. Have you seen the cameras?"

"Cameras?"

"Let me show you." I followed him inside and from room to room. Each room had one or two inconspicuous video cameras up near the ceiling. "It's the same upstairs. One in each room."

"They had video cameras back then?"

"Of course." He laughed. "They probably hadn't made it to Europe yet."

13

WE ALL ASSUMED the adventure would be over in the morning and the retreat proper would begin. Nothing of the sort. We waited.

As we got more and more hungry, we ransacked the house again from top to bottom. There was nothing to be had. Nor were there any provisions in the shed behind the hotel, only more logs, some rusty farming implements, a cylindrical iron stove, and an out-of-commission jalopy. Also behind the hotel we found a staircase leading to a locked iron door on the basement level, presumably the boiler room.

The sun was so strong that by noon it was warm enough for us to sit out on the terrace. "Oh, for a bagel with cream cheese and lox and a glass of champagne!" Jonathan said dreamily. For Meg it was cottage cheese with wild strawberries, for Phil a steak with french fries. Each had his own preference. Mine was two soft-boiled eggs with chives and whole wheat toast with honey. The rule of the game was that it had to be different from everyone else's. I was particularly impressed by Katherine's quail-egg omelet.

But when the game was over, the hunger remained. Not only that, the sun had disappeared behind the clouds and it was cold again. Back inside by the fire we started getting aggressive. What was de Baur trying to pull on us? How dared the van driver fly the coop like that! Why hadn't Jonathan told us that de Baur ran a commune here twenty years ago? Why couldn't Mark do anything? He was a marine, wasn't he?

"If nobody shows up today, we'll have to leave," Mark said with a laugh. "You don't need to be a marine to see that."

"*We'll* have to leave? Why don't one or two go and come back for the rest?"

"We can give them the best shoes and clothes we've got."

"But what if they don't make it and I've got to go it on my own?"

"I can't take any more of this," said Jane. "I'm turning in. May I have your blanket?" I nodded and she stood up. But she did not budge. She was looking out of the window and was so spellbound that we too stood and looked. There was a car moving along the far shore of the lake.

A few minutes later it pulled up. A jeep. Four men got out.

"Hey, don't we know those guys?" Ronald whispered. "Didn't we see them in front of the restaurant yesterday?"

They marched up the stairs, stood there facing us, and asked, "What are you doing here?"

Ronald told them about the retreat and the unfortunate situation we found ourselves in. "We're glad you've come. What brings you here? How far is it to the next town? When are you leaving and how many of us can you take with you? Too many questions at once. Sorry."

The spokesman, a strong-looking older man with chiseled features and a crew cut, heard Ronald out, grinding his jaw and not blinking an eye. He took his time answering. "I don't know where you think you are. It's getting dark now, but tomorrow morning you're out of here."

Pamela introduced herself, ever the efficient, self-possessed lawyer, and explained to him with solicitous courtesy that this was the place designated for our retreat, that our professor had been here earlier but something must have happened to him, that we had no desire to stay here ourselves and would be only too happy to let them stay the night, but also hoped to enlist their aid.

"Pa," one of the others said to the spokesman with a grin, "how about getting the chicks to rustle up something for us."

The spokesman, not turning to his son but keeping his eyes on Ronald, said, "If you want to eat tonight, you'd better make yourself useful. The women can cook, the men give my boys a hand." He turned to Mark. "Who are you? What are you doing here with these types?"

Mark hesitated. I did not know him well. From crack soldier to law student with a special interest in political theory—pretty impressive, and I had always found his comments well informed, well thought out, and to the point. What was going on in his mind during these seconds of hesitation? That he had to decide between us and them? That siding with them would be an easy way out?

That siding with them would be a way to get us off the hook? That nothing really bound him to us? "Mark Felton is my name. I'm here because I'm studying with them. Before that I was in the marines."

The spokesman held his hand out to him. "Steve Walton. Aircraft carrier *Independence*. Pleased to meet you. Want a beer?"

They went into the lounge. The spokesman's son and, as we later learned, nephews, had a grand old time making us carry their luggage and provisions into the hotel and bossing the women around in the kitchen. They commandeered de Baur's suite and the rooms on either side. They were loud and crude, and I imagine that the others were as torn as I was between feeling we should refuse to put up with so degrading a situation and trying not to rock the boat so as to get it over with as soon as possible. No one rebelled. I suddenly recalled a loud, crude boy in my class who had had it in for me, but I kept so aloof that he eventually lost interest.

We had a dinner of hamburgers and potato salad in the lounge, the intruders making it clear all the while that they were under no obligation to feed us. At one point Mike snapped. He was such a dandy that I had taken him for nothing more, but he slammed down his paper plate with its half-eaten hamburger, stood up, and said, "Well, you can shove it, then!"

Mike had gone no more than a few steps when he tripped over the leg Walton's son had stretched out, and fell at the feet of one of the cousins, who bent over him, grabbed his hair with his right hand and with his left forced his face into the plate. He laughed, as did his pals, who pointed to the scene, slapped their thighs, and laughed even louder.

"Enough," Walton said after a while, and the boy let Mike go. Mike stood up—his face smeared with ketchup—and left the room. "They're a little wild, these kids," Walton said to Mark, who was sitting next to him, "the way we used to be." He raised his glass to Mark, who raised his in return.

The rest of us just sat there. Jane and I looked at each other and saw the same helplessness in each other's eyes. I have no experience with violence. I had no fear of being physically attacked and beaten up, but I did feel totally at the intruders' mercy, totally powerless. I would have given anything to leave. Then Katherine rose with the same self-righteousness in her face and bearing she had exhibited when bawling out Mark and Pamela for smoking. The moment she started for the door, Walton shouted, "Sit down!" with such fury that at first she simply froze. But when he put his hands on the arms of the chair as if to get up, she did as she had been told.

"You will finish our food, is that clear?"

We should all have risen and left the room, the food should have stuck in our throats, but we went on eating. We were ashamed and kept our eyes down and hungrily ate everything on our plates.

When we had finished, they told us to clear out. Ronald tried to make our situation clear and to negotiate a compromise, but the two cousins seized him and removed him bodily from the room. For a while we stood freezing in the lobby.

"We've got to get out of here. Tomorrow morning. As soon as it's light."

"Can we make it without Mark? I don't think he'll come with us." Mark was still inside with Walton and the boys.

"Well, I'm not going. I'd rather do the cooking and wait for somebody to come. Or for them to drop me off somewhere. Trudge thirty miles through snow and ice? Not me."

"Or me. The way we're dressed we'll catch our deaths."

"Well, I'm going," Ronald said. He looked around. "Anybody coming with me?"

"I will."

Jonathan shook his head. "There's no point in blowing this out of proportion. I'm going to talk money with them."

Mike had wiped the ketchup off his face but could not look anyone in the eye. "I'm going." Greg and Phil nodded.

When Pamela nodded, Katherine smiled. "As long as you don't smoke," she said.

"I've run out of cigarettes."

"I'd be glad to go with you, but I have a hip problem and can't even walk a mile."

"So that makes seven," Ronald said, grinning, and held his hand out. "All for one and one for all." We shook on it.

Just as I lay down, freezing, on my bed, there was a knock at my door. It was Jane with her blankets and sheet. "Wouldn't it make sense to . . ."

So we crawled under the blankets together. The bed was narrow, so she cuddled up to my back, which was fine by me: better a warm back than a warm belly. Together we heard a voice from the lounge shouting, "We don't want your fucking money! We want a good time!" followed by a crash and a door slamming. Shortly thereafter the sound of heavy footsteps came up the stairs and past our room.

"Maybe I should go with you," Jane said then. "Though it's a crazy idea. We'll never cover thirty miles before dark, and we'll freeze to death, literally, at night."

I told her about Hannibal crossing the Alps, Napoleon retreating from Moscow, and the Germans' attempt to besiege Moscow—in the versions I had heard from my grandfather—until she fell asleep.

14

I AWOKE WITHOUT knowing what woke me. It was dark, I was passably warm, and Jane was breathing peacefully. Then I heard it:

the sound of an engine trying to start up. It must have been the second attempt, the first having brought me out of my sleep. The second attempt failed too. I got out of bed and went over to the window. It was snowing lightly. The third attempt worked. The jeep jerked forward, the headlights went on, and soon it was moving along the road. But it lurched from side to side, had trouble negotiating the first curve and, while taking the second, careered off the road into a ditch.

Doors on the ground floor tore open. Walton's boys ran out onto the terrace. They reached the jeep just as the driver and his passengers were climbing out.

"It's Greg, Mike, and Phil," said Jane, who had joined me at the window. The boys were pushing them back to the hotel, and in the lobby they called for us all to come down. Then one of them ran upstairs and tore open door after door.

Once we had gathered, Walton's son took the floor. He was shining a flashlight on Greg, Mike, and Phil. "All for one and one for all, eh? Your friends don't give a fuck about you guys; they're out for themselves." He laughed. "They were smart enough to jump-start the engine but not to find the four-wheel-drive switch. So which one of you was the hero? How could you be so dumb?" He laughed again. "On with your shoes now, you guys. You're going down there to pull the jeep out of the snow."

"You must be out of your mind!" Katherine said. "Pull it out, when it's got four-wheel drive and can drive out by itself?"

It happened before we could do anything about it. Walton's son grabbed Katherine—a small, slender woman—by her sweater and flung her out of the door into the snow. "Want to go out in your bare feet?" Then he came back in and shouted at us, "Ready in three minutes, you hear?" I went and helped Katherine up. She was shivering and crying, and because I thought she had hurt herself I was very careful. But she shook her head: it was the humiliation of helplessness.

The snow was coming down harder. If it went on like this, we would not be able to find the road the next day. From the look in his eye I could tell that Ronald was thinking the same thing. After a lot of pushing and pulling we managed to get the jeep out of the ditch. We then pushed it over the road and into the parking lot. It was hard work, and Ronald was furious that Greg, Phil, and Mike only went through the motions. By the time the jeep was back in the lot, we were exhausted and soaked through with snow and sweat. Inside, Katherine instructed us to rub ourselves dry, put on all the dry clothes we had, and go to bed.

"Wait a second," Walton said, and when the attention he called for was not immediately forthcoming he took out a pistol, pointed it at the ceiling, and pulled the trigger. We all swung in his direction, and he stuck the gun back in the holster under his shoulder and gave us a stern look. "We're disappointed in you. Here we let you stay even though you don't belong here, we share our provisions with you, and what do you do? That guy"—he pointed to Jonathan—"treats us like cabdrivers to take him where he wants to go. Those three try to rob us. And you"—he turned to Ronald—"you get on my nerves with your talk about sympathy and compromise. What we want is gratitude and goodwill." He raised his voice a few notches. "Your thanks for what we've done for you and apologies for what you've done to us. Tomorrow morning, first thing. Is that clear?" He came up to me. "Is that clear?" When I failed to answer immediately, he gave me a shove. I felt my back hit the wall. He came up to me again, so close that his face was practically touching mine. I was afraid. "Is that clear?"

"Yes."

He went from person to person, and each said yes.

Then he and the boys filed into the lounge, and we filed silently up to our rooms. Jane and I got undressed and gave each other a dry rub, embarrassed because our nakedness awakened no desire.

"Only two nights here, and it seems an eternity," she said in bed.

I could not bring myself to utter the word *yes* again. I was still afraid, but it was no longer a fear of something; it was a physical condition.

"I wonder what tomorrow will be like."

"The snow is coming down harder, and I don't see how we can escape. They won't let us into the lounge. We could try and move the iron stove in the shack into the library."

"We have to apologize."

"We have to do something to get them to go on feeding us."

After a pause she added, "They haven't even told us what they're doing here."

15

THEY TOLD US THE NEXT DAY. They had come to go hunting. At ten it stopped snowing, and they packed some provisions in their backpacks and made a few trial shots on the terrace; at ten thirty the sun came out and off they went. Accompanied by Mark.

"Now's the time," Pamela said.

"Time for what? They've locked the steering wheel."

"Then let's lay a trap for them. Saw a hole in the lobby floor. Or has anybody got sleeping pills? We can put some in their food. Or we can hide all the food and make them negotiate with us for it."

But there was no more food in the kitchen. Besides, the suite was locked, and we had no success breaking the door down or climbing in through the balcony.

"Where did they get the key?"

"Come with me," Greg said, and we followed him to the jeep.

The steering wheel was bolted with an iron clamp, so they had left the doors unlocked. Greg opened the right-hand door and pointed to a leather case lying on the floor. "Isn't that . . . I didn't look into it last night, but doesn't it look familiar?"

Pamela opened it: two books, a sheaf of papers, an engagement calendar. She leafed through it. "It's de Baur's stuff all right."

"What does it mean?"

"I don't know," she said, putting the case back on the floor, "but I don't like the looks of it."

"You don't think . . ." Ronald did not complete his sentence, nor did anyone put into words what we all feared. We moved the stove, sticking the exhaust pipe through a skylight, carried some logs into the library, and made ourselves warm. We heard an occasional shot. Somehow we would manage to break away tomorrow. Today we had to apologize. Who would do it? I walked with the champagne bucket from one person to another, and we drew lots. Katherine was chosen.

"I'll do it, but they may not accept an apology from a woman."

Pamela looked at me. "You should do it."

"Look, Katherine's been chosen by lot. She has to try. If it doesn't work, we'll try something else."

"Why take a risk we can avoid? It makes more sense for you to do it or, even better, all the men together."

"Why should I do it? What was the point of drawing lots if—"

"You've said it yourself. The reason we drew lots was that we couldn't come up with anything better. We hadn't thought things through. Now we have, and we have come up with something better."

Pamela was right. I realized it, but still I balked. I did not want to apologize for something I was not guilty of. As I was passing around the lots, I remembered the time a neighbor had complained to my mother that I had called her a "stink flower" in the street, and my mother forced me to apologize. I was a child and had never used the term before; I was not even sure what it meant. I was terribly depressed after apologizing and could not understand why. It took a long time before I realized that what bothered me was not so much that I had sacrificed my dignity to a desire to make peace with my mother as that all rituals of self-criticism with their false accusations and false apologies are meant to sacrifice one's dignity and that one's self-respect comes apart in the process. No, I refused to betray myself. I would not apologize. Katherine should make an attempt, and if it failed we would try something else.

They came back home with a deer. Katherine was designated to butcher it because she was a doctor, and I helped because I felt guilty about forcing her to apologize. I had no idea what the others were doing: supplying the lounge with logs, kindling the fire, taking the beer outside to get cold, setting up the PA system that suddenly sent high-volume pop music throughout the hotel. During the three hours that Katherine and I spent preparing the venison, Walton and his boys presumably had a chance to have a private chat with each of us, Katherine included, but they did not immediately come out with what they had learned.

Katherine made her apology at the beginning of dinner, and we thought it came off well: she talked about the different expectations they had and we had, about the conflicts that had arisen from them, about our different ways of looking at things and doing things; she was sorry we had insulted them after they had helped us in a time of need, and hoped that the meal would serve as a reconciliation of sorts and that they would enjoy the venison.

But after we had eaten for a while in silence, Walton's son turned to him and said, "Is she trying to say we don't know how to talk good? What does she take us for, anyways? A bunch of yokels? Country bumpkins?"

"I don't know what she's trying to say, but they certainly take us for idiots if they think they can get away with apologizing for the small shit and don't say anything about setting traps, sawing holes, and poisoning food." His voice had been getting louder and louder. "How about some apologizing for that! And this time I don't want to hear no girl neither. Is that clear? You there!" He pointed to me. "Is that clear?"

I nodded, and when that did not suffice I said yes. What is more, I said yes when after dinner Walton and company were sitting in the lounge and we were sitting in the library and I was designated to deliver our apology the next morning. I tried to wriggle out of it by proposing that we draw lots again. Then I could cheat—the way I had cheated the first time around—but no one listened to me. No one was in the mood for talking. Everyone was wondering who had given away Pamela's proposals. Who could trust anyone anymore?

"I think I should come out and tell you," Jane said to Meg after a long pause. "I have no evidence against you—it's only a gut reaction—but . . ."

Meg shook her head sadly.

When the lights went out at nine, one of the cousins came in and pointed to Pamela. "You there, you little slut! On your feet and follow me." He sounded tipsy. Pamela looked around. Katherine, Jane, Ronald, Jonathan, and I got up first. But Walton's son and the other cousin were standing in the doorway, as if having expected something of the sort. Walton's son had a holster draped over his shoulder. It was unbuckled, hanging loose. Pamela looked from them to us and from us to them, then stood and followed them out.

We waited. We heard laughter, then an exchange of words—Walton's loud voice, Pamela's soft one. We could not make out what was being said, but we did not dare move close enough to eavesdrop. Things died down for a while. Then we heard a loud scream, and another. Jane ran up to the lounge door. She grabbed the doorknob. The door was locked. She started pounding on it. It opened, and there was Pamela. She was pale. There were red spots on her cheeks and fear in her eyes, but she said, "It's all right, Jane. It's all right."

16

WHY DIDN'T I GET the picture until my moment of defeat? Because after defeat there is nothing more to win or lose? Because defeat destroys one's illusions about others along with one's illusions about oneself? Because the prime post-defeat question—how could it have happened?—puts everything in a clearer light?

When I got back to my room that evening, I saw that Jane had collected her blankets and sheet. It was Meg she had accused, but she could no longer stand being close to me either. Sitting there on the bed, I realized I was in the same boat: I could not stand any of them any longer—their faces, what they said, the way they moved, their fear. What we were experiencing had not brought us together; it had distanced us from one another. A night without Jane's body and blankets would be terribly cold, and I should have taken my things and gone to the library to lie by the stove, but the thought of hearing the others' deep breathing and smelling their exhalations was so unbearable that I stayed in my room.

I held out until four, when I awoke and the cold became more unbearable than the breathing and exhalations: I went and lay down in the library. At eight they called us into the lobby. Pamela was the last to appear. She came out of the lounge and sat with us but kept her eyes down. They asked what we had to say. When I stood up, they played a game with me. What did I want? To apologize? For the group? Not for myself? Wouldn't it be better if I began with myself?

And so I apologized. Then I went to my room and put all my clothes on; then I went to the library, picked up my blanket, and wrapped it around myself; then I went outside. The snow was still too deep for me to make out the road, but I didn't care: I just wanted to get away from the hotel and from the others. I trudged along the lake until I could see the hotel jutting out of the slope on the other side of the great, white expanse.

What had the commune done here? Everywhere I looked I saw trees. There was not enough open land for the members to grow what they needed. Did they manufacture something? How did they get the raw materials and distribute the products?

Nothing made sense. The commune could not have been an experiment in a new, different, better way of living together, as communes are supposed to be. No, it was de Baur's experiment on the people he gathered here, just as this week was an experiment on us, an experiment whose confrontations, threats, and dangers were as artificial as the promise of a better life proffered by the commune.

How do students, future politicians, judges, executives, and other people in authority perfom under extreme conditions? As team players, as individuals? Do they stick to their principles or collaborate? What does it take to make them betray one another, turn against their own? At what degree of cold, hunger, pressure, or fear does the layer of civilization start to peel away?

Of course none of the subjects must freeze to death or starve to death or be seriously injured. There must be just enough blankets and just enough food for the first night, the intruders must bring just enough supplies for everyone, and when they occupy the room with the fireplace there must be a stove that can be set up in another room. If there is violence, it must look bad but not really hurt: Mike fell on the floor, Katherine in the snow, and I was certain Pamela had not been raped, only given a good scare.

But was this really an experiment? What could our week tell de Baur that he did not know after all the retreats he had staged here? No, he did not want to study us. He did not maintain his distance, as a bona fide experimenter should; he took an active part. Those video cameras did not go back to the days of the commune; he had had them installed so he could spy on us, follow how we behaved. Then he could instruct his accomplices about what to do next. Nobody betrayed Pamela: de Baur had heard what she said, seen her saying it. Steve Walton's son let the cat out of the bag when he derided Greg, Mike, and Phil for thinking only of themselves and not "all for one and one for all," and we should have picked up on it: how could he have known of our pact the night before?

De Baur was not interested in studying us; he was interested in molding us. I suddenly recalled passages from his book and lectures that I had been unable to process at the time: that we had simply repressed things like the joy we find in evil, the pleasure we take in hating, fighting, and killing, the satisfaction that comes from the sinister rituals of fascism and communism; that we did not look evil in the eye, that we turned away from it, but it kept coming back. "Do you think these were the only people who did things like that, this the only time in which they happened?" It had come up more than once in the lecture on atrocities of the past.

The retreat was supposed to teach us to look evil in the eye, the evil in others and ourselves. Each of us had our turn during the week; each of us was meant to experience denying and betraying the principles we professed as good, to experience selling out, doing evil with determination. Anyone who had not fallen yet would fall soon: de Baur would find his weak spot in the videos and give the required nudge.

I had deceived the others when we drew lots, and myself when I apologized. What was that supposed to teach me? That I was capable of evil? That I could turn that ability to my advantage? Was it de Baur's intention to forge the retreat participants into a community that had looked evil in the eye and was now ready to do its bidding, to use it with determination?

I wanted no part in such a community; I wanted nothing to do with it. Nor did I want to wait around until de Baur appeared on the scene to explain and interpret, reconcile and seduce, and send us back into the world convinced that after this very special experience we were very special people. I walked back to the hotel across the lake. In the middle of the great, empty, white expanse I was once more overcome by fear, the fear of the last few days, the fear of falling in and drowning, and a pure, unadulterated fear that needs no object. By the time I reached the shore, however, it was gone.

I went up to my room, stood in front of the video camera, and told de Baur the time had come for him to make his appearance and put an end to it all.

17

THE FOUR OF THEM took me back to New York in the jeep. I went up to them when I saw them climbing in and told them point-blank not that I knew they were leaving not just briefly, as they had told us, but for good, and that they were leaving because they had done their job and de Baur was on his way. They shrugged and let me in.

They were actors. The one who played the Steve Walton part had been a member of the commune many years before and, when retreats replaced the commune, took charge of casting actors to play the unexpected visitors: hunters or poker players or Vietnam veterans. "One year we were a band of criminals hiding out from the cops." He laughed. "It was fun, but one of us hammed it up and it got too much like a movie. By the way, the weather isn't always so cooperative."

"Where's de Baur?"

"Oh, he's at the hotel by now. He's real close, in a cottage on the other side of the hill."

"Watching a wall of monitors."

"Before video we had to do a lot more improvising. John's current dream is that instead of having to phone him now and then we can each have a receiver in our ear and he can tell us exactly what to do. Though he'll have to find somebody to replace me: I'm an actor, not a robot."

He was a careful, steady driver. Once we had emerged from the Adirondacks, the road through the darkness grew monotonous and the others fell asleep. It took me a while to get used to a road without snow, a road of speeding cars, and clear my mind of the images of the last few days.

"What was the commune like?"

"The commune?" He thought a while. "I wouldn't want to have been one of the regular members. I was staff. And even that got to be too much at times. It wasn't just that you gave up your privacy, which meant that unless you were ostracized as a punishment you were always with everybody when you ate, when you slept, when you made love, when you went to the bathroom—that wasn't so bad. But John kept changing the rules, and he never told anybody, so you'd get up one morning and what had been right the night before was suddenly wrong. *We* knew what the new rules were because we were staff and we couldn't enforce them if we didn't. But the only thing the regulars could see was that the old rules no longer applied. Everything was in flux, nothing was permanent, there was no relying on anything. Or on de Baur: he was hot one day, cold the next."

"What kind of rules are you talking about?"

"What time you got up, who made breakfast, who did the dishes, who did all the things that had to get done and who took it easy, who could make love with whom—there were rules for everything."

"What was the point of all the changes?"

He laughed. "You're asking me? It had something to do with the truth of the 'exceptional situation.' When everything is running like clockwork, we don't really experience who we are: we let ourselves be tricked and trick ourselves. But in 'exceptional situations' something happens to us . . ." He paused. "I can't remember what it is that happens in exceptional situations, but what happened to the commune members was that they lost their bearings. He never told them anything about exceptional situations and their truth, by the way; they were supposed to experience it."

"Why did people stay?"

"Only half of them stayed. The other half, the stronger ones, left. One of the ones who stayed cracked up, flipped out. And that was the end of the commune."

"How many years did it go on?"

"Years? Months, you mean. Nine months. From spring to winter."

"Why did *you* do it?"

"John and I had known each other since his days in law school and mine in the theater department. He needed someone; I needed work."

"Who funded the commune? Who's funding the retreats?"

"Some foundation funded the commune. I don't remember its name. And I don't know if it's the one that's funding the retreats."

I was having trouble keeping my eyes open, and there were still so many questions I wanted to have answered. What had de Baur been like as a young man? What had he been like as leader of the commune? What had he told Walton about his life in Europe? What was he like with women? And with friends? Did he have any friends? But I didn't get beyond one important question: did the commune members hate him at the end of it all?

"Hate him? No, the ones who stayed revered him."

18

THEY LET ME OFF AT Times Square. It was after midnight, but the streets were full of cars, the sidewalks full of people, and the neon signs changing color and pattern like nobody's business. It was not cold, and instead of taking the subway I walked.

I passed neon nudes beckoning me in to a floor show; I passed grocery stores that had sandwiches, beer, and magazines for sale; I passed people sleeping in doorways or pressed against a shop's rolling shutter. The farther north I got, the less traffic I encountered in the streets and on the sidewalks. At 72nd Street I switched over to Riverside Drive and was suddenly alone. On my left I could see the lights on the other side of the river twinkling through the park's bare trees, on my right, the tall buildings dark against the city-bright sky.

Was the snow thawing in the Adirondacks? Was the ice on the lake cracking? It was certainly not warm enough to do without the fire in the fireplace. Were they sitting up late in the lounge listening docilely to de Baur's explanation of what they had just experienced and what they should learn from it?

I carried on a mental debate with de Baur. There was nothing to learn, I would argue. Yes, we were capable of egoism and ruthlessness, betrayal and deception, and much else that is heinous. But we knew that anyway. Yes, evil had not been done away with by the wars and crimes of the twentieth century; it lived on. But that was nothing new either. What the mini-artificial, exceptional situation he had set up demonstrated didn't matter. The only thing that mattered was how we established normalcy and how, as time goes on, we became better to one another, more friendly, respectful, and fair.

De Baur would laugh. Better? If I was counting on progress, he would retort, I didn't understand a thing. About the presence of evil in the world or its presence in me. If we knew what iniquity we ourselves were capable of, why were we so presumptuous as to condemn it in others? If we knew that evil lived on in the world, why did we live as if we did not need to confront it, as if we did not need to decide what it was and accept the responsibility to act accordingly?

And you, he sneered, you lack the guts to confront even me! You're on your way to your nice warm bed instead of sticking it out in the hotel. You wouldn't be half so overwrought about what I teach if you weren't so overwrought about having a bad father, who didn't find you cute enough to spend his life with you. Get a life! All you do is play with justice as if it were spectator sport and with politics as if it were a picture book of history. If I weren't your father, I'd be as interesting a discovery for you—no, a much more interesting discovery—than whatever you learned back there in East Berlin.

And you, I sneered back, you have the nerve to invoke responsibility! When it came time for you to accept the responsibility for your decisions, what did you do but run away. And don't talk to me about your responsibility to yourself. Responsibility to oneself doesn't hurt. It's worthless. A joke.

A man walking a dog was coming in my direction. He was looking at me curiously, and I realized I was talking out loud to myself. I put a halt to the dialogue. Besides, shouldn't I be confronting him in person rather than in thought? He would take me on. He would enjoy it even. If I took a light, playful approach, it could turn from a father-son confrontation to a father-son encounter.

He would enjoy following the road that led me from the *Reading Pleasure* novel to him, and would tell me the ending of Karl's homecoming—if he remembered it. Then we would open a bottle of red wine and talk about other homecomings: Odysseus', his, mine . . .

I might actually have gone through with it had he merely been the playful adventurer I had long taken him for. But that playful, adventuresome levity had never been more than a façade for his demons.

I was at home by two. The room was overheated. I opened the window and heard soft music playing. I could tell I would not be able to sleep and wondered what other poor soul was in the same situation, but all the windows were dark. I sat at my desk listening to the jazz, a piano solo, quiet, irresolute, ironic. The combination of the heating, which I could not turn up or down, and the open window made for a comfortable temperature, and I took one of those yellow pads I had grown fond of and laid in generous supplies of and began to write:

THE STORY OF THE YOUTH WHO WENT FORTH
TO TEACH WHAT FEAR WAS

Like thousands before and after him he left behind wife and child and a dark past and came to America from Europe with a new name and the dream of a bright future.

John de Baur made a brilliant career, which eventually took him to Columbia University, where he now teaches political theory. His past is . . .

I recorded his Swiss origins, his studies in Germany, his relationship to Hanke, their flight from Breslau, his time in Berlin, his pseudonyms; I reported the content of his school composition, his war articles in the *Deutsche Allgemeine Zeitung* and *Das Reich*, his postwar articles in the *Nacht-Express,* his novels. I said nothing about my reading of *The Odyssey of Law:* anyone aware of his past could plainly see he was using the book to justify it; I did, however, mention what he had done in his commune and January retreats.

I finished as the sun began to rise. I lay down and slept a fitful hour or two, then went to the department to input the text and print it out. I signed it with my own name. I made an appointment with a lawyer I had met at a law school lecture, and he agreed to submit the manuscript to *The New York Times* with the stipulation that it be published in its entirety or not at all. I could not get a flight out that day but did book a seat on the next flight the day after.

19

THE PLANE WAS late taking off. The sun was already going down as it flew north along the coast. The water shimmered and the snow glistened in the evening light. I did not really believe they were the Hudson or the Adirondacks, but I took leave of them as if they were. Then I saw the lights of Halifax. Then it was totally dark.

I did not call Barbara to announce my arrival: I was afraid. What if she told me there had been some changes during my absence and I had better stay with a friend or my mother. That we would have to see how things went. No, no, she wasn't with anybody, nobody permanent, that is, but she'd met somebody. That, no, no, she still liked me, liked me a lot, but she was a bit confused. Yes, of course she wanted to see me, but in the same apartment? Wouldn't it be a bit claustrophobic?

I had avoided hearing it over the phone, but that was cold comfort. I could just as easily hear it on the stairs, at the door, in the entrance hall, in the living room, from which my furniture had been moved to storage.

For Christmas, Barbara had sent me a teddy bear I received as a child and displayed on the bookshelves of every flat where I lived. "Greetings from Home," she had written, and it made me happy. But how could I be sure she had meant it as a token of her love? What if she had just shrunk from packing it away in one of the cartons she was using to store my things in?

Surely she would have written to me about it! The reason the men in my stories came home unsuspecting was that there was no postal or telephone service, no contact. Well, not entirely. Agamemnon suspected nothing even though he had established contact with Clytemnestra via a messenger. She disguised herself because she intended to murder him, and murder him she did. Was I crazy? What silly, silly thoughts! My furniture and my things were still in place; of course they were: she would have written otherwise. But that was all she would have written. She would wait with the rest, wait until she could tell me to my face.

I was grateful for the diversion provided by the meals and the movie and the prattle of the woman next to me, who had four children and twelve grandchildren. When the overhead lights went out and the woman's snoring head drooped onto my shoulder, the wheel of fear began turning again. I tried to stop it and look at my options. Should I insist on staying if she wanted me to leave? At first I could not imagine doing something of the sort, but then I started wondering what kind of statement my *not* staying would make. Would I be doing it for her sake or mine? Did I want to spare her my presence or spare myself the ignominy of it all? No, I would not make the same mistake twice: this time I would stay. I would be a presence, but an undemanding one; I would woo but not push, I would offer myself; I would not repress my feelings; I would show understanding for her, reveal a tad of self-irony. The longer I played with that option, the more I felt it was the right one and the more I saw it was beyond me. Beyond me.

What would I do if she stood in the door with another man's

arm around her? Fight? I suddenly understood why men used to duel: when two men love the same woman, the world is too small to contain them both. If they truly love her and cannot have her, they would rather die than live without her. Too bad women now stay out of it and sometimes want the wrong one, the one who dies, or even both. Even if I picked a fight with him, I could not predict Barbara's reaction. Let's say he fought back. Let's say I fell down the stairs and lay sprawled out on the landing. She might run and take my bleeding head in her lap. But what if he were the one who fell? Would she take him for the valiant victim and me for the brute?

I had to put an end to my fear. It was spreading like an ink stain over a sheet of paper. Soon there would be no space for me to write "I love you."

It was still dark when the plane landed in Frankfurt, still dark when I got out of the train in my hometown. This was where I would normally have changed trains, but there had been some damage to the wires or tracks or somebody had committed suicide, and there would be no train for another two hours. I took a taxi. I could see the sun coming up over the hills, which I took as a good omen, but there was a bad omen as well: I was coming in on the Autobahn like Karl.

At last I was in front of the house. The bare, wintry garden made it look more massive and dark than usual, and my heart sank. I opened the garden gate, went up to the entrance, and rang the bell. After a while I heard the buzz of the door-opener, pushed the door open, and went up the stairs. The door to the apartment was still shut. I waited on the stairs.

I heard the chain being slipped out of the bolt and falling against the door. The door opened. There stood Barbara in her dressing gown, her hair pulled back as it was the first time we met, her glasses down over her nose. She took off the glasses, recognized me, and her face lit up. She leaned against the doorpost, crossed

her arms over her chest, and watched me come up the last few
stairs, bags in hand. She smiled her crooked, brazen, wonderfully
warm smile. "So here you are!"

20

IT WAS AS IF I had never left. Barbara had to go to school, and
while she showered, put on her makeup, and dressed, I made breakfast. By the time she'd come home from school, I had unpacked,
put my things away, and gone through my mail.

The publishing house wanted to hire me back: they had decided
not to keep my successor on after his probationary period. If I
accepted, I could go ahead with the new series and the new journal. While we ate, I could tell Barbara that we would be leaving for
work together as we used to do. The very next morning. The
longer I waited the more work would pile up on my desk.

None of what I so feared had come about: there was no other
man in Barbara's life and she did not hold my long absence against
me. She was glad to have me back. And yet I could not completely
set aside my fear. Would Barbara eventually tire of the routine of
love that was so important to me? To keep her from noticing it, I
would make off-the-wall proposals she would laughingly go along
with. But what if she saw through me one day? Or did she see
through me even now?

My piece on John de Baur never appeared. *The New York Times*
wanted to have a reporter run through all the facts with me and
find out more about my stake in the story, and that I was unwilling
to do. I had no desire to stir up the relationship between John de
Baur and me.

A few years later the story did come out. It made all the papers,

American and European. I assume the reporter on whose desk the piece landed had gone and done the research himself. That he did not acknowledge me as a source was fine by me. I would not have enjoyed joining in the media hype.

Most of the articles focused on de Baur's biography, the various names he took and parts he played, what he got involved in or let himself in for, his egoism or opportunism or arrogance or whatever the author had decided to call the key to de Baur's character. On television they interviewed the journalist who had broken the story rather than de Baur himself, but he did go on the radio, where he was his suave, charming self, giving a treatment of his youthful desire for adventure and susceptibility to be led astray that was simultaneously bemused and concerned, voicing his understanding of the media campaign and moving quickly on to his pride in what he had accomplished in America and his pride in America for having given him the opportunity to accomplish it. He was so modest, so sincere, so likable that it was impossible to dig into him afterward. I heard excerpts of the program in Germany. He was truly impressive.

The scholarly debate centered on his intellectual integrity and whether he was using deconstructionist legal theory to evade responsibility or had intended to formulate a genuine new way of looking at the law—or both. De Baur's friends held a conference in which these issues were aired, and after his American colleagues had had their say about the difficult or terrible or blind or cryptic or recalcitrant wartime texts and a French colleague had seen in them "embers under flickering flames," de Baur took the floor and deconstructed them with such finesse that it was impossible to censure him for them or even censure him for refusing to take responsibility for them. That too was a brilliant performance.

One paper triggered a minor debate of its own. The author's thesis was that de Baur's attempt to justify his past and integrate it into the present was more intelligent than the traditional attempts by theoreticians and practitioners of the law to talk their way out of such binds: the law is the law, an order is an order, obedience is obedience. It also called the conception behind them something that had long seemed inconceivable: a present-day intellectual fascism. But here too de Baur managed to come out on top.

Not only did he come out on top of the brouhaha, I imagine he enjoyed it. Things quieted down around him once it had passed—in Europe, at any rate—and I did not run across his name again until the turn of the new century, on the occasion of which he wrote a widely read essay full of presentiment and foreboding. After 9/11 he developed a theory of terrorism. I saw announcements of the book and reviews but had no desire to read them. On his eightieth birthday there was a late-night interview with him on television. I watched and listened for a while, then turned off the sound and finally the picture.

A few minutes later my mother phoned. "Did you see him on television?"

"Yes."

"Do you still want to know how his novel ends?"

"You told me years ago."

She gave a spiteful laugh. "You came up with it on your own." She paused for a reaction, but I said nothing. "He was a student here before he left for Silesia. He had a girlfriend. He looked her up after the war. She was married and had two children."

"Was one of them his?"

"He would have told me. He never spared me. He based the end of the novel on the meeting he had with her and the arrangement he made with me."

"Why are you telling me this?"

"Maybe you'll finally get your life together. You still don't know if you want to stay Peter Debauer or be Peter Graf or Peter Bindinger. You're not married. It's too late for you to have your own children, but you could still—"

"You want to be a grandmother?"

"I don't want a thing," she said, and hung up.

It's true. She doesn't want anything from me, which makes things easy and makes me sad. I'm glad I'm still important to Max beyond movies and pizza, beyond school and books. I would like to want more from him than I do now. I will have to work on it.

Sometimes I feel a longing for the Odysseus who learned the tricks and lies of the confidence man from Wenzel Strapinski, set out restless into the world, sought adventure and came out on top, won over my mother with his charm, and made up novels with great gusto and theories with playful levity. But I know it is not Johann Debauer or John de Baur I long for; it is the image I have made of my father and hung in my heart.

Bernhard Schlink was born in Germany. He is the author of the internationally bestselling novel *The Reader*, as well as the collection of stories *Flights of Love* and four prizewinning crime novels—*The Gordian Loop, Self's Deception, Self's Punishment*, and *Self's Murder*—that are currently being translated into English. He lives in Berlin and New York.